I0599419

9mm Press

Raidbyte

Cat Connor

Raidbyte:

A "redundant array of independent disks"; seemed fitting for this compilation of the longer Byte shorts.

These are the extra stories from the boxed sets combined with a few of the other longer shorts.

For information regarding permission email the publisher at 9mmPressNZ@gmail.com,
subject line: Permission.

ISBN hardback: 9798745964824
ISBN Draft2Digital: 978-1-0670072-9-4

For Chrissy: 40/45 because we can.

Lost Highway:

It's a Halloween dance, how bad can it be?

This story comes after Exacerbyte and before Flash-byte.

Lost Highway
1.

"Hungry?" Rowan asked, checking his rearview mirror. Traffic was heavier than usual. The four hour drive from D.C to Rowan's front door had already become five hours and we had a way to go yet.

"A little bit. Could murder a bowl of pumpkin soup."

"In this heat?"

I laughed. "You can tell how hot it is can you with the air conditioning on and the windows up?"

He pointed to the dash. "It says eighty-seven degrees."

"That's pretty warm."

"Indian summer," Rowan said. "Isn't that what they call it when it's this warm in Fall?"

"Yeah."

My phone buzzed in my bag. I reached down and took a quick look. My heart thumped. A text from Mac.

Because that's possible.

I read the text twice.

Mac: *You are dangerous.*

I'm only sometimes dangerous but you're always dead. Another text from beyond the grave could not be good. I dropped the phone into my bag in the footwell and fought to control the rising feeling of doom.

First Mom now Mac. What the hell was happening?

"Ellie, is it important?"

"Nope."

"Okay."

I settled back into the seat. Dead is dead.

"It's supposed to be pumpkin weather and I love pumpkin soup." Ornery edged in. Maybe I was hungrier than I realized. Maybe I just don't like texts from dead men no matter who they once were.

Rowan pulled into a parking lot outside a familiar looking diner. They could've taken Aunt Caroline's diner from Richmond and dropped smack on the side of the Garden State parkway. I felt instantly at home and simultaneously terrified that mom might appear reeking of gin with red lipstick smeared all over her face.

The coffee was good, the roast beef sandwiches were excellent, and the pumpkin soup had the exact right amount of garlic and nutmeg.

"Good?" Rowan asked me, as I finished the last spoonful of soup and the waitress filled our cups for the third time.

I nodded, looked around. "You come here often?"

"A lot more than ever, now it's on my way to and from you."

The waitress popped back a fourth time. "We're good Sally, thanks," Rowan told her with a grin.

"You're welcome Rowan. And this is …?"

Oh, now the attention all made sense. They were protective of their rock star.

"I'm Ellie," I said extending my hand.

She wiped her hand down her apron and shook mine. "You're Ellie!" Sally flung her head over her shoulder so fast I thought it would come clean off. "Yo, Bruce, get out here. He finally brought her in."

A deep chuckle erupted from the kitchen. "I'll be damned."

Rowan laughed. "You were damned along ways back buddy."

"True enough," said the owner of the voice. A large ruddy faced man poked his head out of the kitchen and looked at us, or was it me he looked at?

"Pleased to meet you."

"You too," I called back.

"Time we moved. I want to get home before it gets too late and there is no telling how many more detours we'll come up against."

"Let's go then."

The shadows grew longer as Rowan navigated the roads and detours.

Part of me was looking forward to the weekend. The other part of me was concerned about being around normal people. People who didn't carry guns on their hips and didn't get shot at with frightening regularity. Didn't feel like I had a lot in common with people outside law enforcement fields. Quashing the urge to tell Rowan to turn the car around was difficult but convincing myself new experiences could be fun was damn near impossible.

My thoughts rambled on until they settled on the texts I'd received. The first text arrived at six minutes past six in the morning.

Mom: *You have something that does not belong to you. Give it back.*

Dead people can't text. My mom barely bothered to text me when she was alive, so a post-death text was a bit strange. This was all so different to the messenger conversation I once had with Mac on my laptop. That was deemed otherworldly oddness and Mac's ghost wanted me safe. Very different to the vibe from today's messages. Maybe there was some kind of rift in time that allowed a few messages to get through, or maybe they were old messages now being delivered? Them being old messages almost made more sense than my dead husband and mom texting from beyond the grave but the content disturbed me.

As Rowan turned into his driveway, I considered deleting the messages and tossing my phone into the nearest river. He pulled into the spacious four-car garage and killed the engine. I opened the car door and breathed the air of freedom. It smelled a lot like exhaust fumes. So be it.

Long days, good times, blue skies, sticky nights, we made it to New Jersey.

Rowan slid over the hood of the car. "I wanted to open the door," he said with a flourish. His hand extended to help me out.

"Thank you."

"You're welcome."

He picked up my messenger bag from the footwell, and hooked it up over his shoulder then popped the latch on the trunk. I leaned in to grab my bag.

"I'll get it," Rowan said.

"I can carry my own bags." I gave him a look. Rowan shook his head. A voice came from the depths of my subconscious, 'Pick your battles.' I shrugged and stepped aside. Rowan had my overnight bag in one hand and my messenger bag over his shoulder. His other hand he reserved for me. The warmth from his fingers as he entwined them in mine radiated toward my heart.

It reminded me what a cold dark place that can be at times. I smiled. I knew it was real because I felt it growing inside me. There was lightness, I had to work at it, but it was there. I was on a mini vacation. A whole weekend without work. Everything was okay. Texts can't hurt me. Ms. Conway is on a break and she don't give a fuck.

"Come on," Rowan said. "As great as my garage is, I think you'll like the house better."

I didn't doubt it.

We'd come along way in the last little while, I couldn't remember how long we'd been dating. Why couldn't I remember? A year. Longer? I calculated time and decided it was just over a year.

And it took me until a few weeks ago to finally meet his folks. I am some kind of weirdo. I remembered Rowan damn near bashing down my door one night about four months ago. The image made me smile. He was furious, yelling about all sorts of things all at once. So fired up I didn't think he'd ever calm down. All because I hadn't answered my phone, or my messages, for a few days. I think email may have gone by the by as well.

He stood there in front me and told me how terrified he was. Over reaction much?

No one had ever burst through my door yelling, not ever. Then I thought about it. Mac came close a few times. Maybe I could be better at the girlfriend thing? I could clearly do better with my personal communication skills. Rock stars are dramatic creatures. He finally stopped hollering and listened to my explanation but he then made me promise that I would never disappear like that again. That's not a promise I can make to anyone and keep.

"Hey ..."

I looked into Rowans eyes. Life changes like the weather. I hoped the partly cloudy skies would clear.

"Hey," he said again.

"Yeah."

"Where were you?"

I threw him a smile. "Right here."

"You were miles away."

Time to focus on the present. We were in the master bedroom. Rowan's bedroom. My bags were on a spacious window seat.

"Dinner will be at eight-thirty," he said.

Dinner. My watch said it was heading for seven.

"Dinner? We ate already."

"That wasn't dinner," he said, "That was a snack."

"It was a filling snack."

"I can call down and have chef stop dinner."

"Chef ..." I whispered aloud but really to myself. Of course, he has a chef. He probably wouldn't like being told to stop dinner preparations. "I'm not hungry but I'll do my best."

Rowan chuckled. "Bet you are when it lands in front if you."

Probably. "Yeah."

"Do you wanna see the costumes?"

I'd kinda like to call the office and talk to Kurt about the texts because as much as I'd like to pretend it's fine, it's not, it's weird. Partly cloudy edged into thunder storms and rain. My stormy visualizations scurried into the dark recesses of my mind. A clap of thunder jolted my insides.

Sure. Costumes. Rowan's reason for the four day weekend getaway. His traditional Halloween Ball. The depth of the waters here staggered me. Drowning seemed a real possibility. Drowning in a storm. How very theatrical. The sooner I could speak to someone from Delta A the better.

Rowan took my hand and led me down the hallway to a guest room. He produced the costumes from the closet. King and Queen of Halloween. The costumes reminded me of Game of Thrones. If only I was Cersei Lannister the wife of King Robert Baratheon, and Queen of the Seven Kingdoms. Maybe then I wouldn't flounder in the depth of the waters.

Winter was coming.

I tried the dress on. Rowan laced the back for me. The red dress had long fitted sleeves that came a point on the back of my hand, a small loop secured the sleeve to the middle finger of each hand. The neck was a modest scoop. I swished the skirt behind me and caught sight of the train in the mirror. Regal. A wide red sequin belt hung low over my hips. The dress shimmered under the lights as I moved. Somewhere I heard music. Juice Newton. The gown reminded me very much of the Queen of Hearts which was a welcome change from thoughts of Cersei Lannister. She was a little too close to her twin brother for my liking.

"Ummm?" I said pointing to my holstered weapon sitting on the dressing table. There was no way to conceal my hip holster. The way the dress clung, I couldn't even wear a thigh holster.

Rowan looked at me, bemused.

"You're on vacation. You don't need to wear it."

I could feel it starting, our usual argument. His dislike

of my career and my inability to get him to understand that vacation or not, I was a federal agent. That meant I was armed. Was I going there? No. I could go for a smaller weapon and an ankle holster. There was a moment when that sounded good but it was followed quickly with an inward sigh as my mother's voice broke through my defenses, "It won't hurt you to do what your man wants. No gun. No gun!" I bit my tongue to stop myself answering her audibly.

Steeling myself for a weekend without a weapon my mind tossed the texts up. Dammit. That didn't help.

Reminding myself to remain congenial I waved a hand at the holster. "Then have you got somewhere safe for that?"

"Yes. There is a safe in my room." The smile that radiated toward me told me I'd done the right thing.

2.

I woke wondering where the hell I was and why I couldn't hear the birds in the woods behind my house. It took me more than a few minutes to figure it out. Excerpts from the Wizard of Oz forced their way into my mind as it assimilated my new surroundings.

You're not in Kansas now, Dorothy.

It was true. I wasn't even in Virginia. I rolled over and Rowan was gone.

Gone.

I grabbed my phone from the nightstand. Seven-thirty. I checked my messages. Nothing new. That was a relief. Before the relief took hold my phone buzzed in my hand. Glancing at the screen I saw Cassandra's name. A new text.

Cassandra: *Do the world a favor, eat a bullet.*

Nope. This is bullshit. Now a text from Cassie? We were close. I was there when she died. She'd never talk like that.

"Rowan?" I said. I wasn't sure how loud to be, so I went with something between my normal speaking voice and hollering for my team. A mid-range semi yell.

Nothing came back.

"Rowan?" Slightly louder this time.

I couldn't hear anything.

I called Kurt. He answered on the fourth ring. "Conway."

"Home or the office?"

"Just arrived at the office. What's up?"

"You'll see in a minute." I took a screen shot of the texts and sent them to him. I heard it arrive on Kurt's phone.

"Someone doesn't like you much."

"Yeah. But is it one person or multiples. Three names so far."

"What do you have that doesn't belong to you?"

Not how did dead people text you? But what is Mom referring to?

"I have zero clue." I listened for signs of Rowan returning. The house seemed to be in silence. Would be hard to know though, it was so enormous a party could happen downstairs and I doubt you'd know up here on the third floor.

"You're at Rowan's?"

"I am."

"He has security. Have you spoken with the head of his security team?"

"Not yet." It's on my to do list.

"I'm not keen on the bit about you eating a bullet Conway. Where's Carla?"

"Home with my Dad."

"Lee, Sam, and I are planning on arriving this evening." I could hear his fingers tapping on computer keys. "I'll request some extra police patrols for Carla and your father. Is she staying at your dad's?"

"No, at our place, Dad's staying there with her. They're traveling up together."

"Okay, done."

"Good." I felt better already at the thought of my team being with me, especially with Carla arriving. "Can you pull my phone records and find out where those texts came from?"

"Already doing it."

"Could be spoofed?"

Seemed like the logical answer for deadman texts. Every bone in my body told me Mac, Mom, and Cassie were not communicating from beyond the grave and Cassie did not want me to join her.

"I'd put my money on Caller ID spoofing," Kurt said.

It's not difficult for anyone to falsify the information transmitted to a phone in order to conceal the senders identity and make it look like other people were texting. But why bother? What's the point if this ridiculousness?

"Okay, so, thinking along the spoof line. Can we find out who is behind it?"

"Yes, or at least what the real number or numbers they called from are."

Hunger began to rumble in a more determined way along with the desire for coffee.

"My money is on a burner phone with no ID attached. Get what info you can. Keep me in the loop."

"Will do."

I hung up. Guess we'll find out the who and the why.

Ellie Conway: pissing people off since forever.

Nasty person texting: keeping it cowardly like most bullies.

Hunger rumbled again. It was time to get up and go in search of Rowan and breakfast.

I looked out the bedroom window. One side overlooked the driveway, the other the courtyard. The entire house was shaped like a U, but squarer. An expanse of lawn led away from a natural courtyard in the middle and down to the waterfront and a jetty. Rowan's room was huge, and in the middle segment on the house, or I guess the bottom of the U. It seemed excessive for one guy. No wonder he had staff. The rock star life was a good one.

It was a beautiful brick mansion and I loved the design. But I had a feeling I'd get lost trying to find the kitchen. I hadn't even seen the kitchen. I'd seen the master bedroom, one guest room, the formal dining room, a living room, the garage, and the fabulous sweeping staircase that led up to the second and then third floors. It was all very *Gone with the Wind*.

Frankly, my dear I don't give a damn.

Trying to imagine Rowan saying that amused me. Rhett Butler was an asshole, no, he and Scarlet were conniving and deserved each other.

A door closed somewhere.

I walked to the windows over looking the driveway and

front entrance. The courtyard was deserted.

My phone buzzed. My heart thumped. I glanced at the screen. It was Rowan.

He was in the gym. Gym? Of course he had a gym. He had a chef. He had everything. I didn't know where the gym was or where to begin looking. Temptation rose to jump in my car and go looking back at my place. Yeah. Back where I felt comfortable. But I didn't have my car.

A sigh fell from my lips unchecked and unapologetic.

That was when I decided I needed to explore the house, find my way around, make it less daunting. I opened the room safe and removed my Glock. Instant calm washed over me. Maybe I could wear it for a little while. Was it worth the argument if he saw it? Probably not. I returned the weapon and closed the safe.

The en suite bathroom had everything I could ever need. Fresh towels piled up on a glass shelf. A note above a row of drawers in the spacious vanity unit with his and hers sinks The note said I would find hairbrush, shampoo etc in the drawers. I opened them. Not only did I find hairbrushes and shampoo. It was the brand I used. There was also cleanser, moisturizer, cotton balls, all manner of girl items. Impressive.

Housekeeper? That would make sense. I added find the housekeeper to my internal list of things to do. She'd be the one who knew everything about everything. Definitely the person who would know if there'd been any visitors on the grounds, unannounced door knockers, anything out of the ordinary. I imagined random door knockers were quite unlikely, considering the long stately driveway and gate security, but, wouldn't hurt to make sure.

The voice in my head laughed at me. Mocked by my own brain. Great. The text messages could be coming from anywhere in the world. No one needs to have visited the estate or even be on the estate. Straws fell from my grasp.

A long hot shower washed away some of the feeling of doom. Clean and dressed with my phone jammed in my pocket, I opened the bedroom door and strolled out, trying my damnedest to appear relaxed and calm.

As the bedroom disappeared into the distance and the hallway grew ever longer in front of me disorientation set in. Perhaps I should've carried a ball of yarn and fed it out as I walked, or maybe small pebbles, or breadcrumbs. *Come on, Gretel, it's not that bad.* I passed large windows and could see the driveway in front of the house. The hallway seemed to turn or veer slightly as I walked. On my left, I found a set of double doors, similar to the bedroom doors. I stopped and listened. There were no noise. Wondering what the room contained, I pressed down on one of the lever shaped handles. The door opened inward. I saw weights. On the other side of the room, on a treadmill was Rowan. Sweat glistening on his face, and arms. He was wearing an iPod on one arm and buds in his ears. I knew what he was listening to, because he was singing. He looked up but didn't notice me until the song finished. With a grin and a wave, he removed the earbuds, turned the treadmill off and called me over.

"I don't want to interrupt," I said.

"You're not. I'm done."

"How long have you been in here?"

"Hello." A voice from behind me, made me jump, my hand reflexively touched my hip and came up empty. I frowned and spun to see who it was. "He's been here an hour," said a tall, tanned, well-muscled guy. "I'm Jake, Rowan's personal trainer."

Nice. I have one too. Mine is employed by the FBI, and teaches unarmed combat as well as designing our physical training programs. A little voice in my head spoke loud enough for me to hear above my pounding heart. 'It's not a pissing contest, Ellie. Keep your mouth shut.'

Delta team personal trainer, Carlos, popped into my head, he flapped and cooed. He was almost peacock like. Brightly colored, flamboyant, strutting around the gym admiring himself in the mirrors. Underestimated by most who met him. I would not want him to go to the dark side.

Rowan toweled off and took my hand. "I'm going to shower, you can hang here if you like. Jake said he'd be happy to run you through a training program or whatever you need." He grinned and threw his towel into a laundry basket. "I know how you love to run, wanna use my treadmill." He laughed. That was how we met. Running. I love running but outside in the fresh air.

"I've just showered, so I'll pass," I replied with a smile. Then turned to Jake. "Thanks though, I appreciate the offer."

"Very nice to meet you," Jake replied then turned to Rowan. "I'll be back mid week, Rowan. We'll start on some stamina work to get you ready for the next tour. I want you running at least ten miles daily."

"See you," Rowan said, shaking his hand. Jake left.

We followed him out a minute or so later, and walked hand in hand back to the master bedroom. My mind kept pulling up the texts.

While Rowan showered, I lay on the bed, staring at the elegant canopy above it. I hadn't made the bed, yet it was made. I didn't see anyone in the hallway when I was wandering around. Someone must've come in while we were in the gym. This was a bizarre place. People obviously sneak about doing things without disturbing anyone. I wondered if there were secret passageways to facilitate such things. The phone in the room rang twice, then stopped. Odd.

Rowan appeared rubbing his hair with a towel. Once he was done he dropped the towel into a laundry hamper by the bathroom door and ran his fingers through his hair.

"Breakfast is waiting for us."

"How do you know?"

"The phone rang twice."

I felt my eyes roll involuntarily. "Of course, silly me."

He grinned. "You okay, or is this a bit much?"

"I'm okay. It's a lot much." I moved up a bit onto the pillows more. "I was wondering how the hell you cope at my place."

My four bed, three bath, no staff, regular two-story house dwarfed in comparison to Rowan's mansion.

"I love your place. I love being in New York too. I don't have all this in New York, remember?"

Yeah, I remember. His penthouse apartment in New York, was pretty close to normal. If you ignored the penthouse bit and the Central Park view.

"Why so much rock-type-everything here then?" It was a television or glossy magazine version of life. Removed from reality by staff and massive grounds.

He opened the bedroom door for me.

"This is where I entertain."

Fair enough. I guess when you're a mega rock star entertaining is more than a couple of pizzas and a six-pack.

"You mentioned breakfast."

"It's ready and waiting in the kitchen."

Imagine that? In the kitchen. How very normal. It took about five minutes to get down the stairs, there were a lot of them. I wanted to run down them but behaved.

"We'll take the stairs back up," he said. "But I'll show you where the elevator is."

Oh my god, he had an elevator. Not a fan of elevators. It made sense that he'd have one. How else would you get furniture to the third floor?

I sighed.

Rowan's arm shot out in front of me stopping me in my tracks. His fingers closed around my shoulder and he turned me toward him.

"Are you okay?"

"Hungry."

"Ellie, you need to talk. If there is something wrong I need to know." A cloud of concern settled on his features.

No, you really don't need to know. Not yet. Not until I know what's going on.

I shook the unease away and smiled.

"I'm hungry that's all."

His face lit with a smile. "I get that it'll take you time to unwind, it does me, when I get home from touring."

Yeah, because being a touring rockstar is identical to what I do. Wow, rein that in Ellie. Don't start.

"Yeah. That's probably it."

Not the crazy messages or being unarmed.

His arm hung around my neck, with one smooth movement he hooked me in and kissed me long and hard. "By the end of the day you'll be more settled."

I crossed my fingers behind my back. We'll see.

He pushed the nearest door open revealing a huge kitchen.

A table was set for breakfast in a nook by a window seat. It was nestled out of the way of the commotion and bustle of the large room.

A tall sturdy woman appeared to glide across the room toward us.

"Mr. Grange, breakfast is served," she said in brisk Scots accent.

Rowan introduced us.

"Mrs. MacDougal, This is my guest, Ellie Conway."

"Ms. Conway," Mrs. MacDougal said formally. "If you have any dietary requirements would you let chef or I know."

I extended my hand. "I have no special requirements."

She shook my hand briefly.

"Very well."

She disappeared with the same degree of mystery that shrouded her arrival.

Breakfast consisted of fresh fruit, yogurt, nuts, apple juice, eggs and toast. It was delicious. After breakfast, Rowan showed me the elevator. Maybe it was being fully fueled, maybe it was his company, or maybe I was starting to relax, whatever it was it translated to a smile and a smidgen of peace.

"It's good to see you smile."

3.

The day ran on. I didn't venture to the lower level of the house except to eat. Summoned by two rings of the telephone, and when I didn't arrive within ten minutes, the same two rings were repeated on my cell phone.

It seemed best to keep out of the party planner's way and off the ground floor. The shindig Rowan had planned was so far out of my headspace I would need GPS and satellite imaging to map my way through it.

The upper two floors were plenty to occupy me. The mansion life was beginning to amuse me. I couldn't imagine living in a house where a person could get lost. I noticed there were intercoms or something at several points down the long hallways. Made sense. I explored all aspects of the floors, and came across a suite with two bedrooms and with a nursery attached. Interesting, in a disconcerting way.

I called Rowan on his cell.

He answered after a few rings.

"Where are you?" he asked.

"In a nursery?"

"And you want to know why?"

"I want to know if you have secret children and a wife stashed somewhere in this place," I replied.

"Maybe, but who would know? This place is so big I could've lost half the county."

"Where are you?"

"Guess." His voice changed slightly, it seemed to echo and come from everywhere. "Look left."

I looked right.

"No, your other left," he said laughing.

I turned to my left in time to see Rowan emerge from a doorway.

"This is where Tony stays with his wife and kids."

That made sense. "I never thought of Tony's kids."

He looked at me strangely for a second, don't know what the look was but it vanished and he obviously decided against voicing whatever it was he thought. Rowan pointed behind him, "There is another bedroom off this one, as well as the nursery. Tony and Jemma have three kids now."

"How often do they stay?"

"Usually when they come home to visit family. And special occasions. Like tonight."

"Are they bringing the kids?"

"As far as I know. They usually do, and the nanny. The nanny and the kids will be in this suite ... Tony and Jemma have another room next door."

Children. The thought of small children sent twinges through my gut. If I'm dangerous I should not be near children.

"Your security people are used to having the children in the house?"

"Yes. Do you wanna go talk to Cameron, he's captain of the guard ... or at least that's what dad calls him."

"Can I?"

"If it makes you more comfortable. Come on. You'll have to venture to the ground floor though, his office is toward the back of the house."

"Surveillance equipment?"

"Of course."

Cool. I had a sense of Rowan humoring me, but I didn't care.

We made it to the ground floor unencumbered by party planners and hangers on. Rowan hit a sequence of numbers on a key pad outside a door that announced it was the gateway to the security suite. My phone buzzed as the door opened. I gave an apologetic glance at Rowan and stepped away a few feet to check my phone.

Another text.

Mac: *Go back where you came from. No one wants you here.*

Before I could put my phone away it vibrated in my hand.

Cassandra: *Death surrounds you, embrace it.*

Well, shit that didn't sound friendly. I sent screen shots to Kurt in a message then called him. Rowan was talking in the security suite, it felt okay to talk to Kurt, quietly.

"Find whoever the hell is behind these. I'm not liking the tone."

"We're working on it. All of us."

"Good. Get the feeling people don't like me much?"

"Sure do."

"I don't feel like I'm in much danger from whoever it is. It's easy to be an asshole online or via anonymous text, much harder to pull a trigger while standing in front of someone." Did I really think that? Kinda.

"Let's hope that's the case here."

Yet 'what if's' circled like vultures.

"Kurt ... what if ..."

"Conway, we'll be there soon."

I pocketed my phone, plastered a smile on my face and entered Cameron's office which turned out to be a control room with two adjacent rooms used by the security personal akin to what I've experienced in major hotels and large office buildings. A bank of screens rose up from a wall-to-wall desk. A man sat watching the monitors. He looked over briefly then went back to his task.

"Okay?" Rowan asked me.

"Yep, just checking in with work."

Rowan turned his attention to the man. "Hey Cameron, this is SSA Ellie Conway."

Cameron stood and his hand thrust at me. "Pleased to meet you ma'am. Rowan said you'd be here." We shook. "You're here for four days?"

"I am." I smiled at him. He had an infectious grin that

I didn't expect. His sandy blonde hair was cropped short. He wore dark blue trousers, and a lighter blue shirt, under a dark blue blazer. I put his age about forty-five. About five years older than Rowan, but looked ten.

My attention turned to the other three walls of the room and how they were utilized. On one hung a floor plan of the house. On another a list of names and phone numbers, some photographs, and a current calendar. A rack was attached to the third wall. I counted three shotguns, one Ithaca 37 and two Mossberg 500 ATP. Then three Heckler & Koch MP5's. Further along an Arwen 37 hung. I glanced at Rowan then at Cameron, who I discovered watching me with interest.

"Expecting a siege?"

"I hope not ma'am."

"What rounds do you keep for the Arwen Ace?"

"AR-2 and AR-5."

AR-2 are pyrotechnic rounds that deliver smoke and an irritant into a target area, usually a crowd. AR-5, I knew, were barricade-penetrating rounds, designed to deliver an irritant payload into a structural environment, a house, a building, a shed, anything structural. They weren't messing around.

"Hand guns?"

"Side arms consist of either Springfield .45 or Glock 21."

"You carrying all the time?"

"Yes ma'am." He tapped his hip with the heel of his

hand. "My Springfield."

"Ever thought of carrying less lethal weapons?"

"We all carry stun guns and pepper spray as well, ma'am."

I looked at Rowan, who lounged against the edge of the long desk. He smiled. "Didn't want you to worry. My security guys are ex-special forces or Police."

I raised an eyebrow at Cameron. I picked him as Navy. "You?"

"Bit of both ma'am. Served five years in the Navy SEALS then moved to a police rapid response unit in New Jersey."

That would account for the ageing I detected.

A respectful nod of my head acknowledged his past.

"How long have you been with Mr. Grange?"

"Coming up on two years ma'am."

I scanned the bank of monitors. I could see the driveway, all exterior doors, the garage, inside and out, all the hallways, the main foyer, and some places I didn't yet recognize. There was a lot to keep an eye on.

"How long are your shifts?"

A person can only effectively monitor screens for about sixty minutes, at the outside, before it all becomes a boring blur. Surveillance. I'd sooner watch a Power Point presentation on bathroom cleaning than stare at surveillance screens all day.

"We swap every thirty to forty minutes. There is always someone in here."

Good to know.

"How do you handle security with children in the house?" Or, for that matter, a stir-crazy FBI agent. I could sense restlessness edging in. That'd shake things up.

"Ma'am. Security will be increased with the little ones around. I have a full evacuation plan taking into account the ages of the little people. The security crew for the next three days consists of three shifts, eight men each shift." I looked at him, there may have been a question in my eyes. "By men, ma'am, I mean *persons*. We have two females on staff."

I tried hard not to smile. "Sounds like you have it covered Cameron." I shook his hand again. "I'm pleased to know you."

"Likewise, ma'am."

Without a holster and a weapon I felt almost naked. Without a weapon. The words hung in my mind. Cameron needed to know.

"For your information, I have my Glock in a safe upstairs. Delta A will be armed when they arrive this evening." Because that's how we roll.

He picked up a pen. "Who am I looking for?"

"SSA Sam Jackson, he'll be the big black guy who looks more like a linebacker than a Fed. SSA Lee Davenport, easily recognized, he looks a little like a bigger tougher version on Tony Sharron. Dr. Kurt Henderson, he's kinda Noah Wylie meets Kevin Costner, but taller. Or at least that's how I see them. You may see something completely different."

Cameron chuckled. "I'm sure your descriptions do them justice."

"We'll see. Our SAC, Caine Grafton - he'll be the grumpy old bastard with them. There should be no other weapons coming in other than ours."

"We'll be watching. The problem with costume parties can be determining which guns are real and which are costume accessories. We're all over it."

"You'll be checking invitations against a guest list and asking for ID at the gate and at the door?"

"Yes, ma'am."

Rowan smiled at me. "You okay with this?"

"Yes."

"Can you go back to being Ellie my girlfriend and not Ellie the Fed now?"

"We'll see." I turned to Cameron. "Thanks for your patience. I'll see you tonight."

"Yes, ma'am. Looking forward to it."

Rowan showed me the back staircase. So there were two staircases and an elevator. I'd tried to commit the floor plans on the wall in Cameron's office to memory but missed a lot. Now I knew where to find plans, I could go back and check them out whenever.

4.

Six-fifteen. I knew it wasn't morning despite the alarm clock beeping like a backing truck. I rolled over and smacked the offending alarm clock with the flat of my hand. I slowly rolled back and opted to lie still for a minute or two. Rested but not ready start ball preparations led me to closing my eyes.

"Hey, it's time to wake up," Rowan called from the doorway. I opened an eye. He waved my costume from the coat hanger it hung on. "Your dress awaits my queen."

"Already?" I said with a yawn.

He laid the dress across the end of the bed. "Already." His eyes probed mine. "Don't like balls?"

I grinned. "Wanna rephrase that?"

A chuckle flowed from Rowan. "No." His laughter writhed on the carpeted floor for a moment before he spoke again. "But I should. Don't like dances?"

My smiled faded as a memory edged in. A Butterfly Foundation fundraiser which involved me talking to people who had zero concept of the real world and more small talk than I thought was possible. We were all lucky I didn't shoot anyone. A sigh rattled inside me as I thought about my weapon in the safe. No fear of me shooting anyone this time.

"They're not exactly a regular occurrence in my life. And I didn't much enjoy the last one."

"You'll have fun. I promise."

"You shouldn't make promises you can't keep," I muttered, swinging my legs over the side of the bed and standing.

"Shall I wait?"

"No need. I'm sure you have things to do."

"I do, but I'm happy to wait."

"I'll shower and meet you somewhere?"

A wicked grin spread across his lips. "You want a hand?"

"I have two already," I replied. "I think I'm good."

"I'm pretty helpful," he said the flicker in his eyes told me he was keen to help.

"Go on, shoo." I flapped a hand at him on my way to the bathroom.

From the shower I heard a text alert from my phone and then Rowan's voice from the bathroom doorway. "You got a text from someone called Cassandra."

Shit.

"Okay, I'll be out in a minute." The hot water rushed over my body, swirling soap suds down the drain. I wished I was inside one of the bubbles and whooshing out to sea.

My phone went again. Dammit. I turned the water off and grabbed a towel. By the time I'd wrapped it round me Rowan was in the doorway with my phone in his hand.

"Who is Mac?"

"I don't know."

That was honest.

"You were married to a Mac."

"I am aware who I was married to. It obviously is *not* my dead husband," I snapped, taking the phone from his hand and looking at the most recent text messages.

"They're not nice messages, Ellie. Who are these people?"

I glanced up at Rowan and saw the confusion in his eyes. Here I go again, upsetting people without even trying.

"I don't know, Rowan. I have no idea."

Certainly not my deceased friend and husband.

Cassandra: *Why are you still breathing?*

Mac: *There's nothing for you in NJ. Nothing, for you, anywhere.*

The temptation to reply grew with each message. Do not engage with lunatics. Do not engage. I scrolled back and read all the messages again. Someone was pissed at me and I had no clue why. Another message popped onto my screen.

Cassandra: *Why are your arms always covered. Is it true you cut yourself?*

Nice.

"Did you just get another one?"

"Yep."

"Are you going to reply?"

"No."

The phone buzzed in my hand again. I glanced at the screen and wished I hadn't.

Mom: *You're dangerous. People get hurt around you.*

"Was that another one?"

My eyes met Rowan's. "Uh huh."

"How did those people get your phone number?"

Guess there's a phone book in the after life?

"I'm an FBI agent, my business cards are handed out like lollipops," I said trying to keep incredulousness from my voice.

Rowan shook his head. "I'll leave you to get ready," he said, annoyance eased into the cracks in his words. "Obviously you're not going to tell me what this is about."

The second the door closed I called Lee.

"Are you on your way?"

"Sure are. We're about an hour out. Problem?"

"A few more texts. Seems Mac, Mom, and Cassie don't want me in New Jersey. Or alive. Did y'all find anything?"

"Three different burner phones. We have the numbers but no current location."

"See ya, when you get here."

I hung up, dropped the phone on the bed and carried on with ball preparations. Not much else I could do.

Rowan came back as I finished my makeup.

I tried a smile. It almost worked. "So who is here?"

Rowan sat on the bed. "Tony, Jemma, and the kids arrived about an hour ago. Mom and Dad. My brothers. The band. No actual guests yet, too early for them."

I caught about an inch of hair from the front sides of my hair and pull it back, so it met at the nape of my neck. Ignoring the small sparkly barrette sitting on the vanity in the bathroom I opted for a small blonde hair tie. I doubt there would ever be a time that I'd put a barrette in my hair. Bad memories wriggled out of my subconscious like worms rising from the ground in a storm. With luck a couple of ducks would wander in and gobble them up.

Before too long the King and Queen were ready for the ball, I dropped my phone into a small drawstring purse that matched my dress. Again I heard Queen of Hearts playing. I glanced around the room. The music came from everywhere and no where.

"Do you hear that?"

"There's nothing to hear," Rowan replied, opening the door for me.

I shrugged. "Thought I heard music."

Rowan looked at me for a second, I thought he was going to speak but he changed his mind.

Rowan and I went to Tony and Jemma's rooms.

Their costumes were great, they like us opted for more traditional and less scary. Tony suited being George Washington and Jemma was a stunning Martha Washington.

I met the kids and they were cute. Six-year-old Alex, four-year-old Samantha, and sixteen-month-old Charlie. The Italian nanny took charge and whisked them all off to baths and bed.

The four of us descended the stairs together. I took an instant liking to Jemma. Anyone who could keep Tony the terror in line was okay in my book.

As we reached the last few stairs, a flash went off. I stumbled trying to clear my vision. Freaking flashes. Why? Something touched my arm and pulled me back from the brink of the horror of my life and into Rowans. My eyes focused. I half expected to see paparazzi in my face but then remembered that Rowan had security guards. That wouldn't happen. I looked past the flashes in my eyes and discovered Rowan's mom.

She smiled, and apologized for the flash.

"It's okay," I muttered with what I hoped was a sweet smile. Rowan pulled me aside. Mrs. Grange carried on walking with Tony and Jemma to the ballroom.

Ballroom. Because every self respecting famous person has a ballroom.

"You almost fell."

"A flash went off in my face." I lowered my voice. "What would you have me do? Dance a fucking jig?"

"What the hell is wrong with you?" he matched my tone.

"Nothing."

Nothing he can do anything about anyway. Standing right in front of me breathing my air and oozing annoyed concern wasn't helpful. I bit back a smile. Annoyed concern. That was a great description.

"Is it those text messages?"

"What do you think?"

"Where's your phone?"

"In my tiny little purse."

"You should've left it in the bedroom."

"It doesn't concern you Rowan."

"Really?" He looked over my shoulder then refocused on me. "It concerns you therefore it concerns me. Who are those people and why are they texting you?"

"You wanna do this? Do you? Because if you question me with that tone tonight is over before it began." Music filled the air as the ballroom doors swung open then closed again. "Pretty sure your adoring guests are waiting for you."

His pale blue eyes flicked from mine to the doors.

"Just family and the band so far, they don't mind waiting."

"I have nothing to say. We may as well go in."

He took my hand. "I know there is something going on."

"You know more than me then don't you?"

"I saw two of the messages. It's something. Do you know who Mac and Cassandra are?"

"For all we know it was a wrong number situation."

"Nice try. A wrong number wouldn't come up with a name."

Yeah, well, that's true, kinda.

"Let's just go in there and get this hell over with."

"There we go, the real problem. You don't want to be here."

I rolled my eyes so hard I nearly toppled backwards.

"This is not my ideal way to spend an evening, that's true, but it's happening." I pressed some gravel into my voice. "Shall we go?" I said. I didn't want to argue anymore, it would get us nowhere. I had no answers for him. What am I going to say? Dead people are texting me? That's believable. Such is my life. Does he really want to be part of it or does he want to change it?

He sucked in a deep inward breath. "Yes."

Arm in arm we walked into the ballroom. I just hoped my smile didn't look as forced as it felt.

My eyes searched the expansive room for life, apart from Tony and Jemma there was none. Rowan's mother and father were nowhere to be seen. The entire room was decked out in Halloween finery. Spider webs, spiders, caldrons of dry ice, ghosts, ghouls, mummies, and so forth all lined the walls, or climbed from the tables or out of the floor. It was very cool and very creepy. At the far end was a stage, I saw a drum kit, keyboards, and several guitars on stands.

"Are you playing?" I asked Rowan.

He nodded. "A couple of songs."

"Live band, apart from you?"

"Yes."

The drummer and pianist, Martin and Derek emerged from the wall, or a door disguised as wall. It was a good disguise. They sauntered over looking like they'd come straight from a meeting of the *Sons of Liberty*. I guessed Martin to be John Hancock and Derek to be Patrick Henry. They'd be better suited to *Sons of Anarchy*. I could see them in leather jackets roaring in on Harley's.

"Hi ya Ellie," Derek said with a flourish and a deep bow.

"Good to see you both," I replied with a laugh.

"What time are people arriving?" Tony asked.

Rowan smiled. "Depends how fashionable they want to be. The invites said eight-thirty."

"Time for a quiet drink before hand?"

"Excellent idea. Not here though ..." He looked around for his mother. I followed his gaze and spotted her on the far side of the room. Pretty sure she wasn't there before. "Mom, can you hold the fort?"

"Yes, darling. Will you be in the bar?"

He nodded. His mother hurried away to do whatever she was doing. I imagined it was to organize the last few things and probably make some small suggestions to the planner. I bet she had suggestions for the planner. She seemed the type to have highly important last minute suggestions.

Tony led the way, and I followed with Rowan. Reminding myself to keep my mouth under control and be nice. The bottom floor was mostly unexplored by me. We walked down a long hallway, before Tony opened a door. The room resembled several pubs I'd been in, during my time in New Zealand. Wood panels lined the walls, the bar itself was wood paneled, high round wooden tables were dotted about the floor and there was still left plenty of room for full size pool table.

"What's everyone having?" Tony asked slipping behind the bar. "Ellie? You're the proper guest here, what would you like?"

"I'd like a tequila sunrise, please."

"Tequila, orange juice, grenadine?"

I nodded.

Tony played bar tender until we all had drinks. We sat on bar stool at a table drinking and chatting about life.

For the first time I had a chance to get to know Jemma. I confirmed my initial opinion, I did indeed like her. She was a lawyer. She was smart, funny, and adored by Tony.

Everything began to feel comfortable as the conversation progressed. I suspect the tequila helped. Jemma noticed the sparkling diamond on my finger and made comment, "*That* is a beautiful stone."

"Yes it is."

Rowan caught my eye. There was a hint of sadness in the depth of the pale blue. Jemma didn't miss a thing, she caught our moment.

"Are you engaged?"

Tony looked up at the sound of his wife's voice. "Say that again, Jem."

"They're engaged."

"No," I shook my head. "We are not engaged."

Tony didn't appear to hear me and raised his glass. "So you finally popped the question. About time too."

"No, we are not engaged," I said with a touch more force. The ring sparkling on my finger was put there by my husband. "This is not from Rowan."

Tony stopped, he looked from me to Rowan. "Really?"

"Really," Rowan said. "You think I'd keep that a secret?"

"Guess not."

The small purse on my lap buzzed. I opened the purse and tipped my phone toward me without bringing it into the light. A text filled the screen.

Mac: *There's still time to leave.*

I closed the purse. Rowan whispered in my ear, "Was that ...?"

"It's nothing to worry about."

Rowans mother appeared at eight-thirty saying guests were arriving. We left Mrs. Grange to kick the band out to the bar and hustle them back to the ballroom. She was quite at home overseeing the planner and the band. It was not a life I ever wanted. I would need an entire Youtube series on 'how to plan an event without shooting anyone'. My thoughts amused me but only for a moment. That was not my future.

Rowan and I slipped into the elevator unseen and emerged on the third floor. Back in his room, I took the opportunity to freshen up. Rowan did the same, while he was in the bathroom I checked my phone.

Cassandra: *You brought this on yourself. Die and make the world a better place.*

Great.

What have I brought upon myself, I wondered. The toilet flushed. I could hear the water running in the bathroom sink. Rowan was washing his hands. I sent a screen shot to Kurt and dropped my phone in my purse just as the door opened.

"Time to rock an' roll," Rowan said, with a grin.

"Good." I smiled, hoping it wasn't as fake looking as it felt. "Then let's go and have some fun."

"You're sure?"

"Absolutely."

Let's get down there before I change my mind. Maybe I'll find out what exactly I have brought on myself. My gut twisted and turned, then flopped.

"Come on, Ellie. Let's go knock their socks off."

"It's going to be fun, right?"

He wrapped his arms around me. I should feel safer

than I'd ever felt before. Untouchable. Whomever it was trying to freak me out should not be able to get me, not here, not with Rowan's security and my team. Not even ghosts should be able to reach me here. My brain wasn't buying into feeling secure. It was driven by my gut and that said trouble was brewing.

"You're sure you're okay?"

"Yep. Sorry for being snippy earlier."

His grin broadened with one last squeeze he released me from his embrace, took my hand and said, "Let's make an entrance."

Sure, okay, perfect.

I spent most of my career-walking, cart wheeling, and doing back flips on a knife-edge, this felt like another sort of edge or was it a ledge and I wore slippery shoes? Doris Day spun into my minds eye singing, *Que Sera Sera.*

Doris was right, we can't see the future.

It wasn't exactly comforting.

A thought occurred to me as we walked down the sweeping staircase from the top floor, I didn't know who would be at the party. Apart from Rowan's family, Delta A, and the band, I was clueless. Doris sang louder.

Not helping Doris. Not helping at all. I felt the smile slide off my lips as I contemplated crazy texts, a night without a weapon, and the steady erosion of my confidence and ability. Doris Day relentlessly told me *whatever will be will be*, and dragged the final ounce of anything good into a dark hole.

"Smile," Rowan said, as we descended the last ten steps. The double doors to the ballroom opened briefly. I saw people. A lot of people. Good chance one or more of them weren't super friendly.

"This is a smile," I mumbled.

His hand rested in the small of my back as we walked toward the doors. Two men in dark suits stood on either side. As we neared I saw audio tubes running from their ears. Figuring they weren't robots or bombs, I went with security.

Cameron appeared.

We stopped at the doors.

"Ready?" Rowan asked.

No. I'd like to leave now. My mouth betrayed me and lied to Rowan, "Yes."

Cameron spoke quietly, "King and Queen are at the ball."

Awesome. It didn't matter that it was invitation only. That there was a guest list. Or that guests passed through security on the way in. The only thing that mattered was the flip flopping of my gut.

The hum of voices grew as the doors swung open revealing a vibrant crowd. I couldn't see any I recognized. I looked over at Cameron. He was focused on the crowd. Imagining my Glock and holster hidden in the folds of the dress I wore didn't make it so. Didn't quell the twitchy feeling in my bones either.

I walked into the new hell on Rowan's arm and along a

red carpet that I hadn't noticed earlier. The temptation to add a royal wave was high. That'd probably piss people off so I opted for a serene smile instead. I hoped it was serene. From experience I knew that my serene could look a lot like a scary grimace.

The costumes were incredible and the room was even more enchanting than earlier. Life made the difference. Rowan and I climbed the steps to the small stage. A sudden overwhelming feeling of dread hit me as I looked out over the room and all the faces looking back at me. Rowan had a microphone in his right hand. He held my hand right hand with his left, probably to stop me running.

"It's great seeing so many happy faces all at once. Hope you're all having a good time," he said, with a grin.

A cheer went up. I heard Tony's voice as the noise died down but couldn't hear what he'd said. I think Rowan did, judging by the gesture he made.

"I'd like to take this opportunity to introduce you all to Ellie Conway. Some of you know her already."

Another cheer went through the throng of people in front of us. I looked out I saw Lee, Sam, and Kurt. Lee gave me a small wave, Sam did a thumb up. Kurt smiled. My stomach churned.

The microphone was in my face. I could feel my eyes getting wider and wider. The voice in my head told me to speak another voice told me to run. I took a breath.

No words.

Nothing.

Nada.

Rowan held my hand tighter and removed the instrument of torture.

"Now that you've met Ellie ..." He grinned and paused, then shrugged and pretended to walk away with me. With a backward glance over his shoulder and a cheeky grin he said, "nah."

Facing the crowd once more. He took the microphone and placed it in the cradle on the stand in front of him.

"A toast." Rowan glanced around.

Tony edged his way through the crowd carrying two champagne glasses. He joined us on the stage.

I whispered to Rowan, "This could end badly."

He took the glasses from Tony and handed me one, subtly leaning into me as he did so. "Yes, it could."

Everyone raised their glasses.

"To a wonderful night with good friends and laughter." The toast was echoed by voices below us. Glasses clinked and chimed. Nothing bad happened. "The band and I would like to play a little something, I wrote for Ellie."

I looked down in time to see Martin, Derek, climbing the steps. I made a move toward the steps only to have Rowan grab my hand. "Stay? Please ..."

"I can't, you're going to sing something I don't know about *me* I'll be happier down there with the guys."

When I looked at Lee, he was shaking his head. Sam was glaring at me. I got the feeling Lee and Sam would put me right back up on the stage if I escaped. Then Caine stepped up beside them. I was screwed.

Trapped.

Rowan's joking threat about getting me on stage again one day, wasn't. I looked over at the main doors. Cameron stood in front of them. I watched him for a second, trying not to appear obvious. He stood, feet apart, hands clasped loosely in front, head on swivel as he continually scanned the room. My vision flipped from Cameron to Caine. Who was now positioned with his back to a wall on the right of the stage. He mirrored Cameron.

Something must've happened. They knew something. Kurt had shifted. When I found him and caught his attention his hands moved. I watched. He signed it was okay.

Then maybe they were being cautious. I gave him a discreet thumbs up. My phone buzzed. I wanted to look but I couldn't.

Rowan kept me close. There was no escape. I wasn't close I was a prisoner. Seemed smart to distract myself by checking the guests costumes. Not a vampire, naughty nurse, or school uniform to be seen but quite a high number of historic figures. Not like Halloween parties I remembered.

Rowan's voice broke into my thoughts every now and then. I heard the lyrics of the song and knew he'd written about me. I had no clue if I liked it or not. Hearing a song like that was weird. Can't say I'd ever imagined being immortalized in song. The song ended, applause rang out, and we stepped down off the stage followed by the band. Another band took over. I didn't even look to see who they were. The relief at getting off the stage was great. People were talking. Their voices climbed the walls and clung to the drapes, filling folds and crevices with sound. Another buzz from my purse. Rowan moved ahead of me a few feet. I seized the opportunity to check my phone without removing it from my purse I read the texts.

Mac: *Always stunning in red.*
Cassandra: *If you cut yourself now no one would know.*

I snapped the purse shut and looked around. Rowan turned and held out his hand.

"Come on, time to meet and greet." While Rowan and I moved among the guests I watched everyone and carefully avoiding any conversations that started with, 'so you're an FBI agent'. It's been my experience that that is usually followed by 'ever killed anyone'. And we're not going there.

My refusal to partake in reading of tabloids, glossy magazines, gossip columnists, or watch entertainment TV shows, left me at a serious disadvantage when it came to recognizing people I was introduced to. Pretty sure I was supposed to know a lot of them. When it came down to it

I was just glad none had crossed my radar work wise.

We wound our way back toward Lee and Sam. They mingled with Caine in tow. I noted Caine's posture. He wasn't as relaxed as he tried to appear. I scoured the room for Cameron. For a brief instance a gaggle of women parted allowing me a glimpse. Cameron was still by the main doors. His mouth moved slightly. I looked back at Caine. His mouth moved. I studied him, as he turned I saw the audio tube from his ear.

He and Cameron were working together.

Rowan was shaking Lee's hand. They spoke for a few minutes, giving me time to survey the room trying to find whatever it was that had Cameron and Caine concerned.

Rowan touched my arm. "You okay?"

I smiled. "Yes."

"I'll be around, come look for me ... I need to go say hello to some more people."

Rowan moved away through groups of people, they all spoke to him as he passed by.

I moved closer to Lee "What's going on Lee?"

He grimaced. "That last text message came from the vicinity of this estate."

"And that means what?"

"Pinged off the closest cell tower to the estate. That's all I have." He shot me a wide grin. "Don't worry Ellie, Delta A is on the job."

"I'll raise you a pair." I showed him the last texts I received.

His smile vanished. "Shit. That's gotta be from in here."

"Yes, yes, it does." Keeping a smile on my face and my tone light proved difficult. "Somewhere in the crowd is at least one crazy person."

"At least one."

I almost laughed.

"Any clue who we're looking for?"

"We don't know, but it's not a ghost, that's for real."

"Someone who is pissed at me," I said with a sigh. "That's a fucking long list but I imagine it's a shorter list in this room."

I don't know anyone here apart from the band and my team. My mind revolved over the band and ruled them all out. They were nearby and none of them used their phones when I got the last two texts.

Lee chuckled. "We've got our work cut out for us."

"Thanks."

"Be aware Chicky, eyes open," Lee said with a smile. "We'll find whoever it is."

"Could be three people," I said.

Lee nodded.

On the pretext of looking for Rowan, I climbed the steps to the stage and looked out over the room. The added three feet made a huge difference. A man I hadn't noticed before followed Rowan as he moved from person to person, stopping here and there for longer chats. Another two men appeared to be security and were mingling amongst the guests.

A few people noticed me on the stage, then Tony saw me. Next thing I knew he was standing beside me. He slung an arm casually around my neck.

"What are we doing?" he asked with a cheeky smile on his face.

"Just looking, " I replied. "For Rowan." My eyes hit on another security guy. So far I'd found six.

Tony pointed. "He's over by the doors to the garden ... talking to our manager and the head of the record company."

I followed Tony's finger and saw Rowan and another male Perhaps he should've carried a ball of yarn and fed it out as he walked, or maybe small pebbles? They looked deep in conversation.

"Maybe I should leave them to talk."

"You feeling a bit lost Ellie?"

More threatened than lost but whatever. Tony held my arm as we descended the steps. "Come sit with me and Jemma." Tony's head turned. "Where's Lee, it ain't the same without my double around."

I laughed. "He's that way," I replied with a subtle point of my index finger to the left. "That's where I saw him last. You going to search him out?"

"I wanna get him on stage, that'd be all kinds of fun."

My phone buzzed.

"And freak people out, a doppelgänger will do that."

"Jemma is over there," He said with a nod of his head.

"Can I get you anything?"

"Yeah, a drink please."

"One tequila sunrise coming right up."

We separated. Before I joined Jemma I checked my phone.

Mac: *No one wants you here. No one wants you breathing.*

Delightful. Jemma turned and waved to me. I hurried to her table. She sat with two women who looked to be in their late twenties.

"Ellie! Sit with us." Jemma smiled. "This is Amanda and her cousin Sarah." She pointed to the red head first then the curly brunette.

"Hi," I said, sitting across from the women and next to Jemma. "Are you relatives of Rowan's or friends?"

"Friends, I guess," Amanda replied.

I kept my voice soft. "You are either are or you're not."

She laughed. "Then I am."

I looked around hoping to see Tony and my drink. He could hurry up.

"And you're Rowan's girlfriend?" Sarah said, toying with her drink coaster.

"Yes."

"You're a bit different to his usual type," she said.

"Didn't know he had a type."

Amanda chuckled. "He used to like being fawned

over."

My turn to laugh. They didn't know him at all.

I finally saw Tony weaving his way around people carrying drinks. He handed me mine and Jemma hers. "Ladies. Are we having fun?" Tony slid into a chair on the other side of Jemma.

Jemma leaned close and whispered something in his ear.

They were an adorable couple. He whispered back then excused himself from the table.

"I'll be back in a minute, it's my turn to check on the children."

"What's it like being an FBI agent?" Sarah asked, she stopped fiddling with the drink coaster and took a sip from her glass.

"Bit hard for me to say, I've never been anything else."

She seemed to consider my answer for a moment. Amanda smiled and asked, "Is it dangerous?"

"Sometimes."

Sarah took another sip of her drink, placed the glass on the coaster and leaned forward. "Shot a lot of people?"

Enough with the questions. My turn. "What do you do?"

"I work for an advertising agency."

"And you?" I turned to face Amanda.

"Personal Assistant to Derek."

"Ever been shot?" Sarah asked.

Oh, good, the questions are back.

"It's mostly paperwork and not terribly exciting."

"That's not what we heard." Amanda nudged Sarah. "Is it Sarah?"

"Not at all what we heard. I've seen you on the news a few times. Your husband was killed working with you, wasn't he?" Sarah fiddled with the drink coaster. Her eyes flicked up to meet mine, glinting with delight. "And a friend of yours. Surely that can't be true."

"Sounds dangerous to me," Amanda agreed.

"Didn't your mother die horribly?"

Mac, Cassandra, mom. All the text messages rolled through my head. Didn't seem like a coincidence. My trigger finger twitched. A voice in my head whispered, 'Let it go. This isn't the place.'

Jemma intervened. "Your curiosity is bordering on annoying. How about a different topic of conversation?"

Sarah looked set to ask another question when my mouth got the better of me. "So you work for an advertising agency, ever had a paper cut?"

Jemma laughed. Sarah didn't.

"I imagine it's pretty dangerous with all that paper and hot coffee in a confined space," Jemma said to me but just loud enough for the two women to hear.

"Stuff nightmares are made of," I said, biting back laughter.

Neither Amanda nor Sarah were amused. A switch flipped, their manner changed.

"Where's your gun?" Sarah placed her drink on the table and looked at me.

"Where's your pencil?" I countered. The little voice in my head that sounded like mom cautioned me I chose to override it. "Take a note: Don't annoy the FBI agent, she doesn't like it."

"You shouldn't even be here," Sarah said. "You're not his type."

Had a feeling she thought she was Rowan's type. Didn't stop me wanting to reach across the table and slap the stupid smirk off her face.

Jemma intervened. "I think you two have had enough to drink. I'll get Cameron to call you a cab." Before she could be stopped Jemma rose and disappeared into the crowd.

And just like that Sam pulled Jemma's chair out and sat down.

"Ladies," he said by way of a greeting. "Is there a problem?"

They didn't move or speak.

"Seems they're not my biggest fans," I said.

Sam smiled, leaned back and looked at the women. "Ellie has enough fans she doesn't need you two. I doubt very much that a single fuck will be given."

Amanda sank a little lower in her chair but Sarah sat up straighter.

"She shouldn't be near Rowan. People like her are dangerous."

Sam and I made eye contact. He reached his hand

across the table to Sarah. "Give me your phone. Now."

She shook her head, leaned back and folded her arms across her chest "You can't demand my phone because I don't like someone."

"Hand it over," Sam growled.

Lee crossed my line of vision and stepped up behind the women. His shadow fell over the table. Amanda looked as though she wanted the floor to open up and swallow her. Lee's placed his hand on Sarah's shoulder. "Your phone, ma'am."

She tried to shake his hand off by shaking her shoulder. Didn't work.

"Again, you can't demand my phone. I have rights."

"Yes, you do." Lee hauled her to her feet.

She wriggled and protested, her cries of indignation growing louder in increments. He dragged one hand behind her back then the other. The metallic sound of hand cuffs closing sealed the deal.

Sam hit the table in front of Amanda. "Where's her phone?"

Sarah tried to kick at her and snarled. Lee spun her out of the way.

"Down there," Amanda said, pointing to the floor. "There's a small purse on the floor. It's in that."

Lee moved Sarah out of the way.

Amanda didn't seem keen to help by passing the purse to us. I slipped around the table and picked up the purse while Sarah did her best to evade Lee's grip and kick at me.

Nice.

I tipped the contents of the purse onto the table. Two phones. One was an iPhone the other a much cheaper phone. The last message sent from the cheap phone matched the last text I received from Mac. I scrolled through the messages. All the messages I'd received in the last twenty-four hours supposedly from my dead husband were there. Her iPhone was locked.

"She sent the messages from Mac," I said. Turning my attention to Amanda. "Where is your phone?"

We were doing our best to downplay what was happening but it wasn't the easiest. Caine and Cameron joined the table. Cameron took charge of Sarah and had someone remove her from the ballroom via a nearby concealed doorway. Amanda handed me her purse. Only one phone. I handed it to her. She unlocked it. No messages matching anything I'd received. I handed it back.

"Do you know if your cousin has other friends here tonight?"

She shook her head. "She never mentioned anyone."

I looked at Caine. "She can stay, we have nothing on her. Could be two other people in here though."

My phone buzzed. I took it from my purse and read the text.

Cassandra: *Still breathing but for how long?*

I passed it to Lee. He read all the messages they'd missed out on since arriving. When my phone buzzed again he handed it back. "Your Mom wants you."

"Yay."

Mom: *He's not for you. You're not for anyone.*

A burst of popping sounds came from outside but close. I looked at Sam. "Tell me that was fireworks?" A cold pit developed in my gut. I knew it wasn't. "Rowan?"

I stood, but still couldn't see him. I gathered my dress into my right hand and climbed onto the chair. Rowan was still by the garden doors. Sam took my hand and helped me off the chair. We hurried through the throngs of people toward the garden doors.

Sam brought his mouth close to my ear. "You're not armed?"

"Didn't go with my dress," I said with a shrug. "I can be. I know where the arms are stored."

I overheard some people say that someone must've let off a few fireworks by mistake. I guess everyone expected a display. Let's hope it was one they would all enjoy.

I politely interrupted Rowan's conversation. "A word, please," I whispered.

We walked away leaving Sam to make idle chitchat while surreptitiously maneuvering people away from the glass doors.

"Did you hear the noises outside?"

"Yeah. A car backfiring?" He sounded hopeful. His hope was baseless, the house was so far back from the road that road noises wouldn't penetrate the walls.

"Did you plan a fireworks display?"

His crestfallen look said it all. "It's a surprise. Are you incapable of allowing yourself to be surprised?"

"Pretty much." I kissed his cheek. "Surprises have a way of *backfiring.*"

"I'm sorry. I didn't mean to sound pissy."

"It's okay, I don't mean to ruin your fun."

I love fireworks. Those huge aerial displays the noise, the smell. I love everything about fireworks. Except how they can sometimes sound like gunfire, I don't love that so much.

Another burst of explosive noises resounded, this time closer. It wasn't fireworks.

"That's not fireworks going off by mistake is it?" Rowan said, with rainbows of hope ringing his words.

I shook my head. "I don't think so."

"Is there a problem?" He held me at arms length and looked me straight in the eye.

"Possibly. I need to get to Cameron and Caine, I'll be back as soon as I can." I kissed him. His warm lips tasted like champagne.

"I'm sticking with you." I saw a flash of alarm on his face. "Is this something to do with the texts?"

"It's possible. You should go in the opposite direction to me."

"No. El. We stick together."

There was no time for an argument. "Come on then. Smile, but dodge distractions," I said.

He took my arm, Sam stepped in behind us, and we made our way through unsuspecting dancers and minglers to Cameron's last known position. Snippets of conversation found my ears as we moved through groups of people. No one seemed to pay the least bit of notice to the noises we'd heard outside. Halloween, maybe they expected strange noises. Cameron was back by the main doors. I knew he'd heard the noises.

"SSA Conway," Cameron said with a small smile. "What can I do for you?"

"You can tell me what's going on outside?" I said with a sociable countenance that I hoped would fool anyone over hearing.

"Fireworks malfunction," he replied as the door behind him opened. Two women excused themselves. Cameron stepped out of the way. They carried on, chatting and laughing toward the middle of the room.

"Fireworks, my ass."

My phone buzzed again. My stomach dropped so fast I felt sick. I checked the message.

Mom: *People are going to die because of you.*

I passed the phone over my shoulder to Sam. He pressed it back into my hand as he moved up next to me.

61

"Cameron, how many people have you got inside the house?"

"Eight."

"Outside?"

"Six."

"We in lockdown?"

"Yes, we are, Agent Jackson."

My mind jumped in and out of possible scenarios. Rowan stood next to me. Silent. My phone buzzed again. I wanted to smash it into a zillion pieces. Instead I looked at the screen.

Mom: *This is why you should never be a parent.*

Too late Mom, I've got a kid. And she's okay. Safe, home, with Dad. Because I made the call to keep them away from this potential disaster. I'll wear the wrath of my teen later. There are kids here. Lunatics with guns and children. Two things that should never be together.

"Is there someone with the children?"

Cameron nodded. "I have an armed female guard outside the suite with the nanny and the kids."

"Elevator access?"

"Locked down."

"Stairs?"

"Both sets are guarded."

Rowan found his voice, "Worst case scenario?"

"Gun men break in, taking of hostages, loss of life."

"Don't let that happen, Cameron."

"No, sir."

Rowan pulled me to him, making it look as though we were dancing. Plenty of other couples were dancing, the music was loud. It seemed louder than before.

"Please don't get involved in whatever this is … let security handle it. Please, Ellie."

I leaned my head on his shoulder.

Cameron interrupted us. "You should move toward the middle of the room, and keep away from the windows and doors."

"I'm the target," I replied, with a smile. I looked away as if interested only in Rowan.

"Ma'am?" he said quietly.

I turned my head on Rowans shoulder and spoke to Cameron, "I don't want this night turned into something I can't think about. There's been way too much of that already in my life."

"Yes, ma'am"

"We need this situation contained."

From the corner of my eye, I saw Caine, Lee, and Sam moving quickly toward one of the internal doors.

Rowan's arms tightened around me. "I see them too," he whispered. "Tell me what you want to do."

"I want to stop it. I need to find whoever is doing this and stop it."

"Ellie, can you let Cameron and Delta deal with it."

"Dance this way," I said tapping the top of his right

foot lightly. I saw Tony, he lifted a glass up when I looked over Rowan's shoulder at him. "Tony has my drink."

"That's good, a drink will help," Rowan replied.

"It might, tequila makes most things look better."

We made it to Tony and Jemma's table, they were alone. I could tell by the look on Tony's face that Jemma had filled him in on Sarah and Amanda.

The occasional popping sound interspersed through the music. I saw Tony's eyes flick toward the french doors that led to the garden.

"Something wrong, Tony?" I asked, keeping my voice level.

A quick frown crossed his face. "I thought I heard something outside."

"How odd," I replied and took a large swig of my drink.

Rowan leaned one elbow on the table and did a casual glance around the room. He smiled at some people, waved to others, and then beckoned to his mother.

She made her way to us.

"Darling, having a lovely time?" She crooned and kissed his cheek. "I'd better get back to your father, he's telling stories."

"Oh, Lordy," Rowan groaned and pretended to bang his head on the table.

"Did any of you hear anything outside a few minutes ago?"

We all shrugged. Rowan said, "Fireworks issue. They have it under control."

She left.

It was only a matter of time before someone heard something that wasn't so easily shrugged off, or something was seen through one of the doors. Or worse, someone wanted to leave and then discovered they couldn't. I leaned on Rowan, and draped an arm around his neck, bringing his ear close to my mouth. I whispered into his ear, "Hey Rowan, can we shut the curtains over the doors without anyone noticing?"

"We could," he replied and nuzzled my neck.

I had an idea.

"Yeah, we could, if you and the band got up on the stage and played." Grange were the perfect distraction.

"Clever," he said , his voice husky and low. He kissed me long and hard. When he let me go I leaned back in my chair and fanned my face. Jemma laughed.

"Tony," Rowan nodded toward the stage. "Shall we?"

Tony nodded, with a cheesy grin plastered on his face. "Excellent idea." He let rip a high whistle. Martin and Derek spun around and headed over from the far side of the dance floor. Tony pointed to the stage. They changed direction. Rowan kissed me, Tony kissed Jemma, and off they went.

Rowan called for everyone to gather around the stage. People began to move forward toward the top half of the room. Except for Caine and Sam. We made eye contact.

"Jemma, go on up. I'll be right behind you. I need to say hello to my boss."

"Sure," she replied and headed up to find a space near the stage.

I walked across the room, Sam met me near an external door. Outside, with his back to the door was an armed security agent. I pulled the drawstring and closed the heavy drapes.

"You two need to close the other two, before someone sees what *is* out there."

Sam spoke, "I'm on it." He hurried off.

I leveled a stare at Caine. I stepped back and took a few minutes to watch Rowan and the band. From where we stood near the double garden doors I could hear gunshots outside. Intermittent and unnerving. I listened for anyone yelling but no one did. Scuffling feet, running feet, the occasional pop, pop, pop from what I made to be an MP5, and return fire in singles. Sounded like pistol fire.

Running feet passed the doors again.

Cameron was in plain sight now that everyone was up by the stage. "Caine, we can't keep people hostage and offer no explanation."

"What do you suggest that won't cause a riot?"

"The truth. Or a sanitized version. Let me make a statement."

"We don't have the man power in here. We also do not know if it's one assailant or two. If there is another person and they're in this room, then it'll get ugly fast."

I couldn't believe I was having a conversation with

Caine about the necessity of informing the guests.

"You're missing the point here Caine. These people are guests – friends and family of Rowan's, not general public. Jesus most of them have security issues and bodyguards in their every day lives. Saying we have a problem here tonight is not going to freak them out."

His mouth twitched. I read it as a small smile.

"You're not supposed to be working, you know that?"

"... and you've been out of the field too long."

A double twitch.

"Get me up there with Rowan."

Last minute advice flew out of my mouth. "Try to smile when you're up there. Not that tight mouthed lip twitch thing you usually do."

Caine grimaced and bared his teeth.

"How's this?"

"Frightening, because it's an improvement."

We moved closer to the stage so I could attract Rowan's attention. I managed and he called Caine up. I loved that he understood what I wanted from the look I gave him. As Caine was speaking, I hooked my arm through Jemma's and took her aside. I told her what was happening and stressed the children were safe, they had their own guard. I also promised, if I thought anyone was likely to get near them I'd go up myself. I didn't even have my fingers crossed or anything. She was cool. I mean really cool. God alone knew what was happening in her head, but outwardly, she was a portrait of calm.

From my position with Jemma I could see Caine and Cameron. Caine finished up, as imagined, no one was overly concerned. Tony spun off into a guitar solo as Rowan grabbed the microphone again. Caine walked to the edge of the stage muttering to himself, but not really. Cameron was muttering too. Something was wrong. I read Caine's lips as he moved toward me down the steps. The kids.

Something was very wrong.

I headed for Cameron. Lifted my skirt and ran.

Rowan must've seen me and jumped off the stage. He intercepted me at the door, as I rushed to a stop in front of Cameron. His hand grabbed my arm. "Wait!"

"Stand aside, Rowan."

"Let Cameron do whatever it is you are about to do."

I spun on him. "I have to do this. I can't pull Cameron off the ballroom."

Over Rowan's shoulder, Sam came into view.

"Don't go out there, Ellie." I heard something in his voice that sounded suspiciously like an ultimatum.

"That ain't gonna work. Move," I said and reached for the door handle. "This is who I am. I have to do this. I need you to understand that."

Rowan frowned. "I'm fucking trying."

"Try harder."

Cameron opened the door and leaned toward me. "My office, the code is angel four seven zero."

Sam and I stepped through the ballroom doors. When

it locked behind us, I pointed to the hallway that led back to where Cameron's office was situated. A moment later we were in his office and choosing weapons.

Sam took a shotgun, and an MP5. I took a shotgun, and a pistol from the cupboard below the gun rack. The last thing I did in the office was to take a pair of scissors and cut my dress. I cut straight up the middle to above my knee, then made a cut across the fabric.

"Sam, rip this for me."

He knelt down and took the fabric in both hands, with a quick tearing motion he ripped the skirt completely around. The bulk of my dress dropped to the floor. Good to go.

The door self locked. I checked the door handle to make sure, and we left. I guided Sam to the backstairs. We passed two security men, one near the kitchen taking care of the staff and one at the bottom of the stairs. I told them both to hold their positions. I knew the three kids were on the third floor, and that's where we were going.

"Where are they?" Sam asked as we reached the third floor landing. He shoved the Ithaca into a large vase standing on the floor by the stairs, it was full of dried flowers and grasses. He opted for the MP5 as primary weapon for sweeping hallways and checking guards.

"Down the hall, should be a guard outside."

A gust of wind caught me. The cold forced the breath from my lungs.

Wind.

We both spun around and saw a broken window. On the courtyard side of the house. I pointed to Sam and then the window. He moved closer to the billowing curtain. I moved away toward the nursery suite. Sam caught up. We leaned against the wall. There was a corner in front of us. And I knew that around the corner should be a security guard. I leaned the shotgun against the wall. Feeling more comfortable with a handgun.

Sam smiled. "Okay?"

I nodded in affirmation.

"Let's do it."

Sam stepped around the corner first.

A male voice called out. "Stop. Identify yourself."

A male voice. That was wrong. A female was on this floor with the nanny and kids.

I stepped behind Sam then moved over. I could plainly see a man. He was not wearing the same shirt as the rest of Cameron's people. It was close but the detail on the breast pocket was different. He had a pistol pointed at us. Not much of a match for Sam's MP5.

"Drop your weapon," I ordered. The key now lay in de-escalation. We were right outside of the nursery suite. I glanced around, no sign of the official guard. "This has all gotten out of control," I said.

"Drop your guns," he said. Recognition left a trail of surprise across his young face. "You. You're not supposed to be here."

Really? And yet there I am.

"Where am I supposed to be?"

"Dead."

"Yeah, that's not happening. Why are you here?" Fighting the adrenaline to remain calm and keep things low key wasn't that easy. "Why are you here?" I repeated slowly.

His pale sweaty skin, the way he stepped back when we came around the corner, and the surprise on his face when he recognized me pointed to inexperience. He didn't fire. He held the gun in a two-handed grip yet his hands shook. His stance was all wrong, he wasn't braced correctly, and his legs were too close together.

My mind was having a hard job reconciling this young, inexperienced man someone who'd scaled a wall and climbed in a broken window.

I changed tactic. "Do you know who I am?"

"Yes," he replied. "Ellie Conway."

"What's your name?"

"Dominic."

He didn't hesitate, so either it was his name or he had practiced saying it. I had a feeling it was his name.

"Dominic, I need to check on the children. I'm sure you don't want to hurt them. I need to check they're okay."

Panic flashed across his face and lingered in his eyes. "What children?"

Good, he didn't know.

"The room you are standing in front of, is where the

children are."

He shook his head. "No, no, it's *your* room."

I shook my head.

"Did someone go in there?"

He didn't answer. His gun wavered.

I looked at Sam. He stepped up, he took the gun from his hand and dropped Dominic without a word. Sam dragged him away from the door, used disposable cuffs to secure his hands and feet, behind his back. Hog-tied and unconscious he posed no problem. I'd started to think his only real threat was that the gun would go off when he fell.

Sam had his ear to the door. "There's movement. Like someone's searching the place."

Why would anyone be searching for anything?

I leaned on the wall. "We going in?"

He looked at me. "Wait."

He listened for a few more seconds.

"If you hear the kids, we're going in," I told him. "We've got the element of surprise."

"Is there another way in?" Sam asked.

My mind flipped through the tour I took of the nursery suite. Yes, there was another way in, through Tony and Jemma's room. It had an internal door connecting to the nursery. "Yes, there is."

I ran down the hall. Sam stayed where he was. I went for a fumble on the handle, and drunken giggle outside the other door. Sam thumbs up at me. My next fumble opened the door. I gave it a shove, let go, and hoped its own weight would swing it wide open. With a secure two-handed grip on my weapon I peered into the room from the doorway. There was no one there. The linking door was closed. I stepped inside and scanned the room to make damn sure it was empty. It was.

Silently I crossed the floor area to the internal door.

I counted down from three, breathing slowly, stopping the adrenaline rush from taking over my body.

Two.

One.

I turned the handle with one hand and shoved the door wide. It flung back, and banged into the doorstop. I pushed my right foot forward to prevent the door coming back at me. I adjusted my grip on the gun, following the gun with my eyes as I swept the room. No sign of the kids. I could see the exit door. Sam hollered, "Halt, FBI." The door slowly closed. "Drop the weapon, on your knees."

To my left I spied the door through to another room, I knew it contained three children, and hopefully a nanny. No sign of the security guard.

Knocking quietly I waited for a few seconds. No one answered. I called out, "FBI, I'm coming in."

I turned the handle, the door was locked. Smart. The nanny must've locked them in.

There was a scuffling noise off to my right. I chose to investigate before asking the nanny to open the door.

Everything went quiet from the hallway.

"Hey Sam?"

He replied, "yeah Ellie?"

"You get them?"

"Trussed up like a thanks giving turkey."

Good to know the noise wasn't bad guys. I moved quickly along the wall to double doors, I figured it was a closet. I flung them open and discovered the security guard. Her mouth was duct taped, her hands and feet duct taped, and she was lying on her side.

"You okay?" I asked helping her sit up. She nodded. "Sorry this is going to sting a bit." I grabbed the corner of the tape over her mouth and ripped it off fast.

"Thanks," she replied. I could see a raised red-welted area from the tape on her face. My attention turned to her bound wrists. I began to peel the tape back, and unwrapped it as quickly as I could. They'd used a lot. I had her hands free a lot faster than it felt. She winced as she bent and undid the tape from her ankles.

"What's your name?" I asked.

"Sue."

"You got your phone?" I asked.

She hooked a phone from her trouser pocket and handed it to me. It was then that I saw a spreading dark stain on her right side above the waistband of her trousers.

"Thanks," I said. With the phone in my hand, I looked around for something to mop up the now rapidly growing

74

bloodstain on her shirt. The contents of the bureau drawers lay scattered about. I grabbed what looked like a tee shirt and gave it to her. "Press this against that wound."

She nodded. I knocked on the door to the children's room and introduced myself. Sue joined me, free of tape, and knocked on the door. She had one hand holding the tee shirt and pressed to her side.

"It's Sue, open up."

The lock clicked and sounds of furniture moving came through the solid door. Eventually the door cautiously opened. We found a frightened nanny and three sleeping kids.

"How'd you keep them asleep?" I asked, nodding toward the lumps in the beds and the smaller lump in the crib.

"I saw the men and the guns. I ran in here before they see me and lock the door, I be very quiet. Then I pull the dresser across it. I don't want them to come in and hurt the babies."

I moved closer to the beds, feeling the pulse of each child. Just in case.

Samantha rolled over, her eyelids flitted. The nanny swooped in and stroked her head, singing softly in Italian. The child drifted back to a deep sleep.

So, that's how she did it.

"Everything's okay now. You can keep the door locked if you want to, until Mr. and Mrs. Sharron come up."

The nanny smiled a little. "I will."

Sue and I left the room, she closed the door behind us, and we both heard it lock. I called Caine from Sue's phone.

My patience was at an all time low, and I couldn't bring myself to make nice. "Tell Rowan the kids are safe."

"Will do."

"One gunman and not sure if the other is male or female, about to find out. And let Cameron know Sue needs medical attention."

"Are you all right?"

"I'm okay."

I hung up and handed the phone back to Sue. She sat down on the sofa. "I think one of them cut me."

No kidding?

"Looks like it," I replied. "Bathroom?"

She pointed back towards the main bedroom. I grabbed a couple of clean hand towels and hurried back to her. I wadded one up and swapped it for the sodden tee shirt. "Can you hold this?"

She nodded and held the towel. She was getting shaky. I pulled a blanket from under the up-ended coffee table and wrapped it around her.

"Let's keep you warm."

She smiled.

"I'll be outside in the hallway. Yell if you need me."

Sam waited with the young man he'd hog-tied earlier and another person wearing all black, face down on the carpet.

Sam grinned at me. "Guess what? I found a phone." He handed it to me. "Check the messages."

All the messages supposedly from my mom. Nice.

I leaned down and pulled the head back of the person who'd been in the room. "You don't look like my mom."

The woman tried to pull her head away. "Just leave Rowan alone. He's not for you."

"I suppose he's for you, is he?" I let her head go and it hit the carpet. Then looked at Sam. "There's one more."

Running feet, rushed toward us from the direction of the stairs at the same time the elevator pinged. I heard wheels moving. Sam and I glanced at each other. We moved backwards into the room with Sue. Sam took the left of the door and I took the right.

"Sam! Ellie!"

Lee. Air rushed from my body. I stepped into the hallway followed by Sam.

"Okay?" Lee asked.

"Yeah. The security guard is wounded." Paramedics came into view. "Over here," I said and pointed toward the open doorway. Sam and I leaned back against a blank piece of wall and watched the paramedics. Lee paced the hallway while on the phone. By the time the paramedics wheeled Sue out Lee had stopped pacing.

He joined us leaning on the wall.

"And?"

"They found the third phone."

"Did it have a person attached to it?" I asked, pushing

off the wall.

"It did. Sarah had a friend in the ballroom after all."

"Fuck this shit all the way to Christmas and beyond, someone needs to pour me a tequila."

The End.

Dead Flowers:

A clean up guy, an assassin, and a senator's wife.

We let SSA Sam Jackson take the wheel and this is the result:

Dead Flowers

1.

I grabbed the phone before it woke Sandra. Blurry eyed I saw Lee's name on the screen and tapped the green icon.

"It's the middle of the night ..." I kept my voice hushed.

"This better be life changing in a good way." Rolling over I eyeballed the clock on the nightstand the large glowing red numbers confirmed it was the middle of the night.

"Kennedy is in a bar here in the city. On our turf," Lee said. Ambient noise surrounded his words.

Easing onto my back I held the phone to my ear. "Where'd you say you saw him?"

Sandra stirred next to me. I paused and saw her eye lids flutter for a second.

"Murphy's."

"You're sure it's Kennedy?" I kept my voice low trying not to wake Sandra.

"Bro, it is Kennedy. Something's going down." Lee sighed. "We need to find out what he's doing and why he's in Virginia before the boss hears about it."

He was right. If Kennedy was in town something bad was going down and it almost always landed in our lap and it almost always ended badly for someone.

"I'm on my way." I touched the end call icon, and plunged my phone into darkness.

Without the glow from my screen my eyes worked hard to adjust to the darkness.

Sandra rolled over, her arm snaking across my body.

As much as I wanted to stay and enjoy the heat as her body pressed against me, I couldn't. Lee was right. We needed to know why Kennedy was in town, and we needed to know before Ellie found out he was around. Be good to be ahead of the game for a change.

I lifted Sandra's arm and slid off the bed. Carefully replacing my body with my warm pillow and draping her arm over it. She sighed and rolled the other way.

With my phone held between my teeth I picked up my jeans, boots, tee shirt, underwear, socks and jacket from the floor and tiptoed from the bedroom with an armful of clothing. I pulled the door closed behind me as best I could then hit the bathroom. I'd left my holster and gun on the kitchen table. Five minutes later there was a note on the coffee maker for Sandra saying I was on a call out and I was in the car heading for Murphy's bar.

Every time I walked into that particular bar Irish jokes floated in my head. There was a hint of Ellie in all of us. I glanced around, not wanting to appear too obvious. At this time of night, the clientele was quite different. The usual law enforcement crowd wasn't in residence. I saw Kennedy at a table with a pretty redhead. Lee caught my eye from a booth in the far corner. I sauntered over and slid in across from him.

"Looks like he's on a date," I said. "How sure are you

that something's going down?"

"I got a photo of her when I went to the bathroom. Ran it. She's not a date."

"Enlighten me, brother."

"She's Grace O'Malley."

I let that absorb, knowing I recognized the name but not being able to place it.

Grace O'Malley. With a sudden clarity that I'm sure rivaled one of Ellie's brain farts I placed the name.

"Didn't she die in sixteen-oh-three?"

Lee grinned.

"Not that Grace O'Malley."

"Not a pirate?"

His head shook. "No. But probably not a million miles from one. She's your extra special twenty-first century assassin."

I attracted the attention of a waitress and ordered a Jameson. Then waited for the drink to arrive before continuing the conversation.

"Assassin isn't a job description that comes up very often," I said and sipped my whisky. "Kennedy and O'Malley are looking cozy over there. Could still be a date?"

Wouldn't be a totally off the wall situation. They probably moved in the same circles. Seems I had a low opinion of Kennedy.

Lee got a familiar look in his eye.

"You're shitting me," he grumbled as he passed me his phone. "Take a look."

I read Grace O'Malley's impressive resume.

"She's one helluva piece of work. Doesn't mean it's not a date."

Lee took the phone and scrolled then handed it back. I read some more.

"She's married." I was about to say, 'so what' when I saw the name of her spouse. Cynthia O'Malley.

"It's not a date," Lee reiterated.

"No. Apparently not. Friends?"

"Yeah. An assassin and a clean-up guy just happen to be in Virginia at the same time on vacation ..."

"Probably not catching up for a drink," I mumbled into the glass as it neared my mouth. I tipped the glass and held a swig of whiskey in my mouth for a second before swallowing. I enjoyed the rush of heat that followed it down my oesophagus into my gut. Whiskey makes life taste better. "We could go say hello."

Lee shrugged. "Maybe we should."

I downed the last of the warming amber liquid and stood up. Lee followed.

"Seamus Kennedy," I said, slapping Kennedy on the shoulder. "What brings you to Virginia?"

He looked up with a smile.

"Wondered how long you two would sit there watching us." He looked from me to Lee. "Good to see you."

"Introduce us," I said, sitting in the empty chair on his right.

Lee opted for a free chair next to O'Malley.

"Do I really have to?" Kennedy replied.

I shrugged one shoulder.

"Grace O'Malley, I'm special agent Sam Jackson, this is special agent Lee Davenport," I said, reaching across the table to shake her hand. "Hope you're enjoying your *vacation.*"

"I am," she replied, holding eye contact slightly longer than she needed to. "It's a beautiful part of the country."

"How long are you here?" I asked, leaning back in my chair a little. I felt the need for space. Her intense gaze caused discomfort.

A rush of noise near the door caught my attention. All eyes turned to a scuffle happening between a bouncer and a patron. Lee started to stand. I tapped his foot with mine and shook my head.

Not our fight. Not our problem.

I kept half an eye on the situation while mostly focused on the situation at our table.

"You going to intervene?" Kennedy asked.

"No. The bouncer is doing okay. You two traveling together?"

Lee rested his elbows on the table, and leaned toward Kennedy. "Planning on causing trouble or shooting up any houses belonging to Delta A?" His brown eyes hardened. "Or killing anyone that will drag us into your mess?"

"We're on holiday, Davenport."

Lee and I smiled.

"Sure you are," Lee said. "An assassin and a clean-up guy are on vacation in Northern Virginia."

There's an Irish joke in that.

"What's the punchline?" I smiled first at Kennedy then O'Malley. "That was rude of me, Sorry. I mean who's the target?" I glanced at the door in time to see the bouncer drag the drunk outside. Sirens whined in the night. The sound moved ever closer. I looked at the bar. The manager had a phone in her hand and was talking. "Cops are almost here."

O'Malley stood up. "Back door?"

Because people on *vacation* have an inbuilt sense of self-preservation when cops are around which instantly translates into a need to disappear?

Lee pointed to the hallway with the toilet sign above it. "Down there."

"Go with her Lee, Jackson and I will square up the bill."

2.

Lee and O'Malley were waiting in the alley behind the bar when Kennedy and I emerged through the back door. The world is different at night and tonight was no exception. Dark shadows loomed just outside the shallow rings of light from the sparse street lamps. This wasn't the best lit area in town.

"Any chance you'll spill some truth?" I said to Kennedy as the four of us walked toward the street at the end of the alley.

"Holiday," Kennedy replied. "We're on holiday."

I wasn't going to get anything from him at all. He was a hard man to read. I turned my attention to his redheaded friend.

"O'Malley, I'm sure your wife is delighted you're vacationing with this recidivist troublemaker while she's back in the UK working."

O'Malley's head turned. "Our business not yours, Jackson," she said, her voice rasped like she had a pack-a-day habit. She probably did.

Nice.

Lee made fast eye contact with me. I knew what he was thinking. I was thinking it too. Finding out what was really going on might prove interesting. More interesting than I'd like. Finding out before the boss might be impossible. Seamus Kennedy had a long-standing habit of showing up right before shit got messy.

"A smaller man might take offence at the recidivist comment, Jackson," Kennedy said. "Lucky for you I'm in a jovial mood."

I ignored his bullshit. "Car?" I said.

"Back out front. We'll walk to the hotel and pick it up in the morning."

"I can drop you wherever."

"Thanks we'll walk," he replied. "Nothing like a stroll in the night air to help a person sleep."

"You want company?"

"You mean an escort, Jackson," Kennedy said with a crooked smile. "We'll be fine. It's not far and I'm a big boy." He stopped and turned to me with his hand extended. "Good to catch up, Sam."

We shook. I turned to O'Malley.

"Nice to meet you O'Malley," I said, as my hand swallowed hers. "I'd prefer not to do this again."

"Likewise," she said with a half-smile.

Lee and I watched the pair walk down the dark street. They avoided pools of light and stuck to the shadowy edges of the buildings then disappeared into the night. Vacation? I very much doubt it.

"Now what?" Lee said.

"Let's go find our cars and get out of here."

Lee nodded.

The night deepened and I wanted to be home before morning. There was no chance of uncovering Kennedy's real purpose for being here now.

Hasty footfalls rang out across the street. I spun around. A dark shape took on features as it neared us. Arms waved. Garbled words flew through the air. A panicked male barreled across the road. Huffing in air he stumbled to a halt a few feet from us.

"Something wrong, Bud?" I said.

He nodded. "Call 9-1-1 ..."

Lee flashed his badge. "We're Feds. You all right?"

He shook his head and pointed to where he'd run from. "A woman." He struggled for breath. "I think she's dead. God!" Panic enveloped his words and settled on his face as the color washed right out of his skin.

"How far?" I asked, grabbing his arm to steady him as he wavered. "Sit down, buddy. We don't want you falling."

The man half-sat half-collapsed. I took note of his clothing and hands. No blood. No rips. Nothing out of the ordinary with his appearance. He was dressed like he'd been out for the night. For dinner probably.

Lee crouched down near him. "Can you tell me what happened?"

I tapped Lee's shoulder to get his attention. He looked up. "Hang here with him." I fished a flashlight from my pocket and clicked the switch. Be prepared. Always. Be prepared.

The man's head rose, he made eye contact for a beat.

"My name is Terry, Terry White."

I tossed a smile into my voice. "I'll be back, Terry."

Lee nodded at me. "Stay frosty Oscar Mike."

"Roger that."

I took off at a run. I stopped right where I first noticed Terry moving toward us. Looking left, a dark hole swallowed everything. An alleyway. As a team we weren't fond of alleyways. Monsters lurked in dark crevices. I shook the feeling off. Monsters? Really? Ellie's rubbing off on me more than ever.

The beam from my flashlight shone on the sides of the buildings that created the alley. Five dumpsters sat in a tidy row near the end of the alley. Between the fourth and fifth I saw a dark shape.

With my phone pressed to my ear I approached the shape. Lee answered my call.

"Anything?"

"In an alleyway. There's something on the ground up ahead."

I left the line open and shoved the phone in my top pocket.

It wasn't a woman.

I followed the shape from foot to head. A male dressed in a suit.

My fingers sort his carotid more from habit than the expectation of a pulse.

There was a ligature around his neck pulled tight. Dead eyes stared vacantly up at me. No pulse. With a closer inspection the ligature was a pair of fishnet stockings.

I added that to a mental list of things we've found in alleys.

"Dead guy," I said, knowing Lee could hear me. "Guy not woman."

I searched the body and found a wallet. Opening it I found a driver's license and several credit cards but no cash.

Over the open phone line I heard Lee speaking to Terry White. Terry was adamant he saw a woman and was equally adamant that she was dead.

"I can hear. I'll keep looking," I said. Wasn't like I could help the poor bastard between the dumpsters.

I moved into the dark. My flashlight illuminating the area directly in front of me. I moved my hand to let the beam touch the edges and walls of the alley as I looked for doorways and crevices. Not liking the idea of a surprise made me vigilant. Being in an alley with no backup made me watchful. Both were good things survival wise.

Something caught my eye. I swung the flashlight back to have a better look. Walking closer I saw what it was. A stiletto encased foot.

"Found a woman," I said.

"Condition?" Lee's voice came clear and crisp from my pocket.

"Deceased," I replied checking for a pulse in her neck.

A fishnet stocking and shoe were worn on one leg and foot. The other shoe was missing and leg naked. Without wanting to jump the gun, I was pretty sure her death was connected to the male's death.

"What do you need?" Lee asked.

"Police. The deaths appear connected. We should get Metro down here to deal with it." This isn't for us.

I had another look at the body. No blood. I shone the flashlight in her face. Petechial haemorrhaging.

"Strangled maybe," I said out loud. "Two people strangled. It's not a murder suicide. Police are going to be looking for a third person. Keep Mr. White with you."

I could hear Lee talking.

"Hanging up," he said.

I walked back to the beginning of the alleyway and waited for police. Lee text when they were on their way.

3.

Night and home were fleeting memories by the time police finished with us. We could've left sooner but it was better if we stayed and gave a hand.

Lee and I rocked into work carrying a tray of coffee. I stopped by Sandra's desk. Lee kept going.

"Morning," she said, smiling up at me.

I glanced around, there was no one insight, so I stooped and kissed her quickly before handing her a take-out cup of coffee.

"Sorry about the midnight disappearing act." I watched as she sipped the aromatic brew. She was cute.

"Perils of the job." Sandra placed the cup on her desk. Her email chimed.

"I'll leave you to it."

"Not so fast, big guy ..." Sandra glanced up at me through her long lashes then frowned at the screen. "You and Lee were busy last night."

Part of me wanted to wait and see where she was going with her comment. Then I thought better of it . "Deceased male and female in an alleyway," I said.

"Metro want to speak to you both, this morning."

"They say why?" We spent the rest of our night with Metro telling them everything we saw, no detail left unexplored. I doubted there was anything left to discuss.

"It says here they have questions regarding a potential

suspect in the case." She pointed to the screen. "Read."

I did.

Damn.

I thought I'd see Terry White's name but it was Seamus Kennedy's.

"I'll let Lee know. Can you forward that email to me, please."

"Consider it done. Now give me a kiss while there's no one around and get out of here so I can get back to work."

I stooped, kissed her sweet lips. With a grin on my face I walked away. I'm a lucky man.

Ellie poked her head out of her office as I neared.

"Boss?"

"Sam. Just the man I wanted to see."

Usually that was a good thing but I had a feeling that it wasn't good this morning.

"Here I am," I replied with a smile. "You've seen Lee?"

I saw the coffee in her hand.

"He's here. Joining us?"

"Sure." I knew Ellie well enough to know it was an order disguised as a request.

I ambled through the doorway feeling like my luck just ran out. Lee looked over. I knew that look.

Our luck had run out. Our fearless leader knew something and we were about to hear what that was.

"Sit down," Ellie said, pointing to a chair. Two chairs in front of her desk, Lee in one and me in the other. She sat facing us from across the desk. Her expression gave nothing away. I glanced around. No Kurt. "You were busy last night," she said.

It wasn't a question.

"It wasn't intentional," I replied.

The boss leaned on her elbows and steepled her fingers in front of her mouth.

We were in trouble. She knew about Kennedy.

"You should've called me," she said, her voice calm and controlled.

"I wanted to wait until we knew what he was here for," Lee interjected.

"And do you?"

"No," Lee said.

"He wasn't very chatty," I said, placing my takeout cup on her desk. "He's not alone."

Lee's shoe tapped mine. When I glanced at him, one eyebrow shot up. I shrugged. She already. knows about Kennedy. She may as well know it all.

"The UN?" Ellie said with a raised eyebrow. It was her nickname for Kennedy and his band of merry men. An American, an Irishman, a Brit, and a Russian. They liked to hang out together and trouble followed close behind or trouble was already on the boil and they swooped in guns blazing and fixed it. I'm still not sure which way around it goes. But the four of them sounds way too much like a bad joke. The first time we tangled with them wasn't much fun but they really came through a few times after that.

"Not this time," I replied. "Or if the others are here they're laying low. He was with Grace O'Malley."

Ellie grinned. All traces of annoyance vanished from her face. "She'd be a bit leathery by now ..."

"She's well preserved for an old pirate. Must be the rum," I said, returning her smile. "Neither of them were willing to tell us much of anything."

"It's not a romantic thing is it?" Ellie relaxed and rocked back in her chair.

"O'Malley likes girls," Lee replied. "She's married to one, so she likes at least one girl."

"So, probably not the romance idea then. Do we need to know what's going on here, or should we wait until whatever it is lands in our laps?"

"We'd planned on following them, but then a guy babbling about a dead woman caught our attention," Lee said.

That was pretty much how it happened.

"And about that ..." Ellie looked at me.

"Boss?"

"What is your feeling on the strangling?"

She'd heard about that as well.

"I figured it was a Metro issue. The guy we found could've been the perp." As I said it I felt my head shake slightly.

"You don't believe that." Ellie said, straightening her chair and leaning on her desk again. She knew, I could tell.

"No."

"And who are police looking for concerning the double homicide?"

For a split second I thought about playing dumb. The warning look in her eyes told me not too.

"Seamus Kennedy."

"You two locate Kennedy. Find out if we need to involve ourselves in this strange strangling situation. Kurt and I will tackle the pirate."

"Yes, boss," Lee said, standing and picking up her empty cup along with his.

"One more thing." She paused to pick up a pen. "Find Terry White. I doubt he wandered into that alleyway by accident."

I nodded and followed Lee out.

He dropped the empty cups in the trash in the bullpen.

"How'd you know about Kennedy's involvement in the stranglings?" Lee asked, sitting at his desk.

I pulled my chair out and sat.

"Sandra got an email from Metro, she showed me when I came in."

"What'd they do - kill those two and go for a beer?"

"Looks like it."

"I knew they were up to something."

"I can't believe they'd ID him so fast. Thought he was better than that."

4.

At my desk I read the email Sandra forwarded to me. Moments later I had the lead detective on the phone.

"Yo, it's Sam Jackson. What do you need?"

"Help," he said, "There's another body."

Damn.

"I thought you wanted to discuss Terry White?" Felt prudent to pretend I didn't know anything about Kennedy.

"I did, initially, and then we found something and now we're looking for a British National, Seamus Kennedy. We think you may have come across him before."

Ya think?

"Might need some context on the Kennedy person. I come across a lot of people day to day," I said. "Where's the new body?"

"Same alley as the first two victims."

"And?"

"Deceased male with a pair of fishnet stockings wrapped tightly around his neck."

Sure sounded like it could be connected to the bodies we found last night.

"Send me everything you have, we'll take a look."

"Cheers, Sam. I'll bring everything over myself."

"You got my cell number?"

"Yeah."

"Text when you're at the front desk, I'll come down."

* * *

The cop didn't waste anytime. I met him at the front desk, signed him in, and took him up to our bullpen.

"Lee, this is Detective Sanchez with Metro. He wants us to take a look at this case. Body count is up by one."

They shook hands. "Happy to help if we can. Take a seat. Coffee?" Lee said.

"Thanks but no. I'm trying to cut down to three cups a day." He smiled. "My wife's idea."

I'm sure I had that to look forward to. No doubt Sandra will have a few ideas of her own to implement once we're married. For the greater good, of course.

Sanchez spread photos across Lee's desk then sat down.

Three bodies. Two, we'd already seen. The third was another male in a suit.

"Were they all at the same place?" I reached down and moved photos around. "Two men, wearing nice suits and a woman in expensive clothes."

Lee dropped another photo into the mix, one he'd taken of Terry White.

"He was real quick to give us his name," he said, tapping the photo. "I don't think he came across the first two bodies by accident."

"Nor do I," I said.

We waited for Sanchez to drop something world

changing but he didn't.

"We have nothing to suggest where these three came from. None of them were seen on any video surveillance. There was nothing on them indicating a particular bar or restaurant."

"The guy we saw had credit cards in his wallet. Did you look into his financials?" Policing 101. I lifted his photo.

Sanchez nodded. "He hadn't used his cards for a couple of days. Hadn't even used an ATM in that time. The last thing he bought was a bottle of water from a CVS in Fairfax."

"Who is he?" I put the image back on the desk.

"Raymond Chandler." The boss would have a field day with that. Now we have a dead detective author and an ancient pirate.

"And the woman?"

"Sophie Grant."

"And this guy?" Lee tapped the photograph of the other male.

"Topher O'Brien."

"Topher isn't an every day American name," Lee said. "For shits and giggles, do we have nationalities on these folk?"

Sanchez shrugged. "We have very little beyond what you see. It's very strange. They came from nowhere and did nothing. None of them accessed their bank accounts for a few days. Each of them made a last but small purchase days before they turned up in the alley."

"And Terry White? Do you have him?"

He shook his head.

Lee and I looked at each other. We might know someone who'd know.

"How'd you get Seamus Kennedy as someone of interest?" I kept my voice light. No pressure, just curious.

"We found a business card inside the lining of the woman's purse." He produced more photos from his folder. "See, one of the techs felt something inside the lining of the purse. Was a secret pocket. Inside that we found a business card belonging to Seamus Kennedy."

Interesting. I didn't know the likes of Kennedy carried business cards. The fact that it was hidden was really interesting. If he'd given it to her it must be for a reason. Would he give his business card to someone who was on his radar as a job? I doubted it. Kennedy was teamed up with a known assassin and his business card was in the bag of a dead woman. Those things did not seem to be coincidental.

"Can you hang here for a few minutes I need to talk to our boss."

I left Lee with Sanchez and strode back to Ellie's office. I knocked once and swung the door open.

She looked up and gestured to a seat near her desk.

"What's up?"

"In what circumstances would Kennedy handout a business card?"

Ellie opened her desk drawer and took out a small

black wallet. She flicked through it then showed me Kennedy's business card. "Remember when the UN helped us out of a nasty situation in Harper's Ferry?"

"Yeah. They definitely made a difference."

"Kennedy gave me his card then in case we ever needed help like that again." She put the wallet away and closed the drawer. "I got the impression that those cards are reserved for very special situations and people he's helped in the past." She smiled. "Why?"

"The dead woman in the alleyway. Sophie Grant. She had one of Kennedy's business cards hidden in her purse."

"We need to talk to our Irish pal."

"Do you know where he'd be?"

She nodded. "He has an apartment here. I think it actually belongs to the British Embassy but he's used it every time he comes to town." Ellie closed her laptop lid. "He was at the apartment earlier but not with Grace O'-Malley."

I frowned. "How'd you know?"

Ellie laughed. "I asked."

"And you believe him?"

"Absolutely."

Sun rays bounced off a small crystal vase on her desk and sent rainbows across the wall. It suited her to have rainbows around. Ellie had a way of always holding onto hope.

"Chicky Babe ..."

She chuckled and it was infectious, I couldn't help but smile.

"Okay, I didn't ask. Lee and I might have left a few toys in that apartment a while ago, several of the devices are still operational. I kicked them into life."

"No conversation in the apartment?"

"Nope. Just the usual sounds one person would make. He made a couple of phone calls but nothing worth us getting involved."

"Lee and I will have a chat with him. Any luck finding O'Malley?"

"Not yet."

"She may have left the country."

Ellie nodded slowly. "It's a possibility. I've put some feelers out to Interpol to see if these murders tweak anyone's memory overseas. Could be that this is O'Malley's Modus Operandi."

"The stocking strangulations."

"Uh huh and the rest of this weird situation." Her eyes met mine. "I have the police files. Where were those people before the alleyway, Sam? Where were they?"

"What are you thinking?"

She was thinking something, I could tell by the spark in her eyes.

"Why that alleyway?"

I shrugged. "Don't know, but I'll find out."

"Sam, this one is yours. I'll track O'Malley and be around if you need a sounding board, but I'm pretty sure you can bring this one home without me."

"Thanks boss," I said with a grin. "I'll keep you in the loop."

"You do that. I'll see what I can find out from Interpol and anyone else I can think of."

"You think this could be a cross-border case?"

She nodded. "Get back out there to Sanchez and tell him you're taking point and would like to work with him. Don't shut him out. We're trying to build relationships here."

"Got it."

I left the room and rejoined Lee and Detective Sanchez.

6.

"Okay Sanchez, you're with us," I said, resting a hand on the back of his chair. He looked a little taken a back. "Unless you don't want our help?"

He threw me a half-smile. "I'm happy to work with the FBI on this case."

"Good." I looked at Lee. "Field trip. We need to go back to that alley, then find and talk to Kennedy."

Lee chewed his lip, stuck his cap on his head, adjusted his belt and indicated he was ready to roll. Sanchez stood, gathered his files, shoved them back in the folder and jammed it under his arm.

Lee tossed a coin in the air and caught it. "Heads or tails?"

"Heads."

"I'm driving he said picking the keys up off the desk."

Fine by me.

The three of us walked down the corridor, I did a small wave to Sandra as we passed her desk. She shot me a look that made heat rise. At the elevator doors I pressed the down arrow. The door opened.

Seamus Kennedy stepped out. Holy shit.

He looked unsettled for a second then pulled it together.

"Jackson," he said, stepping around me.

"Don't leave town Kennedy, we need to talk."

I knew he was going to see Ellie. Saved us a trip.

"I'll be right here, waiting."

Everything he said sounded smart-assed. I figured it was the brogue. No idea why women liked listening to his voice. None whatsoever. I'd thought from the first time I'd met Kennedy that he was smarmy and too sure of himself. I came to understand that that wasn't true. He was good at what he did. He was also dangerous. Paid to keep on his good side.

The elevator jerked and bumped to a stop in the parking garage and the doors opened.

* * *

Didn't take us long to get to the alleyway.

Police tape fluttered at the end of the alley in the warm Washington breeze. Police officers stood guard at the scene and forensics techs were just finishing up. We watched them load their SUV.

The alley was quiet. Deathly quiet.

"We need to know where these people came from. Let's get looking." I stepped into the cool sheltered alley. Lee and Sanchez followed.

The alley went a long way but not all the way to the street behind. Three quarters of the way down was another alley. It ran to the right and was even narrower. We could walk two abreast but not three. Looking up I saw several old fire escapes along the length of the small alley. This too was a dead end. Five doors. Garbage bins not dumpsters in this off-shoot. There was no room to maneuver a truck.

Five doors, seven garbage bins. Crates of empty bottles were stacked against one wall, between two doors. I peered into the crates. "Wine bottles."

"That's a lot of wine," Lee commented.

"Thirsty people," Sanchez said.

"Or a restaurant ..."

"The city has no record of any restaurants down here," Sanchez replied. "I thought the people may have come from dinner somewhere and cut through but that's not possible." He looked around. "There is no restaurant that explains them being in the alley."

"An illegal restaurant? We had speakeasy's back in the day could be a restaurant version?" It sounded ridiculous as soon as I said it and yet there it was out there ready for ridicule.

Lee grinned. "It's a thing Sam, trust me. Illegal restaurants exist. Ever heard of the New York *Bite Club*?"

I shook my head. "I've heard of *Fight Club*."

The thought of people soap turned my gut.

"It's an underground restaurant which had bi-monthly eight-course meals and sometimes up to forty-five guests. They ask each person for a one-hundred and fifty dollar donation. Wine is officially donated to avoid selling alcohol illegally. It's been running a few years now and is quite popular."

"You know a lot about it ..."

Lee ignored my comment. "I don't know of any in

Washington, but that doesn't mean there aren't any."

Sanchez nodded. "I read an article in the *New York Times* about underground restaurants."

Lee smiled. "Yeah, that's probably where I heard about *Bite Club*."

I coughed and said, "I call bullshit on that."

"Door knocking, let's go," Lee said. "I choose the door with all the empty bottles as door number one."

I knocked on the door. The wood rattled in the frame. Maybe I knocked a bit hard. Didn't sound like anyone was rushing to answer. Sanchez walked back to the corner and peered down at the end of the alley.

"Where are you going? You'll miss all the fun," I said.

He glanced over his shoulder at me. "I want to know if anyone came this far and thought to knock on doors down here."

"I can save you the trouble, the answer is no. The crime scene is the other alley."

He shook his head and sighed as he walked back.

"Okay, show me this fun."

I bashed louder on the door. The door rattled harder in the frame. I twisted the handle. Locked. I gave it a moment. Still nothing. By bashing the door I determined it did not have a steel core, good news. It was wooden. I can break wood.

"Watch out," I said, before stepped back to get enough room to kick. The wood shattered. A scoff rose. Good strong wooden door. No expense spared. Security was obviously a top priority.

"That was too easy," Lee muttered. "And no one's rushing to see what the noise was."

"Let's find out why no one came to greet us," I said, stepping through what was left of the broken door. Had to duck. I'm a big guy the doorway was not.

In the small entrance way there were stairs leading up and stairs going down.

"Call it," I said to Lee.

"Down."

"All right." I unholstered my weapon and took point.

The stairs creaked in places. Each time I held my breath. Fifteen steps to a landing, then fifteen more to the floor below. It felt like a basement, dark but not dingy and the air held a promise of food. If Ellie were here she'd be able to tell us exactly what had been cooked down here. Her sense of smell was unreal. To me, it smelt like Italian but not pizza.

Doors opened off the short hallway. Three on the right and one on the left. I took a deep breath.

"Let's clear these rooms," I said. Lee was on my left. That's how we always go in. Me, right. Lee, left. Sanchez fell in close behind, Lee. "We got this. Let's go to work."

The first room was a bathroom with four stalls. If this was an underground restaurant at least the forty-five or so people didn't have to use one toilet. That's a good thing.

The next room was dark. I stuck my hand inside the

door and connected with a light switch, flipping it revealed a well-appointed office. I paused to look at some paperwork on the desk. It was right there in plain sight.

"This here is an invoice for fresh vegetables," I said, picking it up for a closer inspection. "Organic vegetables from a farm in Maryland."

Another piece of paper caught my eye. "And here's one for boutique organic honey also from a farm in Maryland."

A laptop sat on the desk but it was closed. Multiple Lever Arch files were in a bookcase behind the desk. The folders were marked: orders; invoices; receipts; recipes; and staff.

"Moving on," I said. The men waited for me to leave.

Next room. I could see light under the door.

I swung the door open. A young male jumped to his feet from a low sofa.

"What the fuck!"

"FBI," I said, pulling my badge from my pocket with my left hand while keeping my weapon trained on him with my right. "You are?"

"Kerry." His surprise faded. "What do you want?"

"Do you work here?"

He frowned. His eyes flicked over to Lee, Sanchez and back to me.

"What if I do?"

"Answer the question, kid. Do you or don't you?"

He nodded.

"What is this place?"

"It's ..." He stopped and appeared to think for a moment. "It's like a ..."

"Like a what?" I smiled. I can be patient until it's time not to be patient.

"A private club. It's like a private club."

"Like one? Or it is a private club?"

"I don't know. People come here and have dinner once a week."

"Is there anyone else in the building?"

He shook his head. "Just me."

I gave Lee a look. He nodded and disappeared.

"Who runs this joint?" I holstered my weapon. He was a kid and I'd sooner not shoot a kid.

"Mrs. Clairvol."

"Spell that for me," Sanchez said. I saw his phone in his hand when I glanced in his direction.

The kid obliged.

"Is there a first name?" Sanchez said.

"Angela."

"All right, thanks, Kerry. Where is Mrs. Clairvol now?" Sanchez said. He showed me the screen on his phone. Fast work. Gotta love Google. Mrs. Angela Clairvol was the wife of a senator. She'd added Mrs to her maiden name. Looked like she used her married name almost everywhere, except for this little enterprise. She was Senator Riley's wife. He was a senator for Maryland, US House and Maryland State Assembly according to

Google. Didn't ring any alarm bells. That was a good thing.

"She'd be at home, I suppose. There isn't another dinner scheduled until next week."

"And why are you here?"

"She let's me stay."

"You live here?"

"Sometimes I stay." He shrugged and sat back on the sofa. "My step-dad is a dick and it's nice to have somewhere to go. She let's me come here."

"Seems like a nice lady," I said.

"Yeah."

"What do you do for Mrs. Clairvol?"

"Clean the kitchen, mostly. She asks me to wait tables if they're short staffed."

"The last dinner, did you see any of the guests?"

Lee arrived back in the room. "Nobody else down here. Rest of the basement is clear. Restaurant must be upstairs."

"Thanks, Lee." I turned my attention back to Kerry and repeated my question.

He shook his head. "I was in the kitchen."

"All night?"

"I came down here for my break, but otherwise I was in the kitchen."

"And the kitchen is?"

"Upstairs with the restaurant."

"Do you know how many people were here?"

He shrugged.

Lee stepped closer. "How many plates did you wash?"

The kid nodded, I could see the cogs turning. His eyes darted about in their sockets as he tried to work it out. "Maybe eleven people."

"Thank you," Lee said.

"Does Mrs. Clairvol know everyone who comes?"

He shrugged again. "I don't know."

"How many people work here when there is a dinner event happening?"

"Five sometimes less."

"Do you know all of them?"

He started to nod, then he changed his mind and shook his head. "There was a new person the other night, a woman. So I knew three people. We didn't have many guests."

Lee unlocked his phone and showed Kerry a photo of O'Malley. "Her?"

The kid smiled and nodded. "Yeah."

"You talk to her?"

He nodded. "Said hello but that's all, she seemed nice, I guess. Her accent is cool."

She's a real charmer. And she was here. That's not at all suspicious.

Three people dead who may have been at the restaurant. They didn't access bank accounts, and no one missed them right away. And O'Malley was at the restaurant. She had to be connected, otherwise why would she be there working? Do assassins need work visas? What are the rules around that? Who would I call to let them know we had an assassin posing as a server in an underground restaurant? Right, that'd be us.

Lee nudged me.

My head turned to see what he wanted. "Yo."

"You with us here?"

"Yeah. We need the senators wife and a guest list and employee records and a reason for O'Malley to be working here. I doubt she needed the money they pay for waiting tables." I turned around and left the room. "Kennedy?"

"I'll call the boss see what she's got."

Sanchez caught up as I walked back to the stairs. "O'-Malley?"

"Not someone we want to tango with but it looks like we will be. She's a killer. Assassin for hire."

"And this Kennedy is working with her?"

I could hear a twinge in his voice that said he thought he was right to start asking about Seamus Kennedy earlier. Maybe he was.

I paused for a second at the bottom of the stairs, one foot resting on a step. "That's the thing I don't get. It doesn't make sense to me."

7.

I sat in the car and called Ellie.

"There's a senator's wife involved. As far as we can ascertain she's running an underground restaurant and that's where the three dead people may have been immediately prior to their deaths."

The tippity-tap of fingers tapping on a keyboard reached me before her words.

"Track down the wife, try not to cause too much trouble."

Time to tell the boss the rest. "O'Malley was a server at the restaurant."

"And Charles Manson is dead."

"The fuck?"

"Oh, okay, I thought we were sharing fake news headlines."

"Boss, for real."

"Wouldn't it be easier to be a customer than try and get a job as a server in a underground restaurant if you wanted to scope the place out prior to killing people?"

Right then I saw her point. Shit.

"This is not good. You still good with me going after the Senator's wife, just for a chat?"

"Yep. Find out how well she knows O'Malley. I've got Kennedy here with me. The woman who had his card, Sonya Grant, she was a client once."

"And now she's dead and he was close by?"

Light footsteps then a hollowness filled the airway, and finally Ellie's voice returned "I'm quite inclined to believe he had nothing to do with Sonya's death."

"You left the room. Don't want Kennedy to know you think he's telling the truth?"

"Yeah," she said, her voice lightened. "There was genuine surprised when he saw the photograph. And he's seething." She was having fun, I could tell.

"I'll keep you updated. Detective Sanchez is with us."

"Good. Keep him safe."

"Yes, boss."

The conversation was over, I had more to consider than when it started. It often went that way with Ellie.

"Sam, we have an address," Lee said, as he shared the address with the GPS.

A twenty-five minute battle with traffic left me mindful of the fragility of life and thankful for the defensive driving courses we do as part of our jobs. We made it to the senator's home intact. Sanchez was quiet and the last one out of the Suburban.

"You good?" I said to him before we walked up the driveway.

"Yeah."

Lee and I exchanged glances.

"You sure?" Lee said.

"I've never questioned a senator before."

Lee chuckled. "Hey, they're people, just like you and me. And this time it's the wife. Come on. It'll be fine."

Sanchez nodded and fell into step as we walked.

I knocked on the large front door.

A woman in a maid uniform answered. "Senator Riley's residence. How can I help?"

I showed her my badge. "Is Mrs. Riley at home?"

The woman nodded. "Wait here." She turned to leave.

"Miss," I said. "It's you that should wait here, with this nice detective. Where is Mrs. Riley?"

Her eyes widened. Guess she didn't like my idea.

Sanchez spoke up. "What's your name?"

"Ava."

"Okay Ava, stay here with me. Tell them where the lady is."

"In the study. Go through the entrance way, down the hall ahead of you, it's the last door on the right."

"Thank you Ava," I said. I nodded my appreciation at Sanchez.

He ushered the woman out to the porch as we followed her directions. The smell of fresh flowers mingled with furniture polish. We passed several sideboards in the hallway. Large vases of flowers sat on small mats on top of the highly polished wood. At the last door on the right, I knocked.

"Yes, Ava," called a pleasant sounding female voice. "Come in."

Lee grinned. I opened the door and immediately saw redheaded woman sat with her back to the main door and in front of a large desk. Another woman faced me across a large desk. I expected that was the senator's wife.

The lady at the desk startled. "Excuse me. Who are you? Where's Ava?"

I held up my badge. "Special Agent Sam Jackson, FBI."

The with her back to me turned toward me. Grace O'-Malley.

I pulled my weapon as Lee stepped up on my left.

"Grace O'Malley. Hands where I can see them."

She smiled over her shoulder. "Mr. Jackson. How lovely to see you again." Her eyes roamed to Lee. "And Mr. Davenport too."

"What's going on here?" Mrs. Riley asked. She pulled herself to her feet.

"Please sit, ma'am," I said, keeping my tone even but firm.

She sat but picked up her cell phone. I shook my head. She put it back down.

"O'Malley, stand," Lee instructed. He'd moved and was in a better position to cover her. "Hands where I can see them. No sudden moves. I'm sure Mrs. Riley doesn't want a hefty cleaning bill."

"It's all rather unnecessary, boys." O'Malley stood and faced me.

"The thing is Grace, it's not. We have three dead people and a visiting assassin. And they all seemed to be connected to a restaurant owned by Mrs. Riley."

The woman's eyes sharpened. "I don't own any restaurants."

"Sorry. I meant to say a restaurant owned by Mrs. Clairvol. Clairvol is your maiden name, is it not?"

Lee reached O'Malley, pulled her hands behind her back and cuffed her. He frisked her and removed two knives, a garrote, and a pistol. He placed the weapons in the middle of the floor. Nice haul.

"You come prepared when you visit friends," Lee commented.

"We're not friends," Riley said. Sinking back into her chair.

That much I figured on my own. It was a working relationship. O'Malley was a hired hand. So the three dead must have ties to Riley or her husband, not to O'Malley?

I whistled and followed it with a holler, "Sanchez. Get in here!"

I called the office and requested back up.

Sanchez hurried into the room, weapon in hand. "Agent Jackson?"

"Mrs. Riley requires handcuffs, she's being held on conspiracy to commit murder."

He looked at me for a second as if my words made no sense. He blinked, the penny dropped, and he propelled himself into action. Flipping cuffs off his belt, he neared the now very pale woman. She stood, slowly, using her desk as support. Moments ago she was much steadier. Funny how frail people become when faced with arrest for murder. Hiring a hitman, not the best move to make.

I heard him read the Miranda to her as he snapped the

handcuffs into place and I smiled inside. People just like everyone else. You break the law you answer for it. We don't care how rich anyone is; how many maids they have; or how fancy a house they live in.

Lee had a firm grip on O'Malley's upper arm. She appeared relaxed, considering. I'm sure she thought she'd skate, somehow. She was notorious for doing so in Europe, that much I gleaned from her extensive record of ill-repute. I watched her as I rang Ellie back. Beautiful and deadly, what a combination.

"You ask Kennedy how much he knew about why O'-Malley was in town?"

"Did you get her?"

"Yeah. Metro or us?"

"Us. She's wanted in five countries, so us. Sanchez is welcome to see it through to the end."

"And Kennedy?"

"He thought he'd convinced her not to take the job. You can imagine he's feeling pretty gutted about now."

"He inclined to help her at all?"

"Not really, he's already given me a statement."

"See you soon."

"Stay safe. Let uniform do the transport."

"Done."

* * *

I rocked on the chair in Ellie's office.

"Sam, I swear, one day you'll fall or break a chair doing

that," she said, with a shake of her head. Her blonde hair partially concealed her face. She tossed it back over her shoulder.

"The dead woman and two dead men ..."

She looked at me. "Carry on."

"The Senator has an appetite and his wife doesn't approve. She made arrangements and invited them to her restaurant after discovering they were with her husband at his beach house for three days for the second time."

"And the husband?"

"Cowering in shame in a hotel, by all accounts. His constituents are calling for him to step down."

"He wasn't involved in the deaths?"

I shook my head. "No."

"How'd his wife find out about the beach house fun and games?"

"A few months ago it got noisy at the beach house and a neighbor called his wife to ask if they had people staying over or perhaps it was now an Air B&B. The wife drove down to find out and saw for herself what he was up to."

"Months ago?"

"Yeah. The planning began. No doubt it takes time organizing hits on three people. By the time the Senator announced his next *working weekend* at their beach house, the wife was ready to put her scheme in place."

"So who was supposed to get the blame for the deaths?"

"O'Malley was supposed to leave evidence to frame the senator, but the wife changed her mind."

"Good work, Sam."

"Thanks, boss."

I hauled myself out of the chair and rapped my knuckles on her desk and turned to leave.

"Murphy's?" Ellie asked.

"Yeah. Sanchez is keen to experience a night at Murphy's with the gang."

"By the way, there's a full account from Kennedy if you need it, I've attached it to the case notes."

"Thanks."

"See you at Murphy's in an hour. I'll go pick up Mitch."

The End

Come a Little Bit Closer:

Mike Davenport disappears from Dulles Airport.

This story kicks off about a month after Databyte ends.

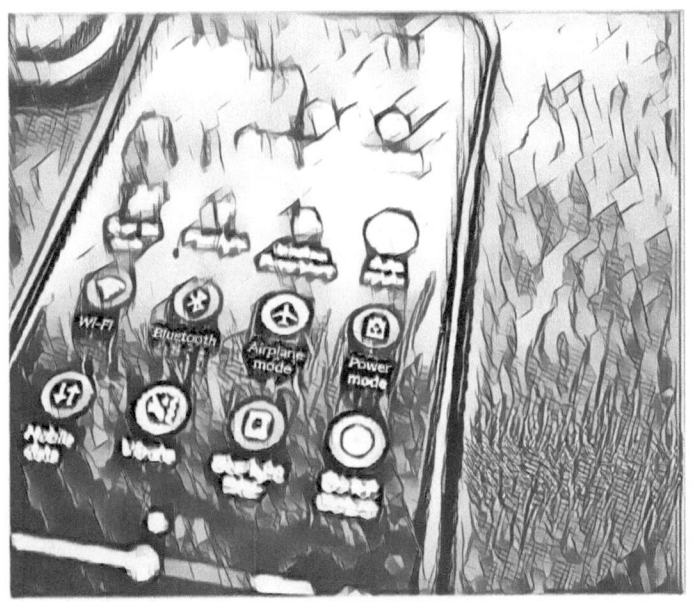

Come a little bit closer.

1.

Lee walked into my office. His shadow swayed across my desk as he moved in front of the window to get a spare chair. He lifted the chair over the area rug, found the best location for it, and sat down.

"Busy?" His right eye brow arched.

"Comfy?" I shot back.

"Indeed I am."

"I was just finishing off some case notes." I lifted my hands from the keyboard in front of me and studied him for a second. "Something on your mind?"

"Have you heard from Mike?"

"Your brother Mike?" He nodded. "Not since he went back to his side of the country."

"Okay then." Lee stood, picked up the chair and put it back where it came from.

"Why?"

He turned and grinned. "Mom drummed into us kids to put things back where we found them."

"Not the chair. Smartass. Why'd you ask me about Mike?"

"He flew in last night but I haven't heard from him."

"You sure he got here?"

"Yeah, I was ten minutes late to meet his flight and he was gone." Lee moved for the door.

"You check he was on the flight?"

"Yep. Spoke to a flight attendant. Mike flew business class. The flight attendant got his autograph."

Didn't think they were supposed to do things like that but knowing Mike he probably offered.

"Maybe someone else met him or he made a friend on the plane?" It's Mike Fisher the actor. He's not exactly unknown and he's a bit of a flirt. He's also currently a grieving widower which makes him hot property. "He knows we can't be seen in public together in case some nosy journalist figures out his *wife* isn't dead. I doubt he'd contact me."

A wry grin settled on his face.

"You don't know Mike at all. He would definitely contact you and I doubt he'd have any intention of being seen in public."

Oh, please.

"He knows I'm seeing someone."

"Without a ring on your finger, that's something my little bro could ignore."

"Moving on. I haven't heard from him or seen him. He's probably with a girl in a hotel."

"Without his luggage," Lee added with a twinge of concern. "I picked up his bag before it disappeared for good."

No doubt he had a carry-on. Probably had essentials in that. He's a traveler. A flirty traveler. And made me smile.

"Nothing from him at all since he got on the plane?"

"Nada."

"Stupid question time: You called him?"

"Of course. Called. Text. Emailed. Then I emailed him using our emergency email via the VA."

"Financials?"

"He used his credit card for a cab to the airport in Los Angeles. I checked a few minutes ago and there were no transactions since that cab ride."

"How snoopy did you get? Did you get a look into his checking or daily account?"

He nodded. "He withdrew five-hundred dollars from an ATM at LAX. Nothing since."

"All right, he has a bit of cash on him. If he wanted to stay under the radar for a night or two, that'd get him a room." She may even be paying. All possibilities should be explored. Somehow that didn't feel right. I couldn't see Mike letting a lady pay for a hotel room.

"You think he's holed up with a lady somewhere?"

"I think, it's Mike Fisher the actor we're talking about, and that's a strong possibility."

"He's also Mike Davenport my brother, who wouldn't leave me twiddling my thumbs at an airport wondering where he is."

Good point.

"Okay, we'll head over to the airport and check the security cameras." We could do it from here, if they gave us access but I felt like getting out of the building. I shut the lid of my laptop, picked up my cell phone from the desk and stood up, grasping my jacket from the back of my chair. I dropped the phone into my jacket pocket before pulling it on. "Let's go find that wayward brother of yours."

"After you," Lee said, ushering me out the door.

A deep voice called out from the direction of the bullpen. "What's happening?"

I turned to see Sam and Kurt walking toward us.

"We're going for coffee," I replied matching Sam's volume level and grinning.

They caught up. Kurt leaned close to me. "Bullshit. What's going on?"

"Fill you in on the way." I nudged Lee. "Both cars?"

"Yep."

I told Sandra we'd bring back coffee as we passed her desk.

2.

"You need to tell me where we're going before I leave the garage?" Kurt said, unlocking the car with a beep.

"Dulles airport."

"Get comfortable, might be more than an hours drive today." Kurt moved the seat back and adjusted the rearview mirror. Telltale signs that I drove last. "Wanna fill me in on the reason?"

I buckled up. Kurt pulled out of the underground parking garage with Lee and Sam following close behind.

"In a minute I will."

I extracted my phone from my pocket and checked my messages. Just in case I'd missed one from Mike. Nothing. I checked my email. Nothing. I searched for all emails from Mike Fisher or Mike Davenport. The last email he sent was over a week ago.

I read it again.

Dear Ellie,

Life as a widower is interesting. You're right, by the way, makes me hot property as far as the ladies are concerned. I'm doing my best but it's a lot even for me. Those women move in fast. No time to grieve in LaLa Land.

Given any more thought to Cotopaxi? It'd be fun. You and me up a mountain, no distractions. Except you. You're a powerful distraction.

I looked out the window for a moment. We were sitting at traffic lights. Cotopaxi. Climbing. Mike was right about one thing, it'd be fun.

"Ready to fill me in yet?" Kurt asked, glancing at me.

"Mike Davenport flew in from LA last night. Lee went to get him but he was gone. He was gone without his luggage."

"You heard from him?"

Why does everyone think Mike tells me what he's doing?

"No."

"I take it there is no answer when Lee calls him?"

"Yep."

"You tried?"

"Not yet. I'm going over old emails in case he said something that might make sense now."

I started reading the screen in my hand again.

I know, I know. You don't have to say it again. We can't be seen together. I've got a lot happening here anyway. Cotopaxi will have to wait.

There's a rumor the show will be picked up for a fourth season. And they want to get a jump on it - we're filming a couple of episodes next month. My publicist mentioned sending me back to D.C for some more promo work sometime soon but no dates yet.

I'll bring you a coffee into work when I'm in town. I

doubt Lee's brother rocking into the Hoover Building would cause a stir.

Think I liked being your husband more than a widower.

Mike

Yep, big flirt. Our pretend marriage lasted all of ten minutes. I laughed. Kurt looked at me.

"What's so funny?"

"Nothing really. Mike Fisher, that's all."

Kurt nodded. "Anything in the email?"

"Not a lot. He mentioned he'd be back in D.C. at some stage for some more promo work. He's filming a few episodes for a new season next month. He talked about not being able to go climbing."

"Did he mention any up coming appointments with Leon Kapowski?"

"Ah, no."

"After that head injury of his, I thought Leon should take a look at him."

"They have very good doctors on the west coast."

"Yes, they do. But we have Leon and he's brilliant."

High praise.

"Hang on. Did you know Mike was coming back here now?"

"Not now, no. I knew he had an appointment with Leon but I didn't know when."

"Maybe it is now?"

"Maybe. Call him," Kurt said, watching the traffic on the bridge.

I found Leon in my contacts and rang his office and put the phone on speaker.

"This is SSA Conway, can you check a patient appointment for me please?" Long shot but worth a try.

"Is it your appointment?"

"Nope. A friends."

"Ma'am we can't divulge that information, you could be anyone."

"Correct answer." I paused and tried to drag up the name of Leon's receptionist. Started with F. Fiona, no. Fran, no. Felicity. That's it. "Is that you Felicity?"

"Yes ma'am. Do you know me?"

"I see you every six months when I come in. I'm a patient. I'm also FBI. I have a friend whose missing and he may have an appointment with Leon over the next few days."

"Ms. Conway, I can't tell you anything."

"Can you say yes or no?"

"Yes."

"Does Michael Davenport have an appointment with Leon Kapowski today?"

"No."

"Tomorrow?"

Fingers tapped on a keyboard then stopped.

"Yes."

"Thank you Felicity. If you see or hear from Mr. Davenport please suggest he contacts me or his brother."

"Yes, ma'am."

I hung up.

Kurt negotiated heavier flowing traffic as we entered Virginia.

"He has an appointment," he said. "Hope he makes it. They're not easy to come by."

I leaned back into the seat with my thoughts. Why didn't he mention the appointment in his email? You can't snap your fingers and get an appointment with a specialist like Leon overnight. Didn't seem like Lee knew either. Why would he leave the airport without his bag? Why would he leave without contacting his brother? I looked at my phone. Silent and ominous in my hand.

Before I knew it I was placing a call to Mike. It went straight to voice mail. I left a message and hung up.

Voice mail.

I sent a text: Where's that coffee you promised me?

I figured if someone had his phone that'd let them know he was missed but not in a threatening way. I wasn't quite ready to channel *Liam Neeson*. I suspected that wasn't far off.

"What are you doing?" Kurt asked, turning the radio on. The announcer waffled on and was easy to ignore.

"Minding my business, how about you drive and don't concern yourself with whatever I'm doing?"

"Conway ..."

"Henderson. Road."

A sudden rush of old music filled the air and surprised me.

"What are we listening too? Radio for ancient people?"

"It's not that bad," Kurt said, turning the volume up. "I like this song. It's called 'Where do you go to my lovely'."

"Who even is this?"

"Peter Sarstedt. This is a late sixties song."

"Well, aren't you widely versed in, what is it? Pop music?"

"I think it's folk music. Give it a chance, not everything has to be Grange, Rolling Stones, or Bon Jovi."

"Whatever." As I listened, the words wrapped around me and told a story. A song about someone who came from nothing sung from the point of view of an old friend that knew her back then. I'd had my fill of Mike's old friends so I really hoped the song wasn't playing for my benefit. Thankfully the song came to an end and something less folksy took it's place. Country. Twenty-seconds in I knew the song wasn't a happy one. I reached to change the station but stopped.

"All right?" Kurt asked.

"Yeah. This song. I've heard it before." The song continued into a chorus. "I remember hearing the story behind the song. It's about Jared Monti, he was a soldier, killed in Afghanistan in 2006 saving another soldier. I can't remember who wrote the song, but it's from the point of view of Jared's dad."

"The family were given his posthumous Medal of Hon-

or? That was him right? He was a sergeant?"

"Yeah."

I let the song finish.

First a song about someone who came from nothing and became someone people adored and then a song about a dead soldier and the grief of a father. Couldn't say the radio station Kurt chose was cheerful. The announcer came back, droning on, a few adverts played and another song started up. This time I leaned forward with different intent.

I turned the volume up.

"Rolling Stones," I said with a smile, the smile slid off my face when I realized which song it was. "Dancing with Mr. D."

"They could play happier music," Kurt said, turning the volume down a notch.

"Hey, it's Stones. Stones means volume," I said. Mick Jagger's voice bounced off the windscreen and dripped off the dash. Leaving behind a number and a place. Forty-four. West Virginia. "A forty-four ..."

"The *Dirty Harry* gun." Kurt grinned. "Forty-four Magnum. See I know movies too."

I laughed. "Seventies movies."

"Something's happening in that head of yours, Conway, share."

"Might just be songs, Henderson."

"Sky might just be blue, Conway."

"Fair comment. Okay. In my head right now ..." It was

going to sound nuts. More nuts than a squirrel can hide for winter. Just say it. Jeez. It's not going to get any less weird. "Someone who came from nothing or maybe nowhere and is now famous, for whatever reason. A families grief at the death of their soldier son. And Mick Jagger dancing with the devil which apparently involves looking down the barrel of a forty-four magnum in West Virginia." My words sank like stones.

"Hmmm. You're reading songs like they're tarot cards."

I felt my eyes widen. Kurt saying tarot cards will do that to a person.

"Maybe I am. What did I just say though?"

"You described Mike Davenport, gave a weapon and a potential location, I very much hope we find him before all those things come together and the dead soldier is part of our extended family."

"West Virginia is a big place."

"Let's hope the security footage at the airport can give us something."

I looked at my phone screen. The email icon said thirty-two unread emails. No text messages. No missed calls. Where are you Mike? Why haven't you responded? What did I know about Mike? He could handle himself. Ex-Army. No slouch. Saved me a couple of times. If he was in trouble he'd hang on. He'd know Lee would be looking. He'd know we'd all be looking. Hell, he'd be looking for a way out. Have a little faith, the guys not an idiot.

The next song to fly from the speakers was 'Help is on it's way', *Little River Band*. A couple of the lines sent twinges through my gut. Could his head be giving him trouble? I hadn't considered that. But he had an appointment with a neurologist and maybe work wasn't the only reason he wasn't climbing now.

"Henderson ..."

"Problem?"

He turned the radio down.

"Mike's head injury. Could there be long reaching issues?"

"Asks the Queen of head injury related phenomena ..."

"Is that a yes?" I watched his profile trying to determine if he felt that way. His mouth set in a grim line. I had my answer.

"If he received another knock to his head since being knocked out, it's even more likely."

It wasn't his first head injury to start with. I didn't want to think about it any more.

3.

My phone rang. Lee's smiling face lit the screen.

"You listening to the radio?" Lee asked.

"Yep," I said. "Some old foggy station Henderson likes."

"We're on a classic rock station. Sitting near 105 FM."

"Great. I'm growing tired of the messages from Henderson's favorite station." I wondered if there was a point to this radio talk but didn't have to wonder long. I fiddled with the radio until I found a station just past 105FM.

"This station takes dedications," Lee said.

"Okay. What's going on, Lee."

"A few minutes back they played 'Dazed and Confused' by Led Zeppelin for Laura because Mike wishes he could hold her again."

"Well, that's fucked up." I sank in the leather of my seat and attempted to ignore the dedication because I didn't know what to make of it. Pretty sure my subconscious would have a field day without my input. "Do you people only listen to old shit?"

"You're one to talk," Sam said with a throaty laugh. "A big shiny gold star for Special Agent Chicky babe and her incredible deflecting abilities."

"It's hardly likely to be a message from Mike to us because it's a radio station, he wouldn't even know if any of us would hear it." I was on a roll. "Furthermore, if he could call a radio station and dedicate a song, he can call one of us and tell us where the hell he is."

Unless there was something very wrong in his head.

At that point I realized we were no longer moving. Kurt had pulled off the road not far from the airport, Lee and Sam were parked behind us.

I climbed out of the car and heard Kurt's door open as I shut mine. Sam, Lee, Kurt, and I met on the shoulder between our cars.

"Something fucky is going on," I said, before anyone else could speak.

They agreed with subtle nods and body language. I could tell Lee was thinking a mile a minute. This was his brother we were talking about. I remember how Mike reacted when Lee was missing. My mind screeched to a halt. No need to go there. No reason to suspect bombs or anything life ending. A little voice in my head said, 'apart from the forty-four magnum and dead solider.' Yeah, apart from that we're golden.

Kurt gave Lee a gentle jab in the upper arm. "This is who we are and what we do. We'll find him."

"I know," Lee replied.

Sam rocked from foot to foot scuffling stones. "Something tells me Chicky Babe might have a few things she wants to share."

Wrong. I absolutely do not want to share. Anything. It will not help.

Kurt looked at me, his gaze seemed to say they were waiting. Like he didn't know and couldn't say?

I sighed.

"They played a couple of songs back to back that kinda made a story, and it made sense to me."

"Songs that everyone could hear, not just music in your head?" Lee asked, plunging his left hand into his pocket.

"Yeah, how's that for different?" Kurt said with a smile.

"Interesting," Lee replied. "And these songs told you what?"

"Mike could be in West Virginia and in danger." No need to mention the gun or the dead soldier part.

"West Virginia?" Sam and Lee echoed.

"Uh huh." I did my damnedest to make it all seem normal. "I want to ask you something Lee."

"Go ahead."

"Did Mike mention any appointments with Leon Kapowski?"

Lee's brow creased as he thought then he shook his head. "Not that I recall. That name is familiar."

"He's my neurologist. His name appears on our calendar every six months."

"Oh, yeah. And Mike has an appointment with him?"

"Tomorrow."

"This some kind of follow up after his latest brain injury?"

Kurt intervened. "I believe so."

"How is his follow up appointment relevant?" Sam was trying to piece things together, I could tell by the pained expression.

"There is a chance that Mike could be experiencing on-going problems since being knocked unconscious. It happens." Kurt tipped his thumb at me. I chose to ignore it. Because he was right. Best not to draw too much attention to some of the less than stellar moments I've had post-traumatic brain injury, if I could help it. I quickly realized I couldn't.

"I think we need to keep open minds here. He may have taken himself off somewhere for some down time," I said, fully aware that everyone remembered me doing something similar after Mac's death which was a post-concussion episode mixed with grief. Made me unreliable for a few weeks and became dangerous. "Airport, check the footage, see if we can see him leave with anyone or leaving alone."

"On foot?" Sam asked.

"Lee checked into his credit card and such, he hasn't used it to rent a car. Doesn't mean he isn't in a car, but, he may also be on foot." I turned and walked back to the passenger door of the car. "Let's just get there and find out all we can." I swung the door open and climbed in.

4.

I took a deep breath as I walked through the automatic doors at the airport entrance followed by Kurt, Sam, and Lee. My lungs filled with a mixture of excitement and trepidation sucked in from the air. Just the usual airport atmosphere.

"I love airports, said no one ever."

"I recall," Kurt said, stepping up next to me. "Airport Police?"

"Yeah." I stopped and looked around. People in all directions. "Can you remember which way?"

"Follow us," Sam said, taking the lead.

People moved aside as Sam and Lee forged ahead, cutting a path for us. A few paused in their hurry and looked at us. Reminding me that the four of us were noteworthy. We sure didn't blend in. Sam held a door open, we filed through. The door closed behind us. Doors opened off the hallway. The first door bore a plaque that said MWAA Police Department. I opened it. Once inside the area resembled just about any police department anywhere. I walked over to the desk and spoke to a sergeant.

"Hi." I showed my credentials. "SSA Ellie Conway, FBI. We're looking for a missing person." I showed him a photo of Mike from my phone. "Seen him?"

"No ma'am. Where did he go missing from?"

"This airport."

Lee spoke, "Between nine-thirty and nine-forty last

night."

"I'll get an officer out here to take you into the security room. If he was here he'll be on at least one of our cameras."

"Thanks."

The sergeant picked up the phone on his desk and made a call. He looked at us and suggested we sit down in the waiting area.

I stepped back, turned, and saw a bench seat extending along the wall near the door where we entered. I motioned to my team. We settled on the lowish wooden bench. Sam, Lee, and Kurt looked a bit awkward trying not to take up the entire floor space with their legs. Three minutes later, and two phones calls answered by the desk sergeant, another door opened and a uniformed officer approached us.

He smiled. The men clambered to their feet; ungainly and awkward best described that maneuvre. I attempted a more graceful rise and failed. The bench was made for midgets.

"Agents. I'm Officer Kantrel," he said, extending his hand to me.

"SSA Ellie Conway," I said with a smile. "Thanks for your help."

"No problem, Agent Conway. Follow me and I'll see if we can squeeze y'all into the security room." He frowned then smiled. "Gonna be a tight fit."

"It's all right, we're used to it," Sam replied, shaking

the officer's hand. "I'm Special Agent Sam Jackson."

"Pleased to know you Agent Jackson." Officer Kantrel turned to Kurt. "And you are?"

Kurt shook his hand and introduced himself, then Lee followed suit.

Kantrel was right about the security room being small.

"I've loaded up the big monitor with the time frame you mentioned," Kantrel said, pointing to the biggest screen above a row of smaller screens. "I've set it to feed through all video from all the cameras for that time frame." He squeezed an arm past Lee and Sam, his body followed, he slipped into his seat and tapped a keyboard. The screen came to life.

"They'll play back to back?"

"Yes ma'am. If look at the bottom right corner of the screen, that tells us which camera shot the footage, I can tell you the location from that."

"Awesome."

We watched. Four sections played before I picked him out of a line of people walking from an arrival gate.

"There he is," I said. "Pause please. Can you zoom in on the blond guy wearing the blue shirt and brown leather jacket."

Kantrel zoomed in. It was definitely Mike. He had a khaki messenger type bag, slung over his left shoulder. Now we knew for certain he had carry-on luggage.

"Okay, let's see where he goes." The camera changed to a different location. I watched waiting to see if Mike came into view.

Ten-seconds later Lee called, "Pause." He pointed at the screen. "Do you see her?"

A woman approximately my build with long red hair, that hung in soft curls down her back she walked away from our camera view. She wheeled a small bag by an extended handle.

"She could be Laura," Sam said. "She's coming from a different gate?"

Kantrel moved his hand a mouse pointer appeared, a menu popped up.

"Yes, different gate and she's moving toward the Aerotrain."

"Mike came from a gate, where should be be going now?"

"To the Aerotrain," Kantrel replied. "Potentially they could've been on the same train to the main terminal."

"Will we be able to see that?"

"Yes. Ready to continue?"

"Please," I said.

We caught sight of both Mike and the redhead at the Aerotrain. She was ahead of him. It was impossible to tell if he saw her. A few minutes later the redhead walked toward the exit, she didn't go to the luggage carousel, and trying to catch her up was Mike.

"Pause," I said. The image that filled the screen was the redhead leaving the terminal building with Mike a few yards behind her. It looked like he was calling out.

The next frame showed her getting into a cab and Mike getting into a different cab.

I exhaled and leaned on the wall behind me.

"Cab. He got in a cab."

Kurt leaned as close as he could to the screen. "Can we get the cab number?"

Kantrel zoomed in. "Looks like six-one-zero."

"Or eight-one-zero," Lee said. "Not the best shot."

"Do you have regular cabs out front?" Sam asked. "Same ones over and over?"

"Yeah, quite a few seem to like the airport."

"Thank you, Office Kantrel, we appreciate your help."

"Why are you looking for him? Is he wanted in connection with a crime? We can alert other airports for you."

I smiled. "Nah, not necessary. He's a missing person not a potential criminal. But now we have a lead. Thank you again for your help."

5.

Lee stepped out of the terminal doors, he pushed sunglasses up on top of his head and scanned the row of cabs sitting at the curb.

"Lee?" He turned his head toward me. "Was it yellow or orange?"

"Orange," he replied, then pointed to a cab that just pulled in. "Like that one."

I spotted the phone number for company on the side of the newly arrived cab and gave them a call.

"Do you have a cab that was at Dulles Airport last night, either six-one-zero or eight-one-zero?"

"Let me look ma'am. Have you lost something?"

"Yes." Not a lie.

The dispatcher came back within seconds. "Cab six-one-zero picked up a fare from Dulles last night at nine-thirty-five. That was his last fare for the night and he won't be back on until five this evening."

"I wonder if that's the cab," I attempted to adopt an innocent confused tone. "Oh, I don't know. Did it go to D.C?"

"That cab went to Shepherdstown WVA ma'am. Probably not your ride." I waved a hand at Sam who strode over.

"Oh, thank you, oh dear." I sighed loudly. "Maybe it was another company. Are you orange or yellow?"

"Orange ma'am."

"Oh, sorry, I was in a yellow cab I think."

I hung up.

"Boss?"

"Orange cab, six-one-zero picked up a fare from here last night and went to West Virginia."

"Where in West Virginia?"

"Shepherdstown."

My gut sank like a rock when I said it out loud. West Virginia was one thing but Shepherdstown meant something to all of us. We only just left there three weeks ago. To be exact it was twenty-two days since our return.

I circled my arm in the air. Kurt and Lee joined us, fast.

"I called the cab company and a cab picked someone up from the taxi rank here last night and drove them to Shepherdstown."

Kurt shook his head slowly. "If that pick up was Mike, then something's up. I'm inclined to think you were right about his head being screwy."

Ya think?

"We saw him leaving the gate and the airport, nothing happened, he just followed that chick out," Lee said.

"He could've taken another knock to the head, doesn't even have to be memorable for it to cause a problem so soon after a TBI."

Lee paled. "If that's the case then we need to get to him."

I considered all the images we'd seen of him walking

through the airport. At no time did he have his phone in his hand. Maybe it was still on Airplane Mode.

"Mike was on a plane with a lot of people. I'd like to know more about the flight," I said and touched the Instagram icon on my phone, definitely worth a look. People Instagram everything these days. Mike Fisher on a plane was definitely more interesting than someone's breakfast. Five hours on a plane, that's plenty of photo opportunity. I entered hashtag Mike Fisher into search within Instagram. Six hundred and two posts were tagged with that hashtag. I opened the most recent photos. There were three photos from the plane and four from LAX. One of the LAX ones was a photo of Mike going through the security at the airport. The other three were Mike drinking coffee. That was still more exciting than someones eggs bene. All the photos were posted by different people at different times. The three photos taken on the plane were more interesting. The first was the back of Mike's head. He was definitely flying first class. The second picture was a side shot of Mike opening an overhead locker. It looked like a bag slid and hit his head. The caption read Overhead Locker one, Actor zero.

"Look," I passed my phone to Kurt.

"That'd do it." He handed my phone to Lee.

Lee gave my phone back.

Sam made a call. When he put it on speaker we heard who he'd called. Sandra.

"Hey beautiful, can you find me the number for Hotel

Bavaria in Shepherdstown, West Virginia."

"For you baby, anything. One sec."

Lee made gagging noises. Sandra giggled over the phone.

"Maybe I should've said you were on speaker, Sandy," Sam sounded apologetic.

"Not to worry. I've got the number for you, my stallion."

Lee went from gagging noises to full on barfing vocals.

I punched the numbers into my phone as Sandra relayed them. Sam finished the call as the hotel reception answered mine.

"Hi, put me through to Mike Fisher's room please," I kept my voice even and professional. Brazen was worth a shot.

There was a pause then a click. Followed by beeping in my ear. I looked at my screen. Call ended.

"You just got hung up on," Kurt said with a note of incredulousness.

I does happen sometimes. My charm isn't infallible.

"Give it a minute and Lee's turn," I said with a grin. "Pretty sure he's there and he checked in as Mike Fisher not Mike Davenport."

Lee leaned over and copied the number from my recent calls list. "Let's see if I get through. I'm asking for Michael Davenport." He put his phone on speaker.

As soon as the receptionist answered he said, "I'm Lee Davenport, can you book me a room next to Michael

Davenport's."

"Are you quite certain you have the correct hotel, Mr Davenport?"

"Yes. Oh, jeez, sorry, Mike probably checked in under Fisher."

"Ah, there is a room next door to Mr Fisher's, how many nights sir?"

"Put me down for two at this stage."

"That's great sir, we'll see you sometime today."

Lee hung up.

I grumbled, "So a man can ring up and get answers but not a woman ... guess she's protecting Mike from crazy fans. Ha." The last crazy person who tried to take him out at that very hotel was a man. The man who killed me, I mean, Laura.

"Let's go get him," Lee said.

6.

The closer we got to our destination the more my head started to ache. That wasn't a good sign. I sent two texts to Mike. Hoping he'd reply and tell me he was okay. He didn't. Again I wondered if it was still on Airplane Mode. I'd know soon enough.

The hotel looked the same as when we'd left it. I didn't know if that was good or bad. I did know I never expected to be back there. We parked close to each other in the parking lot. I rummaged in the glove compartment and found one of my FBI caps. I jammed the cap on my head, pulled my long pony tail through a gap in the back, then adjusted my sunglasses.

I tugged the brim downward, in an effort to get more shadow on my face and to make it harder to recognize me.

Th receptionist looked a bit surprised when I walked through the door, I hoped it was the FBI lettering on my cap and jacket and not my face. I recognized her and could tell by the curiosity in her expression that she didn't quite make a connection. Good news. Let's hope she never put two and two together. She remembered Lee though and he got a massive smile.

"Mr Davenport, so nice to have you back. I've put you right next door to Mr Fisher. Room seventeen, just down the hallway on your left past the desk here." She spun the guest registry toward him so he could sign in. Lee signed the book and handed her his credit card. "Charge both rooms to me. Which room is my brother in?"

"Room sixteen. Happy to charge both rooms to you, sir." She finished the check in process and handed Lee back his card. "I haven't seen your brother. He came in last night so the night manager saw to him, he did ask not to be disturbed today."

"He probably won't mind if I disturb him."

"Of course," she said with a smile as she handed Lee his room keycard. "It must be difficult for him, such a tragedy. I didn't think he'd want to return to the hotel."

"It's not been easy," Lee muttered, making his voice crack a little "For any of us."

"Of course, I'm so sorry," she said, then turned her smile toward Kurt and Sam. "Nice to see you both again."

We're unforgettable. I just hoped she didn't realize I was Laura last time I was there. A bride dying at her wedding dance in the hotel wasn't something staff would forget in a hurry. I moved so Kurt blocked me from view as we headed to the hallway. Staying out of sight seemed smart.

It felt like I should tip-toe past Mike's room and into Lee's. I think I held my breath. Once we were in Lee's room I looked around. It seemed very familiar but don't all hotel rooms? I turned on the spot, taking in the whole room. I knew this room. It was Mike's room. Last time. So the door I saw on the wall in this room was a connecting door to what was my room last time, and became 'our' room. I began to formulate a plan.

"See that door?" I pointed to the wall. "That goes to Mike's room. But it was ..."

"Your room. He's checked into the room he was with you in, when you were dead," Kurt said.

I nodded.

"Right then, I'm gonna go in. Stay out of sight, will ya?" I removed my holster from my belt and handed it to Kurt.

"Good thinking."

"Best not to tempt fate."

I handed my jacket and cap to Sam. Didn't need anything proclaiming I was FBI. Laura didn't wear FBI jackets, she was a PI. She was also dead, so, you know, whatever. I pulled the hair tie from my hair and shook the pony tail out.

"You think he'll recognize you as Laura?" Lee seemed skeptical.

"I do. I think his brain reset to our time here. I also think he'll see who his brain expects to belong to my voice. He's not going to see me as Ellie. He's focused on Laura."

Lee looked to Kurt for confirmation.

"If anyone knows what could be happening in his head it's Conway. You and I were privy to her brain reset. Remember?"

"I'll never forget. We traipsed all over Rockbridge County because Ellie was flipped back into her past, and

155

all we could do was go along for the ride." Lee shook his head. "Not fun. Okay, Chicky, see if you can work some Laura magic and bring Mike back to now."

If this was anything like what I've experienced then he'd need to see Laura.

I knocked on the connecting door, unlocked the door on our side and opened it, face to face with Mike's locked door I knocked again and waited. The three men moved aside, so the only person in direct line of sight from the doorway was me.

Nothing from the room next door.

I knocked again.

Nothing.

"Mike, it's Laura." I looked at Kurt and shrugged. "I can't open the door."

I heard movement near the door. The lock clicked. The door swung open. Mike stood there, bleary eyed, looking like he'd slept in his clothes. He blinked, rubbed his eyes, and peered at me.

"Laura ..."

I wasn't sure if I should say yes or say who I really was. Kurt nodded his head at me from the wall. And mouthed the words, you got this.

"Yes, it's me."

"Lau ... ra," he stumbled over the name as his right hand reached for me. "I thought I lost you."

"I know. I'm sorry." His hand tightened on mine and pulled me close. "I'm here now. It's going to be okay."

He walked backwards into his room, taking me with him. The radio played softly in the background. I pushed the door shut behind us. Seemed a good idea. His mind was struggling enough without Lee, Sam, and Kurt's presence. He led me over to the bed. He must've laid on it, but not been in it. The bedspread was crumpled but the bed underneath was still made. I remembered waking up from the drug Kurt gave me in that bed and seeing Mike crying next to me. He played the grieving widower to perfection. Which is probably why we're here now.

I asked too much of a man with a recent brain injury. The exhaustion on his face told me he didn't sleep much. He needed to sleep.

"Mike," I whispered, to get his attention. He sat on the edge of the bed, I sat next to him. "Why did you come back here?"

"You were here. *We* were here. I couldn't find you when I got off the plane."

Okay, good, at least he remembered getting off the plane. I saw his phone on the nightstand. The screen was dark. I wanted to pick it up and have a look but not yet.

"You found me. I'm here." I glanced around, looking for a gun. Hoping I didn't see one. If he had a weapon it wasn't obvious.

"You looked so beautiful in your wedding dress."

"Brides are supposed to look beautiful."

"You're always beautiful Laura. Always." He smiled, it was almost serene and a little bit creepy. "The way you looked when I put the Hope Diamond around your neck. Stunning." His expression changed, confusion clouded his features. "I said the diamond matched your eyes but your eyes were green that day."

"Yes they were. It was something new I was trying."

"Your eyes are Hope Diamond blue, don't change the color."

"Okay." I touched his hand. "You look tired. Wanna try and get some sleep?"

"Will you still be here when I wake up?" Panic ringed his words in spiky barbs. "Are you really here now?"

"Yes. I'll be right here next to you." I encouraged him to lie down."I'm not going anywhere, Mike. We're in this together." I snuggled close to him, he tucked an arm around me and closed his eyes. Didn't take long before his breathing became slow and even. I couldn't extract myself from his arms, so I closed my eyes too. I imagined Delta A pacing up a storm in the adjoining room but figured if they were worried they'd come on in. It seemed like a good idea to get Mike relaxed and if he wanted to be with Laura then he should be with her, at least until his brain ironed some of the wrinkles out. I knew what helped me and all I could do was apply that knowledge. He needed time. No one, not even me could say how much time he'd need. Faintly over the radio playing on the other side of the room I heard, *Bon Jovi*. Finally something decent. It was hard not to smile as *Jon Bon Jovi* sung, 'I'll be there for you'. I knew all I could do for

Mike, was be there.

An hour and forty minutes, a short nap, and some really good music later he opened his eyes. Mike's hand reached up and touched my hair. "Straight and golden."

"Do you know who I am?"

"Ellie."

I breathed a huge sigh of relief. "Yeah."

"What's going on?"

"You remember anything?" I asked, sitting up.

"I got on a plane," he said, looking up at me. "And where are we? Don't get me wrong, this is very nice. But where are we?"

"Somewhere safe." I wrestled my phone from my jeans pocket and showed him the photo on Instagram of the luggage hitting his head. "Seems you aggravated your previous head injury with a suitcase."

"But where are we?"

"Look around and tell me if you recognize the room."

Mike slowly sat up, then stood, and inspected the room before sitting down a little too heavily.

"It's the hotel in West Virginia, where Laura died."

"You got it in one." I smiled. "You came looking for Laura. Do you remember?"

He went to shake his head but changed his mind. "No. Lee was supposed to meet me?"

"He did but you were already gone. He got your bag though." I watched him trying to make sense of what I'd told him. "You have a headache?"

"Yeah."

"I can get you something for that."

He frowned. "From where?"

"Kurt. He, Lee, and Sam are next door, probably going crazy because they don't know what's happening here."

"The cavalry rode in?"

"Damn straight."

"How'd you find me?"

"It's what we do. Remember? Your brother and I are FBI."

He reached over and picked up his phone. He swiped a finger across the screen. "It's still on Airplane mode. God." One more swipe and the phone came to life in his hands. Alerts chimed. It sounded as though they were piling up because the alerts came through so fast. "Texts. Missed calls. No wonder you're here."

"Your lack on communication and disappearing act was a little concerning."

"How did I get here?"

"A cab. I doubt you've got any cash left."

He was trying to haul events into reach, by the look on his face he couldn't.

"Why don't I remember?"

"You kinda stepped out for a bit," I said, rubbing his upper back with my hand. "I think you're back now." And hopefully back properly. "That knock to your head sort of reset your mind. You came back here to Laura. Could've easily been the top of a mountain and not somewhere we could find you."

"Why here?"

I felt my shoulders move into a shrug and forced them back down. "Just lucky maybe. Or maybe, it was a recent high adrenaline situation, and you were having fun while we were here."

"I was." A bit of spark returned to his eyes.

"Brains are complex things. Maybe yours looked for a time when you were happy recently and dumped you back there for a bit."

I stood up and opened the connecting door.

"Kurt, Mike needs something for his headache. Lee, he's okay."

He really wasn't okay. I could see it in his eyes. He was fucked up and he needed to talk it out and hear from someone who really understood what it was like to live with TBI. Maybe a support group. Yeah, one of them.

I looked over my shoulder to see Kurt giving Mike a couple of painkillers, and flashing his little light of doom in his eyes. Rather him than me. Just the thought of that light made my head hurt. Lee and Kurt talked to Mike for a few minutes. I saw Lee hug him.

Sam nudged me.

"You done good, Chicky Babe."

"It's not over Sam. He's not in a real good place and he's trying hard to pretend he is."

Sam chuckled. "Why don't you talk to him?"

"I think he needs a support group or something ..."

"You're his friend. If anyone knows what he's going through it's you."

But maybe I don't want to go there. Maybe it's too close to home and the wounds are still too fresh. And maybe he's just better off with someone who isn't me. Someone objective.

Kurt came back. "I'm going to talk to Leon and see if I can move that appointment out a bit. He needs to see Mike, but I don't think we can push him to leaving here just yet."

"So, we're staying at this hotel?" That wasn't the cleverest idea ever. I didn't feel like being snapped as a living dead woman.

"We are. He came here for a reason. Let's let him work through some of this, okay?"

"Sure." I'll just keep out of sight as much as possible. "Make your call."

Lee appeared. He was still worried but less so. "He's been listening to the radio or at least the radio is on."

"I know," I replied. Maybe he did call the radio but I know he didn't use his cell phone. "He couldn't find Laura, might've been him that made that dedication after all. Not for our benefit but for his own."

"Hungry?" Lee asked, it was a collective question.

"I could go a steak," Sam said.

"I'm starving," I added. "Probably best if I don't eat in the restaurant though."

"Good call. I'll order room service for you and Mike.

The rest of us can eat in the restaurant."

"Would you have the food sent to this room, and bring it through when it arrives. That way there is no chance of anyone seeing me. I'll go sit with Mike."

Sam gave me a thumbs up.

7.

Lee delivered our meals when they arrived. There was a bottle of red wine included with the meal. Mike opened it and poured us a glass each.

"Nice, dolcetto," I said, tasting the wine. Mike agreed. We ate our dinner without speaking much beyond the occasional appreciative comment.

After dinner Mike rescued the wine and glasses from the cart before I pushed it back into the other room. I checked outside the door to the corridor. There was no one around. So I shoved the cart out the door and left it near the wall. I closed the connecting door on my way back in. Mike had poured us another glass each.

He was lying propped up by pillows on the bed with his glass in hand.

I sat next to him.

"We've done this before," I said, raising my glass and touching his. The clink seemed to echo.

"Yeah. We need to stop meeting like this." He clinked my glass again.

We needed to stop meeting, period.

I took a larger swig than I intended and felt it.

"What?" Mike looked over at me. "You look like you want to say something."

I sighed louder than intended. "I know how hard this is for you."

"It's not. I'm fine."

Another sigh escaped the confines of my mouth, that's my line. "Mike. This is me. I. Know."

"I just got confused, that's all."

Sam's words haunted me. I swilled the contents of the glass like it was water. Mike filled it again. I drank half before speaking. He set his glass on the nightstand.

"Ellie?"

"A few years ago I got confused too. I died for few minutes and it scrambled my brain and my memory."

"You died?"

"Apparently."

"Okay and you ended up like me now, that kind of scrambled?"

If only it wasn't that short lived. My brain was full on scrambled egg territory.

"Yep. I thought I still lived in Rockbridge County. I didn't know who Carla was. When Kurt told me I was dating Rowan Grange, I punched him in the face."

The stunned look on Mike's face gave way to a small laugh. "You punched him."

Twice. Not my finest moment.

"I didn't remember that I knew Rowan. I thought Kurt and Lee were teasing me and I was a mess who couldn't deal."

"How'd they handle that?"

"Like always, they hung in there until I came back."

"What do you remember?" He asked.

A jig-saw puzzle made up of memories filled my mind,

multiple large blank spaces still obvious. Missing pieces. Like almost every old puzzle. The empty spaces were no longer something that bothered me.

"Not much. I know what Lee and Kurt told me. I know I wanted to go home to my house in Mauryville that it was really important that I go home. I thought I still lived there."

"Didn't the new owners find that strange?"

"I still owned it."

"That's not so bad then. Tenants?"

"Ah, no, more a burned out shell of it's former self. I wandered around the burned ruins and all I saw was my home, as it was, before I'd even met Mac. I had no idea I'd gotten married. As far as I knew, I still had both my parents."

"Jeez, I bet that all brought the doctor out of Kurt."

"I guess it did."

"Why did you mind take you so far back and mine only shifted me a few weeks?"

"There's a theory, which is mine, and seems to be the best one I've heard." I smiled as I took a sip of wine. "My mind took me back before a lot of trauma happened in my life. It was an easier time back then, I guess. I'm not saying I was happier. But less traumatized." I'd definitely seen less and experienced less. "You banged your head again, but you were coming to D.C. and maybe your mind went. Hey, D.C. we had some fun there. Then tossed up the wedding prep or the actual ceremony. So, confused

Mike went back to the hotel. To his bride." A high adrenaline very exciting time and far removed from his usual life as an actor.

"That actually makes sense."

"Sometimes I do." I finished the contents of my glass, I could feel so much more truths bubbling up. Things I'd never talked about. And then suddenly I blurted out, "I remember once waking up and my pillow was wet, a big semi-circle of pinkish fluid that was crystalizing at the edges. Turned out to be brain fluid."

"Christ." He flopped onto his back, eyes fixed on the ceiling. "Ellie, you need to be more careful. You could've died."

Yeah, well, I've done that and survived it. Hard to kill.

"You don't get it. The point is ... I. Remember. Waking. Up. A lot of people never wake up from injuries like that. Hell a lot of people don't wake up from regular smacks to the head."

He turned his head to face me. "Is this your way of saying we're lucky?"

I grinned. "Yep."

He rolled his head back and resumed staring at the ceiling. "Lucky?" He whispered to himself. "Sure, we're lucky. I'm struggling to remember lines from one minute to the next."

"It'll get better."

"And the headaches ... do they stop?" He was looking at me again.

"Honestly?"

"Yeah."

"That's where migraines come from for me. They're a leftover from one too many concussions."

Four or five too many concussions.

"How many did you have before migraines became a thing you had to deal with?"

"Three or four. I can't remember."

Back to the ceiling again.

"I've had more than three already."

"I know but it doesn't mean you'll develop migraines. You've got an appointment with Leon. He can talk to you about that and the likelihood."

"I don't feel like myself."

"I know."

A knock on the door startled me. Mike laughed. Jeez.

Lee called out, "Everything all right in there?"

"Yeah, we're talking," I replied.

Mike sat, swung his legs off the bed, but didn't stand. I walked around the bed until I was in front of him and crouched down. "What do you see when you close your eyes?"

He lifted his head, his pale blue eyes met mine.

"I see everything I don't want to see and nothing I do."

"Can I tell you a secret? You have to promise you'll never tell Kurt, Lee, or Sam." I don't need them watching me any closer than they do already. I crooked my pinky and held it out. "Pinky swear."

He hooked his pinky finger around mine with absolute seriousness said, "I swear."

"Some nights I can't sleep at all. Some nights I sit on the chair in my room with my weapon in my hand and imagine what it would be like to put it in my mouth and pull the trigger." I watched the expression on his face, as his head moved in tiny increments from side to side. "Mac died in front of me. Carla committed suicide with her best friend. It's a lot to handle on top of consecutive traumatic brain injuries. Then you add the fun and games associated with my job and there are times when it feels like it's too much."

"Don't, El."

"Where's the gun?"

His eyes flashed to the desk by the window. I walked over and opened the drawer. There it was. A forty-four Magnum. Shit, I was right. I didn't touch it. I went back to Mike and crouched back down in front of him.

"I don't know where I got it," he said, quietly.

"It's all right. I'm just happy you didn't use it. We'll find out and deal with it." Or maybe we won't find out and it'll disappear, either way. Dealt with.

"I don't think I was going to do anything." His voice cracked into shards that stabbed me with their sharp pointy ends and it felt a lot like guilt. Because I caused this.

"You're not the first person to think about it, Mike. You're not. And it's not only you and me that have. I read somewhere that twenty-two percent of people who experienced more than one traumatic brain injury had or have suicidal thoughts." Quite a few of them suck-started pistols, but he didn't need to know that. He was going to get better. We were going to get better.

He tried to smile but it got caught on his memories and never made it to his eyes.

"What stops you?"

"Those three idiots outside the door. Dad. My brother. You. Mitch. All the people I've helped."

"Is it enough?"

"So far." I'm still here. "When all is said and done, I'm a catholic and it's a sin."

"That's a lot of Hail Mary's," Mike said, but he didn't sound totally convinced. "Do you think you'll ever pull the trigger?"

"No. Not on myself. I'm pretty sure about that. Can't guarantee someone else won't get hurt though."

He frowned at me. "Seriously?"

All the truth now.

"PTSD messes with me sometimes, combine that with everything else ... I don't think I'm a danger to myself." I crossed the fingers of my right hand. "I do think there are times when I am a potential danger to others."

And who knows what will happen in the future?

"Can I ask how you handled Carla's death?"

"Badly." I smiled. "I disappeared."

He arched an eyebrow. "Really? Like we were talking

about? Memory lapses and loss?"

"Nope. I dropped off the grid and into many *many* bottles of tequila. And then one day I woke up, hungover as fuck, and I knew I couldn't drink myself to death, because I tried and it didn't take. I went back to work." The events that followed that decision crowded my mind like black fog.

"El? What?" He was studying my face in a way I'd never seen him do before. "What happened?"

"I'd only been back at work a few days when Lee and I ..." I took a breath and tried again. "... when Lee was shot while we were walking back to the office after an arrest. It was a nice night. We walked. We were discussing where to get coffee and he was shot. And all of a sudden, I was wrist deep in your brother's gut trying to stop him dying on the pavement."

I didn't want to talk about any of this. Ever.

"How the fuck do you carry on?"

"This isn't supposed to be about me. I just wanted you to know that I understand what it's like. I really do know what you're going through."

"So tell me how you carry on and how do you get through this mine field?"

"One foot in front of the other."

"I mean it El. How? You see more action than a lot of soldiers."

Some days my office is a war zone. The next memory that launched was me shooting Jonathon Tierney's wife in my office, as she shot and wounded him all within hours of Lee's guts being in my hands. I shook it off and smiled at Mike.

"You know what? You just can't let the bastards win."

"I really thought I saw Laura."

"I know. We saw that woman on the surveillance video at the airport. She really looked like Laura from behind."

"I didn't imagine that part?"

"Not at all." Guilt stomped around in my gut making me feel sicker and sicker. "All this is my fault. You had a head injury and I put you in a situation that I shouldn't have. I compromised your mental health and your ability to cope." I took his left hand in mine. "I'm sorry, Mike."

Because sorry makes it all better. Not.

"You didn't have a choice El. You stopped him before he killed me."

"Yeah, that's what I keep telling myself. But you know what? It doesn't help. I hurt you and now we're here." A tear slid past my eyelashes. I brushed it away before he noticed.

He squeezed my hand and changed the subject, guess he did notice. "How much shit are you all in because you went off the grid to save me and that mess happened and got tangled around you?"

I pulled out a piece of paper I'd been carrying in my pocket for three days and handed it to Mike. He unfolded it, read the contents and handed it back. I put it away.

"The only reason we have to explain ourselves is because of Assistant Director Owen and her shitty and potentially criminal behavior, it's got nothing to do with what happened to you. I expect she'll be neck deep in brown sticky stuff. Roll on the special committee next Friday," I said. "Have you been called to testify?"

He nodded. "Video link a few days after you. Guess they want to digest your information before hearing from me."

Guess so.

I was surprised at the speed in which the investigation into the whole mess was happening. At least it was fresh in our minds. A blast blew across my line of vision. I flinched. Mike's hand tightened on mine.

"All right?"

"I should be asking you that," I said with a smile and hoped it ended the probing look in his eyes. It didn't. I shrugged. Mother of Satan was a hard thing to forget, we were so lucky none of us was killed. "We're okay Mike."

As long as we're still breathing there's a chance that that will be true.

"I was right about you, wasn't I? You are an adrenaline junkie."

"Yeah. If I wasn't I'd be an accountant."

"I can't even imagine what that would look like ..."

Me neither.

"If you're ever not okay again, call one of us."

"I'd like to be able to call you."

"You can. You should think about talking to Lee. He

needs to know when you're okay and when you're not. If he hadn't come to me, we may not have found you. This could've ended differently."

He smiled, this time dimples were involved. Mike pulled my hand, "Come a little bit closer." I lost my balance and fell forward into his arms. "Don't blame yourself for my whacked out brain. You saved my life by giving Laura's and ultimately you saved my life again. I owe you."

"How about we owe it to each other to stay in touch?"

"I'd like that."

And no one eats a bullet.

The End.

Heard it Through the Grapevine:

A lost asset and a jail break.

This is when Agent Argo joined Delta A, this story follows Metabyte.

Heard it Through The Grapevine.

1.

"The fuck she did!"

"Don't shoot the messenger Iverson."

"Don't tell me stupid shit, Henderson."

Exasperated expletive like noises flew from his mouth, swirling steam pumped from his ears. His head had never been closer to exploding. "Is this how it's going to be?"

I shrugged. "Pretty much."

"Rein it in a few notches will you?" He sat in the chair nearest my desk. "All I know is what I told you. We heard from her parole officer that she missed her check in. How do you want to proceed?"

"We activate the tracker in her phone and we bring her in." How far does she think she'll get? Sure she doesn't know about the tracker, it was a clever little addition to her latest Facebook app update, but why she think running from us was a good idea? FBI has a long reach. The only reason Alison was not in jail was because she was feeding us information on her delightful boyfriend Rion Maldorm. He was now known only by his inmate number at a Federal Correctional Institute.

"Just like that?"

"Yep. She's gone a wanderin' we need her back in the

corral," I said.

"All right. Let's see where she is?"

"Yes, let's." I tapped her name into the tracking program we installed on her phone. A message bubble appeared. Tracker offline. Crap on a salty cracker. That's not supposed to happen. I chewed my bottom lip and tried to turn the tracker on. Something that I knew I could often do via the app. Nothing.

"Problem?" Kurt asked, leaning forward with an elbow on my desk.

"Maybe." I opened another screen to see if the phone was operational. Nope. I tried turning it on. It'd be a bit weird for Alison when her phone suddenly turned on but she shouldn't run. The phone remained dormant. "Yes. Problem. I can't find her and I can't remotely turn her phone on."

"Destroyed?"

"Possibly. Could also be at the bottom of the river with Alison."

"Cheery thought, Iverson." He smiled. "The phone might have broken. I've heard that happens."

"Guess not everyone needs or wants heavy duty bullet proof cases."

"I imagine that most people will never use their phone as a weapon," Kurt added.

Our phone cases were solid enough to knock someone out, and the phone inside would be just fine. It wasn't the intention of the case just a useful happenstance. Rugged as fuck.

A laugh tumbled from my lips. "More likely most people don't want their phone dragging their pants down."

"That too."

The mood lightened. Henderson was good at knowing when to do that. Alison was still missing. I sighed. "Social media ... let's have a looksee."

"Facebook stalking?"

"I think we can call it investigating, being FBI."

Kurt laughed. "However you spin it to make yourself happy, Iverson."

I checked the file on Alison. She had Instagram, Facebook, Twitter, and a Tumblr account, that we knew about. I did not want to delve into Tumblr, that place gave me the creeps. So I flicked that link to Kurt. His phone chirped. He read it then arched an eyebrow at me.

"Tumblr?"

"Last time I was there ..." It'll haunt me forever. "I just can't."

Laughter wrapped his words, "You'd think you of all people would know better than to search for Sam and Dean Winchester on the Internet."

I held up my hand. "Shush. I had no idea how sick fans can be." My hand flapped at him. "Get looking."

Kurt's laughter washed over me as I dug into Alison's Twitter account. No mention of the boyfriend or going away. Nothing cryptic. Nothing unusual. I scrolled back through her feed for three months. From what I could tell she used Twitter to keep in touch with friends, talk about books, and TV shows. I moved on to Instagram. She posted photos of food. A lot of food. Delicious food. My stomach complained.

"Hungry, Iverson?"

"Apparently," I replied, without looking up. Didn't realize my stomach was going to impersonate a black bear with quite so much ferociousness.

More food images sailed passed my eyes interspersed with photos of clothes and the occasional selfie. Then I spotted a picture of a lake. It was posted almost two years earlier. Well before Rion's incarceration. No hashtags saying where it was and no location tagged. "Check this out." I turned my laptop to face Kurt. "Where do you think that is?"

"Not sure." He showed me his screen. "Big fat nothing on this site. I'll check Facebook."

"Okay." I spun my laptop back to face me and captured the image of the lake.

"Her Facebook wall has a bunch of posts from friends talking about a night out, last weekend. Photos included. She hasn't posted since then."

"BOLO, time."

I put out a BOLO on Alison Smith and crossed my fingers. A missing asset didn't feel like a good thing. She'd come to us sometime ago with information that linked to a series of home invasions across northern Virginia, over the West Virginia border, and up into Maryland. Her boyfriend was involved. We stopped the violent gang of thieves in D.C. Her boyfriend went to prison for his part and Alison stayed out because she was useful. She uncovered information during visits and passed it on. After a few false starts it began to look like her boyfriend, was running his gang of thieves from the inside and recruiting from the unending pool of reprobates behind the prison walls. His little operation grew and as it grew violence became more of a theme. Turns out I don't like people like him much.

"Did she say if that piece of shit she clung to had any jobs pending?" Kurt asked.

I shook my head. "She was due to bring me what she had by the way of intel. Sometimes she text and other times Alison liked to meet in person. This meet was to be a face to face."

"You think they got to her?"

"Probably," I said.

"Might be a Double A situation."

I looked at Kurt. He met my gaze. "Perhaps we should keep out of train stations then ..."

"Good idea. I don't think Vienna station has recovered."

"Has a bit more ventilation than it used to, that's for sure."

Bullets really make a mess of glass. I pushed the memory of Double A lying facedown in a pool of blood and raining bullets, aside.

"We could do with a more positive outlook," Kurt said.

"I'm positive things are not going to end well for Alison," I replied, checking my email, just in case she'd managed to email me. She hadn't but another forty people had. Woo hoo.

"That's not the sort of positive I was referring to, Iverson."

"That's what you're getting though."

I picked up my desk phone and hit six. Sandra answered fast.

"How can I assist you today O Leader of Troubled Souls?"

"Got a lost asset. Can you put some feelers out and see if anyone has come across Alison Smith in the last two days?"

"Your wish is my command."

"Anything exciting come in?"

Sandra started to speak then stopped. "Yes indeed, it'll be level with your door in three, two ..."

Argo barreled into the room. Stopped. Looked at Kurt, cruised around him and greeted me with licking tongue and wagging tail.

"I thought you were at training school today," I said, rubbing his ears. He sat and rested his big head in my lap.

A voice from the doorway said, "He was, and he came to show you his certificate."

I smiled before I looked up. My husband grinned at me

from the doorway, holding a certificate in his hand.

"He graduated?" I said, petting Argo's head. "That was today?" Dammit. I wanted to be there for that.

"Top three. We have some paper work to do here and then he'll be joining Delta A as a victim support dog."

"High five," I said to Argo. His fuzzy paw hit my hand. "Good job pal."

Kurt stood up, Mitch thrust the certificate at him, with a proud dog owner grin on his face.

"Impressive. And they said you'd never amount to anything boy," Kurt said to the dog. "Just because you're not vicious enough doesn't mean you're not good enough."

His eyes flicked to me. "I think he's going to be a valuable addition to our team."

Kurt excused himself, Mitch took his seat, and Argo lay on the floor at the end of my desk. Near both of us. He didn't play favorites with his humans.

I stood and joined Mitch's side of the desk. After a decent hello kiss I leaned on the desk in front of him.

"Do we both need to do the paperwork?"

"I think that would make it go a lot smoother. They want to fit him with a vest too."

Just like a real FBI dog.

Sandra appeared in the doorway. "O Esteemed Dog Whisperer, the sign is up at the floor entrance saying there is working dog on site. I hear he's official."

"Thanks Sandra." I tapped my fingers on the desk behind me. "About the missing person, please check my

BOLO and make sure I included the tri-state area as well as D.C."

"Consider it done."

Argo's tail thumped the carpeted floor. Thud. Thud. Thud. Sandra left. Argo resumed his resting state.

Mitch rose. He wrapped his arms around me. "How about I do a coffee run before we go do the paperwork. I think he'll want to stay with you."

"Okay. Can you make mine a mochaccino please."

"Of course."

He bent down and ruffled Argo's neck fur. "You stay with Ellie."

I swear the dog nodded. I moved back to my desk chair as Mitch left. The second I woke my laptop, emails chimed and internal messages chirped. A lot of the messages were congratulatory ones from fellow agents who'd heard Argo's news. Our hairy heart thief had quite the fan club.

I checked for any sign of Alison Smith. Nothing. It'd be a while before we got ping backs from the BOLO. It takes time. I opened the case file we had on her delightful boyfriend. There was a chance that held a clue as to her whereabouts. Even as I read the file I could feel a dull niggly notion building into something hard to ignore. Alison might be dead. Positive, Ellie. Think positive. She might have run and gone to ground somewhere.

2.

A familiar voice spoke from the door way. "Agent Iverson. I hoped to find you in."

Without looking up I replied, "Debbie Barnes, what brings you up here?"

A small laugh made me drag my eyes from the file and take note of the person in my doorway. It wasn't Debbie. Argo greeted the man like a long lost friend.

"Sorry, thought you were Debbie, obviously you are not." Although they could easily be related.

"I'm Michael Addison."

"Oh, right." I hauled a memory in from a month back. "You work with Debbie?" Down in the sub basement.

"I do. I was up here in a meeting and thought I'd say hello."

"Come in, have a seat. Don't mind Argo he seems to think he knows you."

Michael sat in the chair Mitch had vacated. The familiarity in his appearance and voice to Debbie was stunning. The shoulder length blond curly hair combined with the identical voice gave me pause. Something was going on. Argo returned to his nap position.

"Nice to catch up."

"You and Debbie job share, I heard?"

He nodded. "She's out for a few days, so I'm the man of the moment. Anything you need regarding new identities just give me a bell." His eyes drifted to Argo.

An idea struck. "Do you have reliable contacts outside of law enforcement that create identities?"

He shifted his line of sight from the sleeping dog to me. "We keep a few. Pays to know whose doing what and for whom."

"I've got an asset who disappeared." I pulled up a recent photograph and spun my laptop to face Michael. "Her."

"I can ask a few people. Is there a BOLO?"

"Yes indeed."

"I'll access that and use the image provided. If she's been asking about a new life or a new identity, then my people might know something."

The smile on my face was real, as I spun the laptop back to it's rightful position. Once again the universe proved that people arrived when they're needed.

"I'd be grateful if you would ask. I'm hoping she's opted for a new life far away from her disappointment of a boyfriend and bad life choices." Because it's better than thinking she's dead in a ditch somewhere. I pulled my top drawer open and took out a small purple envelope. "You'll probably see Debbie before I do." Like when you look in the mirror. "I was planning on popping downstairs this afternoon and delivering this." I handed the envelope to Michael.

"Can I ask?"

"An invitation to my baby shower." I could still not believe those words came out of my mouth let alone the reality implied by the words. Baby shower. For a second I wondered if I qualified for two such events. Or if it should baby should be plural.

He smiled. "I'm sure she'd love to attend."

I wanted to ask if they were the same person so bad but also didn't want to offend. I let it go. No doubt I'd be told if I was supposed to know, other than that, not really my business.

"You had a meeting on our floor?"

"Caine Grafton, well, when I say meeting it was more crowing on my part. I bet him at golf last week and he wants another game."

Golf. Grown men chasing little balls for miles. No thanks.

"I do hope you bet him again."

"Do you play?"

"Nope." That's not even on my horizon. "I run. I like the soothing rhythm of my feet hitting asphalt or grass or dirt."

"Debbie runs," he replied. "If you're still running, maybe you two could run together."

I nodded. "I'd like that. When did you say she'd be back?"

"A few days, I'll get her to give you a bell."

"Thank you, Michael."

He unfolded his legs and stood. "I best be going." Michael hunched over, dragged one leg behind him and said in a rather good Quasimodo voice, "Back to the basement for me."

My laughter followed him from the office.

Argo stretched and ambled over to me. "What do you think boy? Is that why you were so happy to see Michael? Is it because you know Michael as Debbie?"

Argo had no response. No doubt he thought I was an idiot for not knowing immediately. We don't all possess a dogs keen senses. And mine are somewhat muddied by the space invaders.

"Let's go for a walk," I said to the dog. He fell into step beside me, his head level with my leg. Together we walked down the hall and round the corner to Caine's office. I knocked once then opened the door. Argo waited until I moved before going inside.

"Ah, the dog of the hour," Caine said with a lighter than usual growly tone. "Come here boy."

Argo responded happily and allowed Caine to hug him.

"Thought we'd drop in and say hi. Signing all his paperwork soon, then he's official Delta A."

"Best news I've had all week. I'm happier about you being in the field with this dog around."

"He's supposed to be a victim support dog," I reminded him. "All tongue and tail and very little growl." Kinda the opposite of Caine. I halted that thought, it was weird even for me.

"We know that, but the bad guys don't. They're just going to see teeth and fur."

"I guess."

"He's getting the new bullet proof vest?"

"Yeah."

"Good."

"Hey, Caine ..."

He stopped playing with the dog and looked at me.

"Yes."

"Michael Addison. The guy who bet you at golf, is that even a thing? Do you actually beat someone at golf?"

"You win, so yes you can beat someone. And yes, he did."

"Known him long?"

"As a matter of fact I have."

So, he probably knows then.

My tongue rolled the words up into a little ball and spat them across the room. "Is he Debbie Barnes?"

Caine's mouth twitched. First one corner then the other, then a random double twitch that involved an eyebrow.

I waved a finger in the direction of his face. "What is happening there?"

"I smiled," he grumbled.

"Jeez." I sat down. "Don't. I thought you were having a stroke."

A strange strangled gurgling came from deep within Caine's throat. Choking? I stared at him trying to determine if he was struggling for air and needed assistance. Then it happened, the noise flowed from his mouth as a laugh. I didn't even know he could make happy sounds.

Argo jumped and hid behind my chair. I wanted to join him.

Caine controlled himself. The twitching continued.

"In answer to your question," he said with a massive twitch. "Yes. Michael has days when he is Debbie."

"Well, that explains a lot." The voice thing, the appearance, how Argo knew him.

"Sometimes, Ellie, you're a bit slow to the party."

I rolled my eyes. "That's unfair. I'd only ever met Debbie." More unaccustomed laughter fell from Caine's twitching mouth. "We'll leave you to your amusement. I have paperwork to complete for the hairy beastie."

3.

The paperwork didn't take as long as I imagined it would. Argo behaved beautifully even though I knew he was bored. Mitch and I walked him back to my floor sporting his new vest that proclaimed him an FBI agent. He had a badge attached to his vest. It filled me with joy.

"I'll see you two later, I've got to get back to the office," Mitch said, giving me a kiss. "You're not going to be late tonight, right?"

"Definitely not late tonight."

He said goodbye leaving me to contemplate the missing asset and Argo settling for a nap. I rocked back in my chair, aimlessly tapping a pen on my desk. Music. I needed music. Or Chance. Maybe Chance would know something.

I sat forward and read the file again. Perhaps there was something I'd overlooked. Maybe I knew something?

Music called to me. I opened my phone, dragged the bottom of the screen up, scrolled left, and hit play.

"Come on, brain. There has to be something here." The mouse pointer wandered over the file like a spider building a web."Oh,what a tangled web we weave when we fuck with people and intentionally mislead."

Argo woofed in his sleep.

My office door opened. A fresh breeze rushed across my desk. Papers rustled. Odd. I glanced up in time to see the room fade into muted colors and a black pencil sketch outlines around everything. A tornado of lines and color swirled around me. Sucking me and Argo into the pages of a comic book. The wind dropped. We fell through newsprint paper landing in a large office space. Argo lay on an area rug. I was seated in a leather chair. In front of me, a glass topped desk and Christopher Chance.

"Nice of you to drop in," he said with a smile that lit his eyes.

"Don't think I had a choice," I replied, adjusting to my surroundings.

"You were thinking about me ..."

"I was wondering if you knew anything."

"Nah, ah. You needed me." He seemed to enjoy that notion way too much.

"Whatever. Do you know something?"

The smile became a grin. "I know a lot of things. What in particular would you like to know?"

"Where's Alison Smith?"

He looked at his phone then back at me. "That I don't know."

"Then I'm here why?"

"Because, your brain needs a hand." His eyes flicked to the sleeping dog. "Nice that you have the dog around now. He's going to be useful."

"So everyone says. Can you help me or not?" I was trying to be patient. I was trying to be appreciative. But, it was Chance and he annoyed me on a visceral level.

"You have a partial answer, I heard you say it."

Jeez.

"I said it?"

He nodded.

I pressed rewind on my day, hoping I'd hear myself say that partial answer. Nothing jumped out and made me want to stop and push play. A sigh escaped. Chance waited.

"I don't know what I said ..."

"You butchered a Sir Walter Scott quote."

"Did I?"

"You sure did, but I think you meant to say, 'Oh! What a tangled web we weave when first we practice to deceive.' Instead you colorfully commented on Alison's intent to mislead."

"Okay, and?"

"You know the poem, yes? Marmion."

I shook my head. "No. Must've slept through that class." I was surprised he did. "You didn't just read The Art of War at military college then?"

Chance smiled. "Here's a quick overview for you: Lord Marmion wanted to do away with a lover, his former page Constance de Beverley. Side bar, Constance was posing as a page and therefore not supposed to be a girl."

"Great."

"Anyway, Marmion wanted to get rid of her because he wanted Lady Clare. He betrayed Constance to the church where she was walled up alive."

I yawned. "That's a cruel way to kill someone. Is this

going to take long?"

"Your education is lacking. Just filling in a gap."

"Will it take long?"

"It'll take longer with interruptions."

I groaned. "I hope there's a point to this."

"Shush and listen!" Chance said preparing to tell more of the story. "Lord Marmion framed Lady Clare's suitor, speared him and left him for dead, then he saw Lady Herron and thought he wanted some of her which annoyed King James, she was *his* mistress. Clare was captured by the Scots, the guy Marmion speared turned up during a battle and he was a bit pissed. Understandable, I thought. Anyway the crux of the poem is that deception never ends well."

Everything Chance said meandered around a pasture in my mind. A herd of words with no leader. Until Lord Marmion's name morphed into a name I recognized. Rion Maldorm. Alison Smith's low life jailbird boyfriend. I grabbed a pen off Chances desk and reached for a piece of paper. My fingertips met the edge of a memo sheet he pushed toward me.

I wrote the names Rion Maldorm and Lord Marmion on the paper, then folded it, and put it in my pocket. I didn't want to forget what Chance told me. His stories usually had a point and this one seemed to have embedded clues.

"The boyfriend," I said to Chance. "He's a dick. Alison is his Constance."

Chance nodded.

"See, amazing what you've got stored in that big brain of yours."

My lip curled. "Thanks, I think."

Rion was sketchy from day dot. I imagined him shaking down the other babies in the hospital nursery for their milk.

"You good now?"

"Uh huh."

A puff of wind lifted the edge of a page as it curled Chance grinned and waved. "Take care, El." A stronger breeze came from my left. The room spun, sucked upward by a twister.

The debris and dust cleared to reveal my office. Everything as it should be. Argo slept on, oblivious.

"You with me Argo? We got something."

He opened an eye and looked at me for a second before stretching and standing. I walked out my door with Argo on my heels, still trying to wrap my head around what exactly it was I had. From my pocket I pulled a piece of folded paper. I opened it. Rion Maldorm's name and underneath was written Lord Marmion. Weird. The paper was white memo paper. I turned around and stared at the pale green memo paper in a container on my desk. Well shit, that's strange.

4.

Halfway to the bullpen I stopped and looked at the paper again. Rion Maldorm was an anagram of Lord Marmion. Holy shit my brain is a weird place.

I swung the bullpen door open. Noises floated in the air above the desks. Typing. Phones. Voices. Photocopier. Water dispenser. Drawers opening and closing. Life.

From just inside the doorway I scanned the room. No Lee. Where was Lee. Kurt was leaning on a desk talking to the SSA of Delta B. I waved to attract his attention. He joined me.

"What's up?"

Then I remembered Lee was on vacation.

"Forgot Lee was away, wanted to talk to both of you about Alison."

"Dane and Stewart are around, if you need to assemble a team."

Do I?

Not really. Not yet anyway.

"You, me, and Argo?"

"Lead the way."

Back in my office I filled Kurt in on the gymnastics of my brain. He took it in his stride, as always.

"Where do you want to start?"

"I want someone in the prison talking to Rion."

Kurt regarded me for a moment. A small smile settled. "You don't want to do that yourself?"

"Nope." I made a promise to Mitch that I'd take care of myself. Wanting to choke the life out of a smarmy asshole like Rion was not a healthy situation to put myself in. "I'd like Caine to go in."

"Good choice."

I called Caine. He'd stopped laughing.

"I need you to talk to a prisoner for me, he's prisoner number six-five-nine-one-three-six-five his name is Rion Maldorm."

"Where is he?"

"Federal Correctional Institution Petersburg, Richmond."

"How important is this conversation?"

"It's worth you spending three hours in a car to get to him at FCI Petersburg."

"What do I need to know?"

"His girlfriend, Alison Smith, has disappeared. She's also an asset of ours. I'd like to know if he knows anything about her disappearance. Currently have a BOLO out, and Michael Addison is asking his contacts on the outside." I gave him a moment to digest the information. "Good chance Rion figured out she was working for us. He's set himself up quite nicely from what we've gleaned and his home invasion gang is still active and recruiting from within the prison and more than likely beyond."

"How active?"

"Every time Alison gave us intel it was solid and arrests were made. We're spreading the info to law enforcement agencies and police departments keeping us as far away as possible. Hoping that it takes longer to connect the dots."

"How long did it take?"

"Thirteen weeks and four days or thereabouts, if, that's what's happened here."

"I'll drive down. I'll be leaving within the next few hours."

"Thank you."

I liked having Caine working with us. It took some getting used to, having the SAC back in the field but it was working well. If anyone could scare information out of Rion, Caine could.

"And us?" Kurt asked.

"Let's go visit her house, and her job." And then find the friends who posted pictures on her Facebook page after their night out. "Argo is with us."

Kurt smiled. "Figured as much, does he need a leash?"

Good thinking. I'm so used to him being right by me I never think he needs to appear as if he's being controlled. I fished his short leash from my drawer. Argo watched. He didn't care either way. Leash or no leash. He behaved the same.

In an attempt to cause less worry I opted for the elevator. Running down the stairs caused Kurt to launch into a doctor diatribe aimed at pointing out the dangers of stairwell running and potential falls. No one wanted to hear that.

The car beeped as we walked toward it across the shiny concrete floor of the parking garage. Kurt opened a back passenger door for Argo. Then leaned in and clipped his harness to the seat belt attachment in the middle of the backseat. We had the same attachments fitted to the middle of the backseat of all three of the Delta A cars. Safety first.

5.

From the car window, I took in as much as I could about the area. Alison's street was pleasant in a suburban working class way. Lawns were mown. Front yards tidy. A few driveways had older model American cars parked in them. A quiet working class area. There were no children playing in the street or in front yards. With a glance at my watch I determined most children would be at school. Alison's rented home was white clapboard with navy blue on the window sashes and the front door. No garden, but neatly mown grass with two large rhododendron trees sprouting from each side of a concrete path leading to the front door. We parked at the curb outside her house. Didn't seem to be any need to hide our presence. Argo waited in the car. Kurt headed around the back to knock on the back door and I opted for the front. I peered into the windows but saw nothing but my own reflection.

Several knocks and no answering noise later I called Kurt's phone.

"Anything?" I said into my phone, while watching the street for signs of life.

"No. Curtains are closed, can't even see inside from here."

"Front curtains are open but I can't make anything out through the sheers. I'm going to check the mail box."

I hung up and walked down the path. The mailbox was locked. No way to sneakily remove mail without opening it so I used my handy lock picking kit. Ten-seconds, thirteen at the outside, and I had access. I pulled out the few letters inside and checked post marks. Not very helpful. All the mail was from the other side of the country. So the postage date didn't tell me much except it took five days for the letter to end up in my hand. I stuffed the mail into my inside jacket pocket and went to join Kurt around the back. He'd just opened the back door when I reached him.

"FBI, Alison are you here?" Kurt said.

No noise.

Kurt stepped inside. "Alison?" He shook his head at me. "Don't think she's here."

"I'm coming in, let's do a thorough search. I've cleared her mail box." Something made me stop. A tug, a pull, an urge to go no further without Argo. My gut said get him. "Kurt, wait one. I'll get Argo."

Didn't take me long to get back to the car, his working leash was under the backseat, I took that before I let the dog out. I unclipped his short leash and pushed it into my back pocket. He sniffed around the front yard a little then followed me to the back. Before we went in the door I clipped his long leash onto the D ring on his vest instead of his collar. Walking for fun we used his collar and a shorter leash, working we used the vest and the running leash. Distinct difference so he knew what was expected. I gathered the bulk of the leash length into my right hand. Argo looked up at me. I nodded. Kurt stood just inside the door. He waited for us to pass him before closing the door. Once inside I pushed my sunglasses up on top of my head.

"Room by room," I said. Argo and I moved first, leading the way. I let the leash out so he could go into rooms before me. Argo would tell us if anyone was hiding anywhere. Using him was quicker than us clearing every room.

At each door my heart pounded. Argo went in, sniffed around, came back. Kurt went in and came back. Once we were sure the house was empty we began to look for anything that would tell us where Alison was or what she planned to do.

I took her bedroom, Kurt started on the unused bedrooms. Argo sat in the doorway of the bedroom while I opened drawers, shook books, and rifled through the contents of boxes. I sat on the bed and stared at the closet with the doors wide open. There were two empty clothes hangers among the hung clothes. What was missing? Maybe a jacket or a coat or both.

The dresser attracted my attention. It required a closer look. I moved to the dresser and looked at the what was sitting in plain view on the top. A hair brush, moisturizer, sunglasses, and a jewelry box. If she'd gone away on vacation she'd take her hair brush. She'd probably take her sunglasses and moisturizer too. Same if she was planning on running. I opened the jewelry box. Silver glinted in the light. Necklaces, a few rings, and two bangles. Nothing particularly expensive looking but it all probably contained sentimental value. The sort of things you'd take with you into a new life. Or wear on your way to the new life. What was missing? Her watch. I knew Alison wore a watch. It was silver *Guess* watch. Her father brought it for her before he died, was her last birthday present from him. I checked the dresser drawers, no watch.

I poked around looking for a handbag or purse. She often had a dark green leather cross-body bag when she met with me. I found two handbags on the shelf above the rail in the closet. Didn't recognize either. There was light backpack up there as well. Suitcases? I couldn't see any in the closet or under the bed.

"Hey Kurt, you find any suitcases or luggage?" Pretty much everyone has suitcases or travel bags.

"Yeah, in the guest room sitting on the bed," he called back. "You should and come see this."

Argo and I marched into the bedroom. Kurt was bent over an open suitcase.

"She was packing," he said, straightening up.

"Did you open it or was it open?" I moved closer and looked into the bag.

"Open, looks like she was in the process of packing."

A pile of neatly folded clothes sat on the bed next to the suitcase. A toiletry bag gapped open by the clothes. I lifted it up for closer inspection. Travel sized shampoo and conditioner, soap in a case, toothbrush still in the wrapper, small toothpaste tube. The sort of things you'd pack if you were flying and planning on buying proper sized stuff at your destination. Or the sort of things you'd need for a weekend getaway. What was missing? Perfumes and body sprays, deodorant, makeup, and lotions. Hair brush. That was still in her bedroom on the dresser.

"She was planning a trip," I said, flicking through the packed clothes. "What interrupted her packing?"

I put the toilet bag down and looked around the room, opening the closet and checking under the bed. Just in case there was something that indicated a struggle.

"Did you find her cell phone or laptop?" Kurt asked, walking out to the hallway. "Did she have a laptop?"

"Yeah, and I think a tablet of some description. And nope, I haven't found any of them yet. Her handbag is missing too."

I glanced at the suitcase, there was a jacket poking out from a packed pile of clothes.

"We need to search for anything that suggests where she was headed," Kurt patted his thigh, "Come on, Argo, let's go check the living areas."

Argo glanced at me. I dropped his leash. He picked it up and trotted to Kurt. Kurt laughed and took the leash from his mouth.

I went into Alison's bathroom and opened the cabinets. Toilet paper, tissue boxes, full sized bottles shampoo and conditioner, body wash, a basket of soaps, a tray full of makeup. I rummaged in the tray. Everything I'd expect to see was there. The shower was dry. I lifted the lid on the laundry hamper. No wet towels. No dirty laundry. I went back to her bedroom and looked at the bed. Made, neatly. I lifted a pillow and saw folded pyjamas.

From there I went to the laundry. A washer and a dryer, side by side. I lifted the lid of the top loading washing machine. Empty. I bent down and tugged the dryer door open. Empty.

Looking out the back window I saw an empty washing line.

What did that tell me? That she'd dressed, folded her pyjamas, made her bed, and put the pyjamas under her pillow. She may have showered and then washed, dried, put away her laundry. I couldn't tell. She's clearly a tidy person. She was also planning on leaving. You don't want to leave wet towels around to start stinking. Why would she care unless she wasn't leaving for good? Kitchen.

"You checked the fridge yet," I said from the doorway.

"Nope, going through drawers and found her receipt drawer."

I opened the fridge. Nothing perishable. A jar of pickles. Two jars of olives.

"She was going away, all right ... or she doesn't eat fruit, vegetables, dairy, or eggs."

A door slammed. The vibration rippled through the floor and the walls. Argo stood, hackles twitching, slight growl in his throat. My hand slipped to my hip and contacted the butt of my Glock. Kurt had his weapon in hand. The three of us faced the direction of the noise. Listening.

Argo rumbled in his throat. He heard someone.

I looked for cover and found a space next to the refrigerator. Kurt moved to the other side of the room, glancing out the door as he did. Once by the wall he showed his hands. He held two fingers toward the hallway and pointed twice.

Two people. He pointed at himself twice.

Both male.

It didn't feel like they knew we were here. Yet our car was outside. Maybe they thought it was someone visiting a neighbor. Maybe they didn't care that there was a big black Chevy Suburban with federal plates outside. Guess we'd find out soon enough. They're either stupid or scary. Who knows? Lucky for us if stupid was the case.

Kurt still had hold of Argo's leash even though the dog was up against my leg. Doors closed. Something hit the ground in the one of the rooms. Then another bang. Argo rumbled again. I touched his head.

"Ssh, it's alright boy," I whispered. "Stay with me."

Another thump and the noise of smashing wood followed.

They weren't searching so much as wrecking the place.

I nodded to Kurt, held up three fingers and dropped them one at a time. We moved together, he passed me Argo's leash, I gathered it into my left hand, allowing Argo room to be in front of us. My gun was nestled in my right hand.

Argo took the lead. He knew exactly where the men were and led us right to them. Kurt and I stood on each side of the doorway of Alison's bedroom. Argo planted himself right in the middle of the open door and let out a low menacing growl.

"Fuck, dog!" One man said.

"She don't have a dog, dumbass," the other male said.

"... the fuck is that then?" Panic ringed his words.

That was our cue. I stepped forward next to Argo, now I could see the unfortunate soul. "He's my dog," I said, smiling while taking aim. "And he doesn't like you or your friend."

"Who the fuck are you?"

"Your worst nightmare."

The other male came into view. "Nah, lady, that'd be me." He pointed a gun at me, then at Argo. Waved it around a bit then pointed it back at me. Great, another dumbass.

"Drop it, or I let him go. One of you will get bit the other shot."

Kurt spoke from next to me. "She's never missed and he's got forty-two teeth. Your choice."

"Who the fuck are you?" The tough guy's gun flopped around in his hand. Giving the impression he was less gangster and more retard. He seemed to have zero control over his hand, wrist, or arm.

"FBI."

The other male dropped to the ground with his hands

on his head. Good choice.

"Don't lady. I surrender," he said, his voice muffled by the rug. "Put the gun down Clarence!"

I arched an eyebrow at the noisy, gun toting fool in front of me. Clarence. Like the cross-eyed lion.

"Houston, you fucker, Don't say my name!"

You're freaking kidding me. Houston, you have a problem. I sucked down the urge to laugh. These two were a comedy duo. Idiots with guns are dangerous.

"Drop it, last warning."

He regained control of his wrist and pointed the gun at me again. I adjusted my aim, from his head to his shoulder. Squeezed the trigger. The bullet tore into his shoulder. His gun and jaw dropped at the same time. Confusion clouded his features for a few moments as his brain processed what had happened.

"Sit down," I said. Argo punctuated my words with a growl.

Clarence crumpled to the floor groaning and clutching his shoulder. "I could die!"

"That's what happens when you wave a gun at the FBI. Consider yourself schooled."

Kurt moved toward the other male, Houston. He cuffed him then turned his attention to the wounded, Clarence.

After a quick inspection of the hole in his shoulder he gave his opinion. "You'll probably live." He picked up the gun. "Unless you continue to irritate, Agent Iverson."

Kurt's eyes flicked to me. "Iverson?"

Saliva built up at an alarming rate. A cold sweat prickled. I shook my head as grey fog encroached. Pass out or puke were my choices. Shit. I spun on my heels Argo moved with me.

"Stay," I said and took off for Alison's bathroom. Flipping the lid up of the toilet I retched hard, vomit powered from my mouth, some caught on the the end of my ponytail as it fell forward. Yuck. Satisfied the vomiting had stopped I hauled myself off my knees using the porcelain as support. My right hand held my hair off my shirt. I did not want to walk back into that room reeking of puke. I flushed. Turned the facet over the basin on and rinsed the end of my hair. It didn't pass the sniff test. I took Alison's shampoo from the shower and washed the last three inches of my hair, rinsed well, sniffed again. Flowers. I smelled flowers. Using a towel from the rack I squeezed as much water from my hair as I could. Minimizing the dripping. I saw mouthwash on the vanity and used some.

A knock startled me. I exhaled and took a slow breath before answering.

"Yep?"

"You okay?"

"Yeah."

The door opened. Kurt's concern evident on his face.

"Sure?"

"Absolutely. Think adrenaline has a new way of leaving my body."

He nodded. "Bodies change when they're already under stress."

That made sense, in a weird way. Vomiting to release adrenaline might become annoying. Think I liked it better when my hands got the shakes and I needed physical activity to burn off the excess adrenaline.

"I have all the fun."

Kurt touched my wrist in the hallway. "You're definitely feeling okay?"

"I am."

He walked into the bedroom. Argo remained vigilant. Watching the two men from near the doorway.

"Houston - let's talk ...," Kurt said, hauling the cuffed man to his feet from his prone position. He gave him encouragement to sit on the edge of the bed. "Why are you here?"

Houston looked at Clarence as if he needed to know what to do next. Clarence was too busy moaning and clutching his shoulder to take any notice.

"You two are wasting our time. Speak, make it good," I said.

"We ... didn't look like anyone was home. We broke in, is all." Houston's voice wavered. He didn't seem super sure of himself. "She has good stuff."

"You know whose house this is?" He already said she, so I'm picking he did.

Clarence became aware, he stared at Houston. I knew the look in his eye. It was the 'don't say anything' warning look.

Houston paid zero attention or maybe he didn't understand non verbal communication.

"Okay Houston, why are you in Alison Smith's house?"

"No reason."

Jeez.

"Do you work for Rion Maldorm?"

May as well just get that out in the open.

Clarence gasped and tried to cover it with a groan. I turned my attention to him. "Something to add?"

"I need to go to hospital."

"Might be a while," Kurt said. "You're not urgent and paramedics are busy people."

One look at Kurt's face told me he hadn't made the call yet. I bit my lip to keep from smiling.

"Rion. Maldorm. Ring any bells with either of you?"

Nothing.

I wondered if they knew by another name. Something told me they were out on parole so this would get them both thrown back into prison to finish their sentences.

"We don't have time for this. We'll have you escorted back to jail."

Total panic writhed on Houston's features muddling them into a contorted mess.

"How'd you know? I can't go back. I can't. He'll kill me."

"Who'll kill you?"

"Him," he tipped his head at Clarence who glared at

him. Clarence tried to move but Argo stepped closer, bared his teeth and uttered a low menacing growl. "He will."

Okay, interesting turn of events. Not worried about anyone else. But by the look on Clarence's face I'd say he was.

"Someone needs to talk or you're both going back to jail, today. In fact you'll be there by tonight."

Do not pass go. Do not collect two hundred dollars.

"I needed the money," Houston said. "We were gonna rattle her a bit. Fuck. I need the money."

"Well, it'll be real useful inside, I guess." I made a call to police. "Hey, it's SSA Iverson. We have a pick up. One needs medical attention, but both need returning to jail. Parole violations." I gave them the address.

"Sending a squad car over now, Agent." There was pause. I knew the officer hadn't finish with me. "Seen your BOLO and we might have some info, it just came in from a homeless gentleman down by the Holocaust Memorial Museum."

"Is he still there?"

"He camps around the area. Good chance he's not moved far. His name is Terrence Whitehall. Old Terry is a drinker. Might not be anything."

"Thanks. As soon as your officers arrive we'll see if we can find Mr. Whitehall."

6.

Kurt and I finished our search of Alison's home once police took the men back for processing. I found a ziplock plastic bag in the kitchen, took her pyjama tee shirt from under her pillow and zipped it into the bag.

Kurt smiled. "That for Argo?"

"Yeah," I replied, shoving the bag into my jacket pocket. A shudder ran through me. Felt like we'd need him to find her.

"Her handbag is gone, her phone is gone, her laptop is gone, no sign of her tablet and her car is gone," I said. "Why did she leave in the middle of packing with all her electronics?"

"Good question," Kurt replied, leaning on the kitchen counter. "She'd certainly been preparing to leave. The house is ready for her to walk out. Something must've interrupted her."

"Something that meant she needed to take her laptop ... and tablet, and cell phone."

"Work?" Kurt offered.

"Certainly a place to go next." I knew where she worked from her file. She worked at Macy's in the women's clothing area. She was a retail assistant. Retail assistants tend to be on the shop floor not in an office. Why take the laptop to work? Time to find out. "We'll drop by her work on our way to see the homeless gent who might have info."

I opened the back door and took the leash off Argo then let him out to do his business and watched to make sure I knew if he left a deposit. I had dog bags ready. He didn't. He watered a couple of trees then came back.

"Let's go," Kurt said, jingling the keys in his hand.

Macy's greeter smiled brightly as the three of us walked through the doors.

"Would you point me to Alison Smith, please," I said with a matching bright smile.

"Alison works in women's wear," the man replied and pointed left. "I'm not sure if she's on today but someone over there will know."

"Thanks." Kurt led the way, Argo and I followed.

Two small kids squealed with delight as Argo leveled with them. The mom smiled.

"Could they say hello to your dog?" she asked, holding one little boy by the hand and trying to catch the other before he dove at Argo.

"Of course," I said. Meeting and greeting was part of his job. I crouched down next to Argo, who sat. His tail swished back and forth across the floor. "This is Argo, he's an FBI specialist trauma dog."

"These two are Troy and Carl," the mom said. "They're three."

"Pleased to meet you," I said to the boys. Argo lifted his paw ready for shaking. They giggled and one by one shook his paw. "Good boy," I whispered to the dog, ruffling the fur near his right ear with my fingers.

"What does he do?" the mom asked. "Is he a police dog? A working dog?"

"Yes, he's an FBI agent just like me. Today he helped with an arrest but his real job is comforting victims of crime."

"Oh," she said. "That's a great idea, having a dog that can provide comfort."

"We thought so. A lot kids and adults respond better to animals than people after traumatic events."

The boys petted Argo. One wrapped his arms around Argo's neck, getting a generous lick for his trouble. More giggling followed.

"Was nice to meet you boys, but we have to go to work now."

One boy looked up at me with his wide brown eyes. "Does he live with you?"

I smiled. "Yes, he does."

"You are lucky."

"Yes, I am." I touched Argo's head. He stood. We were ready to move on. "You two be good for your mommy."

They nodded.

Kurt waited near the customer service desk for us to catch up.

"He's gathering a fan club," I said.

"That's a good thing," Kurt replied. Two women eyed us with suspicion from behind the counter. Their gaze softened when they saw Argo. He was going to gather a huge fan club.

I tipped my head toward them while looking at Kurt. His right eyebrow rose. I matched his look. He got the message and spoke to the women.

"We're looking for Alison Smith." He didn't bother showing his badge or credentials.

"We've already had someone looking for Alison this week," the older woman said. "She's popular all of a sudden."

I read her name badge. Aziza.

"Who was looking for her, Aziza?" I hoped my pronunciation was correct. Judging by the smile, I nailed it.

"Her boyfriend. Rion. He came in yesterday. Nice looking but he had trouble written all over him."

"Had you met her boyfriend before?"

She shook her head. "Alison told us about him. She visits him in Richmond once a month."

I pulled up a mugshot of Rion Maldorm on my phone and showed Azzia. "Is this him?"

She studied the image. "Yes."

The other lady stepped up to the counter. "I am Nailah the duty manager for today. Alison took a leave day. She told us she was going to visit Rion."

I showed Nailah the photo on my phone. She confirmed it was the man they saw.

"You haven't seen her at all today?" Clarifying the situation.

"No," the women said.

"Thank you." I handed them one of my business cards

each. "If you see her, or if Rion comes back, call me."

"Yes ma'am," Aziza said, pushing the card into her pocket.

I didn't speak until we were in the car and then I called Caine.

"Have you left?"

"About to," his voice rumbled. "Change of plans?"

"Yeah. Hold off. Sounds like Rion is in town."

"He's not due for release for another five to ten," Caine replied, his growl deepened.

"I know."

"I'll make some enquiries and get back to you."

"Thanks. We're going to talk to a homeless man who might know something."

"I'll be in touch."

Kurt turned the key. The rumble of the engine reminded me of Caine's voice.

"Holocaust Museum, yes?"

"Yes."

I settled into the seat and closed my eyes. Fifteen minutes with my eyes shut would work wonders, I just knew it.

The stop start trip made napping difficult. But it didn't stop my brain for conjuring up it's own special brand of crazy. My eyes opened revealing pencil outlines encompassing my world. A sigh caught behind my teeth. I glanced at Kurt. He turned his head and looked at me. Not Kurt. Chance.

"Nice nap?"

"Not really," I replied. "Is there a reason you're back?" I looked around with more interest. A black pencil drew new lines. A sofa, a large comfortable looking arm chair, a fire place. This wasn't the car. As I watched a paint brush blended the lines and another added color.

Chance walked across a furry rug in front of the fireplace. He crouched, flicked a lighter, and lit the fire. Flames flickered and mesmerized me.

"Ellie … you still with me?"

I turned my head to the sound of Chance's voice. He was next to me on the sofa.

"What's going on?"

"There's a construction site down by the museum you are going to. I think maybe you should look there."

"Seriously?"

"Remember what happened to Constance in the poem?"

Flames leapt from the fire, engulfing the room.

My eyes opened and focused on the dashboard. Solid. No pencil drawing. No flames. Good. When I was last down by that museum? Months ago. I didn't recall a construction site.

"Kurt?"

"Iverson, we're almost there."

"Chance said there's a building site near the museum."

"Look out the window." The car slowed as I looked out onto a construction site. Whatever they were building was big and the walls were cinderblock and what looked like slabs of granite or something rock like. "Across the road, Iverson. I see a homeless encampment."

"Could be our guy is over there."

My phone rang. Caine.

"He's still in prison. Or at least they thought he was."

"Wait, what?"

"A few days ago Rion's lawyer came to see him with his brother."

"I take it the brother looks very like Rion?"

"Yes. He's older but they're very similar to look at."

"And they were in a private room, I take it?"

"They've just sent a guard down to his cell to get his fingerprints. Sounds like the brother is in jail and Rion is loose."

"How embarrassing for the facility."

"Indeed. As soon as they confirm we'll move on the lawyer. He aided and abetted a prison break." Caine ended the call. My screen dimmed before turning off.

I leaned my head on the head rest while I thought about the situation for a second.

"You okay?" Kurt asked, he'd pulled over. The engine was off.

"Rion might be here."

"There's an older gent watching us with open curiosity, might be Mr. Whitehall. Shall we go say hello?"

I nodded.

I climbed out of the car then opened Argo's door. He

jumped onto the sidewalk and waited for his working leash. Argo and I waited for traffic to slow then hurried over the road with Kurt right behind us.

"Mr. Whitehall?" I said to the man sitting outside a rough shelter made of cardboard boxes and plastic trash bags.

"Yes."

Argo sidled up to the man and sat.

"We're looking for a young woman who went missing." I showed him a photo on my phone. Argo leaned on the old man's leg until the man petted his head.

"Friendly fellow aren't you?" he said to the dog. Mr. Whitehall looked up at me. "That girl was over there." he pointed at the wire fenced building site across the road. "With a man."

"Thank you," I said and I meant it. "When were the construction workers last on the site, do you know?"

"Work stopped about a week ago."

"Know why?"

"Developer went bust." He gave Argo a hug. "You got a good dog."

I smiled. "He is good. Thanks for your help."

Kurt had been observing. "We're going to go check the site out, then we're coming back. All right?"

"I'll be here."

Argo joined us. We crossed the road. Kurt went to the car and took heavy duty bolt cutters from the back. We travel prepared. He cut the chain off the gate and pushed the gate wide open. I dropped Argo's leash on the ground, all I had in my hand was the loop at the end. From my pocket I took a plastic bag containing a tee-shirt that belonged to Alison and held it under Argo's nose.

"Seek." He put his nose to the ground and ran with us running behind to keep up. He was all over the place, up and down hills of sand and stones, in and out pallets of cinder blocks. Then he stopped. We were in the middle of the construction site. Scaffold rose above us and all around. We were standing on a concrete slab. They'd started building rock and cinder block walls. I looked at Argo. He was sniffing around what looked like a wall.

Shit.

Constance.

"Kurt."

We joined the dog. It wasn't a wall. The cinder blocks were staggered all the way to the top, like a staircase on both sides. It was a structure built above a pit. Kurt climbed up one side and shone his torch into the hole. "Alison!" he hollered.

Argo whined and scratched at the cinder blocks.

I climbed up the other side of the cinder stairs so I could see. His torch illuminated something and that something looked like a human shape.

"Alison!" I yelled. "If you can hear us knock on something!"

Silence fell. I was about to yell again when a faint tap resounded.

Kurt swung into action. He was on his phone to emergency services and running to the car at the same time. Argo sat still at the bottom of the wall I was standing on.

I talked to Alison. "We'll get you out. Just hang on."

She didn't move, she didn't speak.

I saw Kurt running toward me carrying a bottle which I guessed was water, he had his medical back pack slung over one shoulder. He stopped near a hut and kicked the door in and disappeared. Moments later he emerged with a coil of something.

He called out to me as he climbed back up the cinder blocks. "She talking?"

"Nope," I replied, watching him. He had a coil of conduit and bottle of water. Kurt undid the bottle of water then did it back up, tight enough it wouldn't leak but loose enough for an injured Alison to be able to open it. He tied one end of the conduit through a cinder block, then the other end to the water bottle and lowered it down to Alison. She didn't react.

"Alison - water!" I called down the hole. It felt like a well. Maybe we should've called Argo, Lassie. What's that Lassie? Alison's stuck down a well? Stop it brain.

It felt like ages before she moved her hand. But she did move. She managed to open the water and drink. A few sips later she tried talking.

"I ... knew." Silence for a beat. " ... you ... would."

"Hang in there, emergency services are on the way. We'll have you out and safe soon."

I could hear sirens coming closer.

My phone rang just as the first fire truck pulled into the site.

Kurt signaled them. I spoke to Caine.

"Confirmed a prison break. Police stumbled upon Rion at the airport."

"Ha, flying somewhere was he?"

"Trying too. He was using his brother's passport."

"Thanks Caine. We've got Alison. She's alive." I peered into the hole. Barely.

"We can trace his little gang of thugs from prison records and conversations with other inmates and newly released parolees. Won't be long before we have them all in custody."

"I take it there won't be any visitors for Rion in the near future?"

"Not in solitary at a federal penitentiary. No more medium security for him."

"Hanging up now, see you when we get back."

Fire personal joined me at the top of the blocks.

"Ma'am, we need you to go down to safety. We'll take it from here."

I nodded and walked down the blocks. Kurt reached for my hand at the bottom, helping me off the last step.

"It's going to take them some time to get her out," he said.

An ambulance arrived on the scene, followed by more fire trucks, and police. Uniforms and activity filled the area.

"Argo!" I yelled. The dog ran, dragging his long leash behind him. He bounced at my feet.

"Good job pal," I said, giving him a hug. "Extra dinner for you tonight." I gathered up his leash in my hand. Kurt steered us toward Mr.Whitehall who'd crossed the road to see what was going on.

"Mr. Whitehall, you helped us. We recovered a missing woman," Kurt said, as he opened his wallet and handed the man three hundred dollars. "This is a token of our appreciation."

A tear slid down the old man's craggy face. "I didn't know she was there. I just saw a woman with a man."

"She was, she is. Thank you for paying attention and making that call."

They shook hands. Argo waited patiently for his turn.

The End.

Undivided:

D&D shouldn't be fatal.

Undivided comes a little while after Metabyte and six or so months before Qubyte.

Undivided.

1.

He stared straight ahead. His mud brown eyes fixed on a point behind me.

"Might be a while before your lawyer arrives. You are quite within your rights to sit there and say nothing." My back twinged. I moved a little in the seat to ease the annoyance. "If I were you, I wouldn't say anything either."

He blinked slowly and adjusted his line of sight. Staring into my eyes he said, "You will never find them."

I rose, pushed my chair in, leaned over the table and with quiet control said, "That's where you're wrong. Not only will I find them but I'll see you fry."

"Not this time, Agent." I detected a bit of cockiness in his voice. Although I didn't have a decent base line so that could be how he operated on a regular day or his goto when challenged.

"Watch me," I said over my shoulder as I walked to the door. I pulled the door toward me and delivered a parting shot. "Enjoy breathing while you still can."

Lee stood near the wall on the opposite side of the hallway; feet a shoulder width apart and hands behind his back. Parade rest. The door locked behind me. His posture relaxed a smidge.

"We wait?"

"You can wait if you like," I said with a smile. "I've got

things to do. He's not going anywhere."

"The room is monitored, yeah?"

I nodded, and opened an app on my phone. Our guest sat smirking at the table. "No sense hanging around in the corridor when we have perfectly good offices." I clicked the screen closed and pocketed my phone. "Coming?"

"Yep."

Silence rolled in behind us. Our footfalls quieted. The ding from the elevator bounced off the ceiling and hit the floor causing a lurch in my guts. Lee ignored the elevator and swung the heavy stairwell door open and held it for me.

We ran, shoulder to shoulder, down the stairs to our floor. The annoying twinges from my back dissipated with each stair. With grins a mile wide we exited the stairwell into the reception area of the Delta floor. Sandra looked up, shook her head, and gave a finger waved from her desk.

I paused by her desk. "Any word from Bletchman's lawyer?

She passed me a square of memo paper. I read it and handed it to Lee.

"He's in court all day," Lee said giving it back to me.

"Guess Mr. Bletchman will be our guest for longer than he imagined."

Sucks to be him.

Argo looked up as I entered my office, thumped his tail

once, and almost instantaneously fell back to sleep.

"Nice life you have, pal."

I settled at my desk and thought about the lawyer. Seemed odd that Bletchman's lawyer didn't arrange for someone else from the firm to meet with him. Usually they can't wait to spring clients from our hospitality suites. The strangeness of making a client wait all day niggled.

I leaned back in my chair and tapped at the keyboard of the laptop in front of me. Then began rereading the case notes for Operation Dungeon Master. Everything we had. Every piece of data. The undisputed pieces of DNA evidence that linked Bletchman to three murdered boys. His skin found under their fingernails. Not to mention the survivor.

He didn't deny the crimes.

I scrolled back a page and scanned the list of names. Fifteen boys vanished over a two-year period. We had three bodies. Where were the others? I was sure all fifteen of the missing boys were Bletchman victims. They fitted a type. Bletchman favored a certain kind of boy. Boys that played Dungeons and Dragons. Boys that spent hour after hour in fantasy worlds with their fantasy world loving friends. Average height for their age group, socially awkward, not really athletic; probably the kids who were chosen almost last for sports teams at school. They weren't overweight. They weren't scrawny. The kids he chose were in the middle of the road body shape wise but they were more interested in playing games than being outside playing sport. He didn't count on his final victim being more athletic than the rest by being the kid who paid attention in self-defense class. Mickey Splincott was a smart kid.

Lifting the phone receiver from the cradle I pressed a series of numbers and waited. Five rings. Six rings. An out of breath female voice. "Yes."

"Mrs. Splincott?"

"Yes. Who is this?"

"Agent Ellie Iverson, Mrs. Splincott. How's Mickey today?"

A door closed. A lighter flicked. I heard the unmistakable sound of Mrs. Splincott drawing on a cigarette. Just the thought of it made me feel ill and pleased I wasn't nearby.

"Better than I expected, Agent. Is that all you wanted?"

"No. I'd like to talk to Mickey today, if that's possible."

She took a long drag on the smoke. "Sure. When?"

"Within the hour."

"He's tired."

"I imagine he would be."

"Bring the dog," she rasped and hung up.

Argo snored on his bed in the corner of my office.

"Field trip, Argo."

The dog woke, sat up, and tilted his head to one side. Waiting.

"You heard right, we're going out. Time for you to do

some work," I said with a smile. One ear twitched and rotated toward to the door. Someone was coming.

I closed my eyes and conjured an image of the visitor.

Dane. It was Dane.

Argo and I watched the door. One knock and then it opened and in walked Dane. The dog jumped to his feet and intercepted him for a pat. I opened my top drawer and took out a packet of mints. They might alleviate the potential nausea of being near a heavy smoker.

"Want company?"

"Sure. Heading over to see Mickey Splincott."

"He's home?"

"Yeah."

"He's okay?"

"Traumatized but otherwise in one piece."

I handed Dane the dog's leash. He snapped it onto his harness. My back twinged as I stood up. Maybe I'd walk down the stairs like a normal person. This pregnancy body is starting to be annoying. I pulled my jacket on and my shoulder holster disappeared. It was a new thing. I'd always appendix carried but that wasn't feasible with the noticeable growing bump created by our twin girls.

2.

The drive was inner city stop-go at its finest. We hit every traffic light. Our destination was not too far across the Anacostia River. I needed the GPS to navigate those streets.

I pulled the car into the driveway of the Splincott residence. Tidy house and garden. Someone paid attention to the lawns and small flower beds. The street on a whole was pleasant.

"Dane ..." My phone rang before I could continue with my thought. I answered, "SSA Iverson."

"Ellie, it's Josh Konstram. Another boy was reported missing an hour ago," he said.

"Damn. When was he last seen?"

"When he left for school. He never got there." Josh paused. "Copycat?"

"Or partner ..."

"Shit."

"Yeah. I'm about to talk to the survivor. I'll text when I'm back at the office. Meeting?"

"Yes."

I hung up.

Dane and I looked at each other. "What were you going to say before the phone rang?" Dane said.

"Maybe Bletchman isn't working alone."

"I was thinking along those lines."

We exited the car with Argo and were ushered into the

233

living room of the Splincott home. A cloud of smoke hung in the air. I popped a mint into my mouth and tried not to breathe in too much.

Mickey stared up from the worn sofa. The colorful bruising on the side of his face and stitched cut above his eye made him look tougher than his diminutive frame suggested. He patted his leg to call Argo to him. Dane unclipped the leash. The dog sat in front of the boy, his paw raised ready to shake hands. Mickey smiled and shook the offered paw and then rubbed Argo's head.

"I do not know anything else, Agents," he said, taking care to annunciate every word. Rehearsed?

A side-glance revealed the mother's head nodding in the smallest of increments at her son. Damn it. He was a minor so talking to him alone if the mother was coaching him wasn't going to happen.

My lower back twinged, I rubbed it.

The annoyance continued and gave me an idea. Water.

"Mrs. Splincott could I trouble for a glass of water?" I said, with a smile.

"Come along to the kitchen. It comes out the faucet."

Dane caught my arm as I moved. "You okay?"

"Yeah, thirsty. You chat to Mickey."

"Will do."

I followed Mrs. Splincott from the room, down the hall, and into the kitchen.The cream paint on the cabinets could benefit from a touch up but other than that the room was bright and clean. Water ran for a few seconds before Mrs. Splincott plunged a glass under the streaming faucet and filled it.

She handed it to me, her eyes probing, questioning. I took the glass and sipped the cool water.

"Are you feeling all right?" She asked, perching on a stool by the counter.

"Yes."

"You're looking paler than when you came in."

Yeah, well, the house is leaching tobacco smoke from every surface and that smell turns my gut faster than *Opium* perfume.

Instead of denying it I went with some truth. Mother to mother. "I'm pregnant. I'm sure you remember what that's like."

"Miserable from my memory," she said, with a sympathetic nod. "You must be early days." She tapped a cigarette from a packet on the counter, and stuck it between her lips.

"Not really. Twenty-eight weeks, yesterday."

A lighter flicked.

"Wow," she said, turning her face she exhaled a cloud toward the window. "You can't hardly even tell."

"I've been lucky so far."

Good genes, luck, whatever. She was right. Unless you knew or I wore tight fitting tee shirts it was hard to tell. I don't advertise my growing belly during work hours.

"Must be hard doing what you do, seeing the evil in the world, and, you know ..." She waved a hand at my stomach. "It must affect you."

Of course it does.

"I find running helps."

Her eyes widened in horror. "You run and you're pregnant. Lady you should be resting."

A small laugh erupted. "Plenty of time for that when I'm dead."

Her head shook. A frown settled on her face. Deepening the already prominent lines. Smoking did the woman no favors.

"How are you coping with Mickey and the situation?" Keep it general. Keep it mother to mother.

She tapped the cigarette pack. "I'm going through these."

I bet.

"Were you given a number to call if you need to talk to someone?"

She shook her head, then changed her mind and searched through a bunch of papers at the end of the counter. With a nod she produced a letter from Victim Support.

"I haven't ..."

"You can, any time, even if that call is a year from now. There is no time limit on you getting help to cope with what happened to your son."

She sucked in more smoke. "I feel like I shouldn't need help. It didn't happen to me. It was Mickey that went through hell because of that, that ... asshole." Smoke surrounded every word. "It isn't about me."

"Can I call you Sherie?" She nodded. "Okay, Sherie. First, this *is* about you. He's your son. What impacts his life, impacts yours. You nearly lost him." I smiled and touched her arm. "Even though you got him back, there is a grief process surrounding the near loss, the trauma, and an adjustment to the new normal, and you need to take care of you to be able to take care of Mickey."

"Thank you," Sherie said and grasped my hand in hers. "Thank you."

"You're welcome. I think you're doing great so far." I paused and gathered my thoughts. "Has Mickey said anything much to you about his ordeal?"

Tears filled her eyes. One escaped. She brushed it away before it reached her cheek.

"The man, Bletchman, he grabbed him when he left the community center after a Dungeons and Dragons game. It was one of those marathon games, you know, played over the whole weekend. The kids took their sleeping bags and the organizers provided meals."

"Has he been before?"

"Uh huh. The same people run these marathon weekends every few months. The boys had been three times."

I could imagine the delight of the boys. A hall full of smelly tweens and teens playing table top games all weekend.

"Was it just table top play or did they dress up and act out the quests."

"Both I think. I know Mickey had a cloak with him and a wand."

Not my idea of a good time but I imagine it would be fun if that was your thing.

"Bletchman, he ever see him before?"

"Mickey saw him watching some of the games earlier in the weekend. Said he was with another man. But he never saw the other man again."

Another man.

They weren't watching games, they were picking a victim.

"He was held in a house?" I knew the answer. I'd been to the house but she didn't know how much I knew.

She nodded.

"Did he mention anything about the house, or being in the house, anything at all?"

I could see her thinking. Trying to piece things together, trying hard to haul in information that she really did not want to think about.

Sherie swallowed hard and looked at me. "He asked me what sort of food *long pork* was."

Fuck.

"Why would he ask that?"

"Bletchman told him they were having Long Pork for supper."

We found no evidence of human remains in the house. This was the first time there was any suggestion of cannibalism. My mind spun over possible scenarios the worst

being the boys were fattened up there and killed somewhere else?

"Did you tell Mickey what that is?"

Her head jiggled into a shake. "If he looks it up himself
it's going to be bad." She sucked harder on the filter of
her cigarette. "He said, supper was always nice and
Bletchman even gave him desserts every day."

The kid was missing four days.

"Did Mickey mention other meals. What he ate?"

"Cooked breakfasts every day of sausages, bacon, eggs
and pancakes. That sort of thing. Mid-morning snacks of
cheese and crackers and fruit. A cooked lunch and afternoon snacks. He said he was allowed whatever he wanted
whenever he wanted, he just couldn't leave or contact
anyone."

I recalled the kid saying there were no televisions, ra-
dios, stereos, or computers in the house, that he saw. And
no telephone. He was kept in a bubble and fed.

"And he never saw the other man again?"

"No."

Images popped into my head of two men watching
teens play table top games. It was akin to us choosing a
lobster from a tank in a restaurant. I wondered for a split
second what made Mickey appear tasty. What was it they
looked for?

Nausea rose in waves. My back twinged. I needed to
get out of the Splincott's home.

"Agent, are you all right?"

I sipped the water. "Yep. Just a bit of nausea. You know how to reach me, if you need anything. And know you can always call the support people. They are awesome."

She smiled. "Yes. Thank you again."

"No problem."

I hurried from the room and rejoined Dane, Argo, and Mickey.

"Sorry Mickey, I haven't had much time with you but we need to get back to the office."

The boy smiled and rubbed Argos ears. "It's okay, thank you for bringing him by."

"We'll bring him back, promise."

Mickey grinned.

Kids bounce back so much faster than parents.

Dane clipped the leash to Argo's harness and we left.

I chucked my jacket into a bag in the trunk of the car in an effort to get rid of the smell of smoke before climbing into the drivers seat.

Before we were out of the street Dane said, "The kid ate people."

I swallowed hard to no avail. I pulled over, flung my door open and vomited on the side of the road.

Dane handed me wet wipes as I straightened up and pulled the door closed.

"Sorry," he said.

"Not your fault. I'd been fighting that since we stepped foot in the house."

"Smoke."

"Yeah smoke and then Sherie Splincott saying Mickey had asked what *long pork* was."

"You know how forensics said the house wasn't a murder scene ..."

"You know how we found no evidence of human remains ..." Even in the freezer.

I drove, just leaving my contribution out there. We both knew there was a crime scene somewhere and it was potentially a butcher shop or a slaughter house, and meat was more than likely stored on the premises. And the other man, I suspected he was the butcher.

As I pulled into the underground parking garage at the Hoover Building Dane said, "Why didn't they eat the three boys corpses we do have? Not a bite mark on them."

I preferred to think they didn't gnaw the flesh off their bones while they were still alive.

"Dunno. I think we need to find out."

Choosing the lab phone number on the way up to my office I pressed the call button. Charlie answered faster than expected. "Hey Charlie, I need you run some tests on the boys from case HQ-309-3245DeltaA."

"What are you looking for?" Fingers tapped on a keyboard. "Helps me determine what tests to run and if they're even possible at this stage."

"A reason that took them off the menu."

Silence for a beat.

"Did you just say menu?"

"Yeah."

"Fun case," Charlie muttered and blew out air. "Are you thinking disease?"

"I don't know, but I think something was wrong with those kids, something that meant the guy we have in custody didn't want to eat them."

"Okay, I'll see what turns up. You know this could take a while. Backlog and all."

"Of course. I'll see what I can dig up my end."

"Back to it then."

Charlie hung up.

Another nagging pain encompassed my lower back. Maybe I did need to rest. By the time I reached our floor the pain was gone and forgotten. I hurried to my office with Dane and Argo in tow. Argo lapped up half a bowl of water then flopped onto his bed. Dane dragged a chair closer to my desk. He produced an iPad from his bag.

Our eyes met. "What would make meat unpalatable?" I said. Easier to think in terms of meat not people.

"Mad cow disease?"

"That'd do it, if they ate brains, and if they knew Prion disease was part of the genetic code."

Dane raised his eyebrows at me. "And that's off the top of your head?"

Laughter bounced across my desk at him. I reined it in. "Yeah, nah, let's not start with the puns ... it'll end badly."

Dane smiled.

"Mad Cow Disease is probably not the cause. But something made those three less palatable than the others, potentially."

We looked at the photos the parents supplied then the photos from the body dump sites.

"Maybe there was something unpleasant about them ..." I flicked from photo to photo. "Carl went missing two months ago and Rick vanished on his way back from a D&D game a month later, two weeks before Mickey was snatched, that's recent. The third boy, Skeeter - he's been missing for five months."

"Skeeter was unthawing when the body was located," Dane said. "But neither of the other two exhibited signs of freezing. They were fresher corpses. Although, Carl was killed about twenty-four hours before Rick."

"Which brings me back to my thinking that a butcher shop or slaughter house is the actual crime scene. We need to find that place. We also need to work this out. From the photos the parents gave us, those kids looked like any other pasty gamer."

"And they hold one at a time?"

"I'm seeing cross over, but maybe not at the house?"

"Yeah, they move one to the chop shop, for want of a better word, and bring another to the house?"

Chop shop.

Jesus.

"Could they be testing them for transmittable disease

while fattening them up a bit. Are the meals and snacks just to occupy the boys while they wait for test results, rather than the old Hansel and Gretel type fattening for the cook pot?"

We looked at each other.

In unison we said, "They're testing them. They have access to a lab."

A loud bell rang in my head. A blurry figure wearing a white forensic suit carried a rack of test tubes from one room to another. The reflection in the window looked very like the FBI seal. The bells rang on and on. Dammit, that's not good.

Dane's eyes widened.

"What's with the ringing?" He said. "There are a heap of labs, El. What do you see?"

So he could pick up on the noise in my head but not the images. Interesting.

Stewart knocked on the door and walked in. Argo thumped his tail on the ground.

"She sees a lab that we know," Stu said, smiling. He placed a hand on the back of Dane's chair. "Someone in the FBI lab is running those tests."

His words hung above my desk like a guillotine ready to fall. I leaned back. Not wanting my neck caught.

My mind slipped sideways. Karl sloped from a class-room, furtively glanced around the corridor then snuck out a door. He hurried along a path between the building and a row of trees, then ducked around a corner. There was no one around. He secluded himself behind some dumpsters, took something from his backpack and lit it. A plume of smoke rose.

I reached for my phone and dialed a number on the screen in front of me.

"Mrs. Green, this is Agent Iverson. I have a question about Karl."

"Yes."

"Did he smoke cigarettes?"

"I never saw him and he denied smoking when I asked. But I smelled it on his clothes sometimes after school." She sighed. "I was just relieved he wasn't doing drugs."

"Thank you."

"Why did you ask?"

"Just tying some loose ends."

I hung up.

"He smoked?" Dane asked.

"Yeah, I want you to find out if the other two smoked as well, and what they smoked. I don't think we're talking weed, I think it's cigarettes with all of them."

Sandra buzzed me.

"Josh is here."

"Send him in."

Stewart grabbed two more chairs from the back wall, Dane moved over making room for everyone. Josh grinned as he strode in the door.

"Hey y'all. Where are Lee and Kurt at?"

"Kurt is an expert witness in court and Lee is on vacation," I said, ushering him to a chair with a gesture.

"Let's get to it. We got another missing kid but you have the suspect in custody."

"I think there is a partner in crime." I paused for a split second because we hadn't told anyone about the true nature of the crimes since getting back from the Splincott residence. "It's possible the boys are menu items. They are being consumed."

Josh leaned back but my words hit him anyway.

"Cannibalism. I didn't think that. I thought ... shit ... so this isn't a sexual thing?"

"Didn't say that, Josh. The three bodies we have showed no sign of molestation or sex, but that doesn't mean the killers don't get off on butchering boys and consuming their flesh."

"Thanks for that mental image," Stewart muttered.

I shrugged. Sorry, not sorry. I can see it why shouldn't they?

"It's also possible that they're selling the meat." Better to think in terms of meat and cuts of meat than children, ideally I'd like not to think about it at all.

No one wanted to comment on my observation.

My back niggled, making me move in my chair. It didn't help. I stood and walked around the desk, perching on the edge nearest Dane. Thinking a change in posture might do the trick.

"How do we find the accomplice?" Josh asked.

"We need to find the crime scene," Stewart said.

Yeah, and the butcher.

Another thought occurred. A lot of boys have potentially been taken, more than I imagine two men could eat. What if they actually are selling the meat. Blackmarket human flesh trade. Different to the black market organ trade, but whose to say that this isn't a by-product or that organs aren't being traded as well. It would make sense. Maybe they are 'all of the buffalo' type criminals.

Nausea slammed me. I pushed off the desk and ran for the door with my hand over my mouth and pounding in my ears. When I slammed through the bathroom door Argo was right next to me.

Vomit sprayed into the toilet bowl. When the retching stopped and I straightened up I realized the pain in my back was gone. I flushed and walked over to the sink. Argo stood by the door, watching me. A few splashes of cold water on my face helped. Cupped my hands and drank a few mouthfuls of water from the faucet before staring into my own eyes in the mirror.

"Maybe it's time for maternity leave," I whispered to my reflection.

My pale reflection whispered back, "Two more weeks and then you'll be a lady of leisure."

The dog whined again. I glanced at him. "It's okay Argo. We got this."

I took a deep breath.

3.

Heads turned when I appeared in my office. Argo resumed his position on his bed and licked his paws.

"You all right?" Dane asked.

"Yeah," I said, moving past the men in front of my desk to sit in my chair. "Let's see if we can find the accomplice and the kill zone."

Stewart waved a finger in the air. "There's a bunch of chat rooms on the web that are dedicated to unusual meats products." He was scrolling. "There are literally hundreds of these type of rooms."

"I don't even want to ask," I said, fishing a box of mints from my drawer and popping one in my mouth.

"You really don't," Stewart replied, showing Dane the screen.

Josh leaned in to see. "Definitely a no. Wish I could unsee that conversation."

An image of a word popped into my mind: Placenta. That was followed by: Fetus. Crapadoodledoo. Stewart sent a swift mental apology for not shutting me out of his thoughts fast enough. I chewed the peppermint, swallowed and popped another one. People talked about eating unborn babies and placentas. Talk is one thing, the deed is something else.

Don't think about it.

My left hand rested on my stomach as one of my babies kicked. A timely reminder of life.

"Dane, get a list of all the places within fifty miles of the dump zone that could be used to butcher meat." I shifted my gaze to Josh. "Can we count on Metro to help?"

"Yes. I'll head back and deliver a briefing. Make sure everyone is aware that we're looking for premises and a butcher. Also, we're investigating the latest kidnapping. You want in or ..."

"Metro can handle it. We're here if you need support."

"Thanks, Ellie." Josh said his goodbyes.

"Stu, monitor the chatrooms, see if you can dig around and find something here in D.C. Get Sandra to help."

Stu rose and left the room.

I leaned back in my chair and considered our options. We didn't have much. One survivor who only saw the male we had in custody. Three bodies with the DNA of our suspect under their fingernails.

Why?

If he's not the butcher, why did they have his skin under their nails?

"Dane, how were the boys killed?"

He looked up from his iPad, small frown lines wrinkled his forehead. "Suffocation."

Horrible way to die. So they fought, hence the skin under the nails. That meant our suspect did potentially murder them. Did he murder all the boys or just the ones that they chose not to eat?

The ache in my back returned. This time I ignored it

and hoped it'd stop without me moving. Visions of butcher shop windows and men in blue and white striped aprons were projected from my mind to the surface of my desk. The images continued to form under my gaze. What was I seeing? Old time butchers. None of it was familiar. Breathe. Just breathe. Let your mind work. The desk surface wobbled and shimmied. Images changed from photo realistic to pencil drawings. I lifted my eyes. My office was not my office. I sat in a comic book sketch of a similar office. Sitting in front of me was Chance. He smiled.

"You called?"

"Didn't think I had, but, here you are." I swept my arm across the space between us, palm up.

"I am. Lay it on me, El. What's going on? What caused this summoning?"

"It's possible that an unusual slaughter house is operating somewhere in the Beltway or maybe just outside."

He ran a hand across the top of his short blond hair. "How unusual?"

"*Long pork* unusual."

Chance stared at me, his pale blue eyes searching mine. "You're not kidding."

With a shake of my head I said, "Nope, 'fraid not."

"If you're chopping up people then neighbors would be a security risk." I picked up a pen and wrote notes on the pad on my desk as Chance talked. "This operation wouldn't be in a suburb or a commercial area, maybe in an industrial park, although there is a certain amount of stench involved in butchering and disposal of ... leftovers ... you'd want a good furnace."

Our eyes met.

"A funeral home," Chance said. He was right. It doesn't need to be a slaughter house, it just needs to have cold storage, disposal facilities, and a room that could be used as a slaughter room. A funeral home with a crematorium. It would need the functional furnace but it wouldn't necessarily have to be an operational funeral home. "El, it could be operational."

"So while a funeral is going on someone is in the basement butchering a kid?"

His eyes widened. "You never said this was about kids."

"Sorry. It's about kids. Young teen boys in particular."

"If someone was in the basement butchering a kid in the embalming room then I'm going to suggest whoever is conducting the service or owns the funeral home knows what's going on downstairs."

"Good point."

You wouldn't want to be interrupted mid-slice and dice.

I lifted the lid of my laptop and typed Bletchman's name into a search engine, one of ours not a public one. While that ran I plugged his name into a database that stored weird and wonderful snippets of information about people. A smile flickered in my mind. I shut it down before it reached my eyes or lips. The nifty database didn't officially exist.

"What are you looking for?" Chance said, leaning forward in his chair.

"A straight up connection between Bletchman and a funeral home."

Screeds of information came back regarding many people named Bletchman from the search engine. Including his Facebook page. Nothing of interest to the investigation and it was a public page. Nice. I'd still want to get into his messages though. That was a job for Sandra, later.

The database chucked up several references. The very last one, was an educational reference. Thirty years ago Bletchman graduated from Tidewater Community College with a degree in Funeral Service and Mortuary Science.

"I got something," I said, spinning the laptop to show Chance the screen. "But there is no mention of him working for or of any involvement with a funeral home, so far."

"He could be using a different name."

Yeah. I thought about how he reacted when I told him his lawyer was delayed. He didn't react. Why?

"He's sitting in an interview room, because his lawyer is too busy to come in."

"That's weird, right?"

I nodded. "Real weird."

"Why would a lawyer leave a client hanging?"

"Said he was in court and couldn't get away. Weirdest thing is he didn't arrange for someone else from the firm to handle Bletchman's case."

"El ..."

"Yeah, the lawyer, he knows."

Chance grinned and stood up. "Make an appointment with your obstetrician for later today, El."

"I'm seeing her tomorrow."

"Today," he replied firmly. "Take care."

Chance walked toward the door then melted into the sketched floor. A vortex of muted color twirled around me and vanished into the puddle by the door. I blinked. Real life stared back at me.

"You okay?" Dane asked, from the exact spot Chance had occupied.

"Yeah. Funeral homes. They're killing in a funeral home." I showed him the information on my screen.

Dane grabbed his phone from the edge of the desk and called Stu.

I called Josh Konstram. "Josh, the lawyer for Bletchman - get someone to pick him up. He's wanted for questioning regarding the murder of the boys."

I searched for a name, usually names were easy for me but not this one. Names flew inside my mind finally I saw one that I recognized as belonging to the lawyer.

"Might need a name, El."

"Lee Barrington."

"Spell that?"

I obliged and hung up.

The ache in my back increased. I added Lee Barrington to my database searches. Didn't take long for a connection to appear.

"Dane, we're going, get your gear. The lawyer, Barrington, the family owns Barrington's funeral home has done for three generations."

We needed back up. I tapped a number on my cell phone while pulling my jacket on.

"I need a team," I said as soon as Andrews answered.

"When?"

"Now. We're moving on a funeral home, heading out the door as I speak. Texting the address to you."

"Funeral home. Zombies?" A smile leaked into his words. "Was only a matter of time."

"I wish. Slaughter house for human meat."

He blew air out. "We're rolling."

I ended the call, text him the address, and clipped Argo's leash. Dane grabbed the keys from the desk. I paused at Sandra and Stu and asked that she get cyber warrants, fast, and check out all social media especially messages from Bletchman. I wanted to know if he communicated with Barrington and said anything incriminating. I doubted it. A lawyer should be smarter than that. *Should be.*

From the car I called Josh back with the address of the Barrington Funeral Home and told him to meet us there if he wanted to be involved and that SWAT were on route.

Then I settled into the seat and noticed with relief that my annoying back pain had subsided.

4.

The funeral home sat well back on immaculate mani-cured lawns. The rolling landscaped grounds extended to the left and right of the building and the whole area was surrounded by a brick and wrought iron fence. We drove through the large open gates with two SWAT vehicles be-hind us. A carpark area near the double story sprawling red brick building contained one car. I climbed out of the car and opened the back door for Argo. Big white pillars on either side of the front door gave the building a stately air. Lavender and rosemary grew in planters either side of the path to the main entrance.

Dane handed me a bulletproof vest. I removed my jacket and shoulder holster to accommodate the vest. It was uncomfortable. Irritation tweaked. I threw my jacket into the car, took the Glock from my holster and chucked the holster into the car. It landed on top of my jacket. With a sigh I closed the door.

Andrews joined us. "We good?"

"Yep. Let's see if Barrington is in, shall we?"

"You hang here with the furry guy, Dane is with us," Andrews said. There was no room for argument.

Something was off, I didn't feel like arguing. I shoved the weirdness away.

Argo and I watched SWAT deploy. Once everyone was in place, Dane and Andrews approached the front door. Dane swung the door open then disappeared into the interior.

I wrapped Argo's leash around my hand. "Come on pal, let's go see what's happening." Hang here, my ass.

From the doorway I listened. Doors opened and closed. From my right I heard someone say, "Clear." Another door closed.

I text Dane: *I'm in the foyer.*

A low growl came from Argo. He looked left, his ears twitched and fur bristled. Whoever was there wasn't one of our guys. My phone buzzed.

Dane: *Stay put.*
I text back: *Going left, there's someone there.*
Dane: *SWAT are in and moving toward your left from the back. Stay put.*

I read the text and smiled.

"Argo, SWAT are coming. We wait."

Whoever was in the building was being driven toward us.

We moved back a few feet into the doorway, out of view of the main areas of the reception and foyer.

Argo growled. The person was still coming. We were blocking their escape. With that a grey haired man rushed into view. He pulled up, startled, and tried to turn. I let the leash go. Argo launched through the air and grabbed him by the arm.

"Don't move. He will not let go," I said.

"Call him off! Get the dog off me!" Panic permeated his voice. "I work here. For Gods sake call him off!"

"Argo." He dropped the arm but didn't move away. His lip curled up over his teeth. A low snarl reminded the man who was in charge.

The man rubbed his arm. He appeared shaken and jittery. A confrontation with a dog will do that to a person.

"Name?"

"Barrington. Thomas Barrington."

"Do you know Lee Barrington?"

"He's my son."

"Is he on the premises?"

"I don't think so." His eyes remained fixed on Argo.

"Last chance Mr. Barrington. Is Lee on the premises?" I had my phone in my free hand, and dialed Dane's number. Dane answered but I didn't. I knew he could hear me. "Mr. Barrington is Lee here?"

"He might be in the basement."

"What's in the basement?"

"The embalming rooms and storage areas."

"Get that," I said into the phone.

"Yep. We can see stairs and an elevator."

"Go."

I hung up. Argo stepped forward as I did, Mr. Barrington stepped back.

"Stay still," I cautioned and moved toward him. I

stepped behind Barrington, pulled his arms back and cuffed him, then guided him to a chair near the reception desk. "Sit down here and wait."

With one gesture Argo went back to the door and waited. No one was getting through that door. I sat near Barrington.

Adrenaline thumped through my veins making it hard to keep still. Ten-seconds later I was on my feet and pacing. Phone in one hand and Glock in the other. I paused in front of Barrington.

"Your son's office told a legal client he was in court all day today."

The man looked confused.

"That can't be right."

"Why?"

"He doesn't have any clients. Not live ones at any rate."

"Excuse me, what?"

"He's not a lawyer."

"What does he do?"

Barrington sighed. "He has a trust fund, he doesn't have to do anything."

"Didn't go into the family business then?"

"He keeps his hand in, I suppose. But no, not really."

"And he has a degree in Mortuary Science?"

"He does. We, his grandfather and I, thought he'd take over the business one day."

"Why did he go to a community college?"

Seemed curious for someone from money to go to a

community college.

"When you get asked to leave your chosen college, then your second and third choices because of bad behavior there eventually comes a time when you exhaust your options."

"What did he do that was so terrible?"

Barrington looked away and shook his head.

My phone went. Dane.

"Yep."

"Down the hallway on your right, first left, second right, down the stairs. You need to see this."

"Okay." I hung up.

I beckoned Argo. He came.

"Stay. Guard." I touched his head. He sat in front of Barrington. He wasn't going to move and no one would get past the dog. Not in one piece anyway.

I said nothing to the man and followed Dane's directions. At the bottom of the stairs the air was cool. Voices came from somewhere in front of me. I walked toward the sound.

Near an open doorway I called out, "Iverson coming in!"

"Come through," Dane hollered.

When I walked in the first thing I saw was a man in handcuffs face down on the concrete floor. Beyond the man and the stainless steel table was a cage built into the room. A jail cell.

Andrews was unlocking the cell door.

"What the actual fuck," I muttered at Dane as I stood next to him.

"What we can ascertain is, that while they prep the room and so forth, check the orders on their ordering system, because yes, they have one." He flipped a thumb toward a laptop open on a counter. "They keep the victim in that cage over there." He gave the man on the ground a nudge with his booted foot. "I'm sure this gentleman will tell us if we're wrong."

The man on the ground groaned as Dane nudged him again.

I was on my phone before the third groan and talking to Josh. "Argo has the owner in the foyer, arrest him, conspiracy to commit murder and kidnapping."

"You got it El."

I shoved my phone in my back pocket.

No way in hell did they build a fucking cage without the old man knowing about it.

Family business.

A shudder ran through me. A dull ache in my back kicked up a gear. Maybe Chance was right, maybe I should call my doctor.

Dane grabbed my arm. "You need to sit down, you don't look so good."

I ignored him and spoke to Andrews just as the heavy cell door swung back into the wall. "Come on. Let's get out of this place. It's giving me the creeps."

Andrews took the young man in the cage by the arm. I

could hear him talking but not what he said. My back was killing me. Time to go.

I made another call. "I want a forensic team to my location now."

When I hung up I remembered that I thought someone was testing the kids. It seemed like a random thought at the time. Dane hauled our guy to his feet and I got in his face.

"What lab are you using to determine their blood type for organ harvest?"

The guy leaned away, as if he was trying distance himself from my question. Yeah, it's not that easy.

"Barrington, answer the fucking question," I growled.

He swung his head around to look at me with a small laugh he said, "Yours."

Fuckadoodledo. Charlie.

Time to call Stu. I walked into the hallway. "They've been using our fucking lab to type the blood. Find out who, I won't be surprised if it's Charlie."

I hung up before he could say anything.

Back in the room I addressed Lee Barrington. "What was wrong with the three boys you didn't butcher?"

"They wasted our time. One was marinating himself in Axe body spray, one was smoker and the other kid had a diet issue." He shook his head. "What thirteen year old eats asparagus and curry on a daily basis, and eats raw garlic as a snack?"

One who plays D&D and is scared of vampires? May

you rot in hell you utter bastard. I looked at the unrepentant horror of a man in front of me. Evil hides in a personable exterior. Evil walks among us and most people have no idea.

Nausea rose. My back ached. I had a bad feeling. Neither baby had moved or kicked in almost two hours.

"Dane, I gotta go."

"Yeah, you do go, call Mitch or I will." He threw me the keys. "You okay to drive?"

I nodded and hurried away.

My call to Mitch went to voice mail. I left a message. "Meet me at the hospital."

I knew Dane would get back to the office, Andrews would let him ride with SWAT. On the way back to the city the feeling of dread and that something was wrong grew with every ache. By the time I reached the hospital and saw Mitch's car I knew our babies weren't waiting any longer. I called Kurt and told him where we were.

The End

Telephone Line:

The past revisits Delta A with horrible consequences.

This story comes after Cryptobyte and before Vapobyte.

Telephone Line.

1.

She sat opposite me. Her ankles neatly crossed, her knees together and legs tilted to the left. She wore a calf-length skirt, and round-necked unadorned taupe top. My first impression was that of a modest woman. I'm sure my father would appreciate her. Carol was a woman of a sensible age, she even had a sensible name. It went well with her flat heels and no nonsense hair style. The greying at her temples added to the over all image. She held a stenographers notebook. Old school. Most people recorded conversations with their smart phones and had done for the better part of my working life, and before that, dictaphones.

Carol adjusted her grip on her pen. Disappointment rose when I noticed it was a ballpoint and not a fountain pen.

"Shall we start with your childhood?"

I gave a faint smile. "No."

Her hazel eyes flashed gold at me. Perhaps she had some fire in her?

"High school?"

I shook my head. Nope. That would bring out the whole *Son of Shakespeare* debacle and I didn't want to go there, yet.

"College?" She sounded hopeful.

My head moved from side to side in the smallest of increments.

"Your job is to tell people about my career, or at least, that's the brief I was given by HR that came from the publisher. Has that changed?"

She blinked, frowned, and then set her thin lips to a determined line. She reminded me of a deputy principal who taught me at high school. Humorless.

"I was commissioned to do research for a biography of one of the most decorated female FBI agents in the Bureau. *You.* Can you allow me access to do my job?"

Uh huh. A misguided publicity stunt to try and entice more women into a career that eats lives for breakfast or a publisher who thinks this crap will sell? There are no soiled blue dresses in my closet. I've just got a few medals and whatnot shoveled into my bottom drawer. That's not what my work life is about.

"It's still my life and I will talk about the parts I feel are relevant."

"You didn't emerge an FBI Agent from thin air ..."

"Correct. I emerged from Quantico a freshly minted agent with no real clue what life I'd chosen for myself. Everything up until that point is irrelevant."

The pen scratched at the paper as she wrote. It grated on my nerves. Not a good quality ballpoint then.

She looked at me. What did she see?

"Why the FBI?"

"Because they wanted me."

"Why?"

"If you'd asked me when I was twenty-one I would've said it was because of my degrees. They were useful."

"Were they?"

I shook my head. "Not really." I paused. "Maybe, psychology was useful and I guess accounting meant I could add." And holding a double degree after three years at college meant I was a high-achiever. "FBI was a better career move than McDonalds drive-thru. And I doubt I could've handled the Navy." I thought the FBI liked rules but they're nothing compared to the Navy. Also, I like to think for myself not be fed regurgitated information from archaic handbooks.

"Navy?"

"Yeah, back in my college days, the Navy tried pretty hard to get me interested in a career with them." Or maybe it was Dad that tried hard. Whatever.

She smiled. "Why did the FBI want young Ellie Conway?"

I don't know. Nope, that wouldn't do. Come on, El. Just say it, but don't refer to criminals as fucktards. Do not say fucktards.

"Because I was driven to find the answers to questions posed by ... crime and the criminals who committed crimes. Because I see things other people miss. Because I pay attention to the details." Because I had zero fear. Had. I've plenty of fear now. Because I was six feet tall and bullet proof. Only I wasn't. I opened several veins and an artery or two for my job.

"What sort of things do you see that others don't?"

"Depends on the situation." I tapped my fingernails on the arm of the chair. "I have an ability to read people and situations."

She wrote then stopped. "Can we talk about what it was like for you in the early days of your career?"

"Yes, to a point."

A frown crossed her brow. "I thought I had unlimited access to your life as an agent?"

"As an FBI agent, but, I was seconded to another agency and worked off-shore for some of the time during my early years."

"And that's classified?"

Oh, fuck, yes.

"Yep."

She changed her line of questioning. "Why did you live down in Mauryville yet work out of Washington?"

"Mostly because I like small town life." To a point. "Also because my parents were in Richmond at the time and it wasn't that far from Mauryville. The team travelled a lot up and down the Eastern seaboard so, even if I'd lived in D.C. I never would've been home."

"That must've been difficult? You were young with a demanding career. What was your work/life balance like?"

A laugh rolled from my mouth and covered her feet in giggling yellow ducklings. As I watched a duckling snapped at a thread on the carpet. He pulled and the carpet began to unravel. As the thread grew longer and longer more ducklings joined in. All of a sudden the thread broke. Ducklings tumbled backwards and disappeared in a ball of yellow fluff. I shook the interlude away.

"I don't think I ever really got the hang of a work life balance. When you're a young agent, it doesn't occur to you that you're missing out on life and, anyway ..." I looked at her for a beat. "It's a vocation not a job. I wouldn't want my life any other way."

"What was it like for you leading a team of men like Lee Davenport, Sam Jackson, and Kurt Henderson and more recently Stewart Smith and Dane Wesson?"

"Don't really know how to answer that." A carousel of images of the team, my team, filled my mind. The laughter; tears; shock; blood; inappropriate grins; the way we had and have each other's back, always. I pressed pause on the stream of images. A group photo hung in the air. I was in the middle of the photo with one arm around Kurt and the other around Lee, Dane crouched in the front. They made me feel short and I am not. Carol waited. I took a breath. "I've never really felt like I am any more capable of making decisions or whatnot, than any of my team. I've never felt like the *leader*. We were a team. We are a team. We fit together and we work as a cohesive unit, always."

"But you are the team leader. Their boss. You are the

Special Agent in Charge of Delta."

"I thought we were talking about when this started. When I was just a special agent."

Carol smiled. "Why do I get the feeling you were never *just* a special agent?"

"I started at the beginning like every agent," I replied with a smile.

"You had a close relationship with the former Director Cait O'Hare. How did that come about? Surely for a young agent like yourself it would be quite unusual to have someone like Caitlin O'Hare as a friend and confidante."

Oh, right, here we go, looking for dirt.

"Very unusual. I met Director O'Hare when I graduated. She took an interest in me and my career. She mentored me." May as well go for broke. "We were also neighbors for a few years down in Mauryville."

Carol smiled, it was the smile of someone who'd stumbled on something tantalizing. "How well did you know O'Hare?"

"Quite well. Although not many people in the office knew the extent of our friendship and she was still very much my Director."

"How did that affect your ability to do your job? Was it easier? Was it harder? Did you make a point of keeping your relationship quiet?"

I shook my head. "There was absolutely no cover-up of our friendship." Breathe. "Work was work. We got on well at work but we also had our moments and disagreements. Everything was legit. I didn't get special treatment, if that's what you mean."

If I had I would've been able to get Owen off my back instead of putting up with her nasty shit for years. And then Owen died. Nope, still couldn't feel sorry about that outcome.

"Was the relationship downplayed in the office setting or within the FBI?"

Thought I'd covered that. I could feel frown lines deepening on my forehead. "Not at all. We were always professional during work hours and cases." A smile crept in. "Behind closed doors there was a bit more freedom but not that much. O'Hare was an excellent Director and mentor."

"Your relationship, by which I mean your friendship, with O'Hare wasn't general knowledge was it, Agent Iverson?"

"I can't answer for other agents as to what they may or may not know about my life, Carol." Why did I want to say Karen?

She flipped a page in her notebook and sat quietly for a moment before asking her next question. This time she framed it with a setting.

"When you lived in Mauryville ..."

Great here comes the son of a bitch case. Son of Shakespeare. Son of Shakespeare. Don't say son of a bitch.

She watched me as she continued, "When you lived in

Mauryville you ran a poetry chatroom. How and why did that get out of hand?"

Fair enough.

"Bearing in mind that we cannot look at that incident from today's point of view," I said. "Technology twelve years ago was different. We did not have the surveillance cameras on almost every corner and outside or inside businesses that we expect these days. It was easier to go undetected."

"That's what happened?"

"Yes, for the most part. The whole nasty episode was constructed by someone who I honestly had never given a moments thought. I had no idea that he hated me so much as to bide his time putting himself into a position where he could attempt to destroy me and my family."

"What triggered his behavior?"

"I don't know. We were at the same high school for a few years. I bet him at everything but not on purpose." I shrugged. "I've always been an overachiever but I'm not competitive as such. I'll do my best for me but not to purposely beat someone else. Does that make sense?" I didn't crow about it, I just did my best.

She nodded.

I continued, "He was an unstable genius." Whereas I've always been a stable one. I bit my lip to stop a cackle of laughter.

"How did he manage to kill so many people and get so close to you and your family?"

I just said he was an unstable genius. Come on, Ellie, play nice. I let that settle for a beat.

"He played a long game. It took him years to get himself into the required position. While he worked at placing himself within the FBI, not as an agent, but as a civilian worker. He was simultaneously ensconced inside poetry chatrooms and one of them was mine, it was all very well thought out. He did not make a play for me immediately."

"Can you tell me about the chatroom?"

"I can." I waited. That's not the right question, lady.

She knew. "Will you, please," Carol said with a smile.

"It was a supportive fun place for me to hang out after work. Most of the poets didn't know each other in real life and we were mostly anonymous simply using nicknames instead of our names." I stretched my right leg out then pulled it back. "I'd been a regular for a few years before taking the room over with my poet buddy, Galileo."

She read something in her notebook and then looked up. "Cormac Connelly?"

"Yes."

I could see her stick a mental pin in a thought. Weird.

"Carry on."

"Mac and I ran the room. Whoever was first in to open the room on whatever night was in charge. We basically just kept people on track and allowed sharing without anyone being harangued or bullied. Not a strenuous exercise at all, usually."

"Usually?"

"We ran a safe space and we had rules. Not everyone appreciated our rules. Some got nasty. Some got stupid and made threats. Some were banned. And one became a serial killer."

"What happened to him? What do you call him?"

"Let's be clear, he called himself the Son of Shakespeare not us. I would prefer if you referred to him as Charles Boyd and not to use the name he cultivated for himself."

"What happened to Boyd?"

"He spent ten years of his years on death row appealing his convictions. We won. He was executed by the Commonwealth of Virginia two years ago."

"How did you feel about that?"

"His death?" She nodded. "It was deserved."

Chance's words echoed in my head. *No one deserves to die.*

"Let me re-phrase that. Justice was served."

"He killed your mother, is that correct?"

"Yes."

That also was a form of justice.

"Your mother had some deep seated mental health issues, how did that affect you?"

"It affected me enough to set up a Foundation with Mac to help the children of mentally ill parents."

"That's the Butterfly Foundation?"

"Yes. My father and Mac's father run the Foundation

and have done so for several years."

"There was a rumor you stepped down as the chair after your adopted daughter committed suicide. Is that true?"

"Yes."

We're not discussing that.

"I've heard people say that you talk to your dead husband and can converse with other dead people."

Well, that's not a question, that's a statement. People say all manner of things. Think I'll leave it alone.

"I think we need to concentrate on my role within the FBI rather than gossip."

"The public need a rounded view."

'Off you fuck' nearly rolled from my tongue.

"People do not need to know anything about my private life, this is supposed to be about the work I do. My vocation."

"Is it true that your former mother-in-law accused you of killing your husband?"

I bit my lip. "Yes."

"Why would she do that?"

Because she was fucking insane. Why else? Memories snuck in under my warning system, evading the radar and bring that entire horrible time into the spotlight.

"She did and said a lot of things that made little sense to the rest of us," I said, with care.

"She was quite vocal about you causing his death, that must've been difficult for you and your daughter."

Breathe. Just breathe. "It was unpleasant."

"How long after he was shot did he died?"

Words rolled around in my skull then formed a sentence I didn't want to see. She has his death certificate otherwise she wouldn't be asking. Fuck! The spotlight shone bright and relentlessly on the breach within my mind.

That was my cue to get some air.

"Coffee?" I said as I stood. Argo stood and stretched. He was a super patient dog. He tipped his face upward and looked at me. I nodded. Argo spun around and trotted to my desk. The bottom drawer opened. A few months ago I had added a rope to the drawer so he could pull it open. I heard him take his leash from the drawer then drop it on the ground. He took the end in his mouth and dragged it to me. "Good boy, Argo." I gave him a good pat on the side and clipped the leash to his harness. I looked at Carol. "Are you coming or would you like to talk to Agent Sinclair?"

"I'd like to talk to all of Delta A."

No hiding the smile at that statement. It grew into a grin. "I'm sure they'll love that. Would you like to start with Sandra while I go for coffee and let Argo take a pee break?"

"Yes. That would be helpful."

"How do you take your coffee?"

"Mocha with chocolate on top please."

Of course.

"I'll send Sandra in on my way."

Argo and I stopped at Sandra's desk. She pushed her glasses up the bridge of her nose and looked up at me. "How can I be of service, O Leader of the Stir Crazy?"

"Delta being a bit annoying?"

"One by one they pop out here asking what's happening."

"I'll take one of them for a walk with me ... meanwhile, Carol would like to speak to you."

Sandra grimaced. "Do I have to?"

"It'd be rude not to."

"But do I have to?"

"I suppose not."

She smiled, adjusted her glasses again, and flicked her locked screensaver on. "Okay. I'll make sure she's getting good information."

I laughed. Argo strained against the leash. "Better go." I let out a whistle, a split second later Dane ran toward us. Keen.

"Boss?"

"Let's go, coffee run."

Lee and Kurt paused in the bullpen doorway. "You want us?" Lee asked.

"Nope. Dane'll do. As you were."

Dane, Argo, and I ran down the stairs to the entrance foyer. "Hey Frank," I said as I passed his desk.

"Take care out there, SAC," Frank replied. "Americano on your list?"

"You'll get your coffee Frank," I said stepping outside into sunlight. I took sunglasses from my pocket and put them on. Dane did the same.

2.

"El?"

"Yeah?" I turned to look at Dane. "What?"

"There's something wrong, I can feel it."

"That woman, the researcher, she has Mac's death certificate."

"Okay, why is that causing this amount of unease?"

"Because ..." Argo whined and pushed my leg. I knew what that meant. He wanted me to sit somewhere, anywhere, before I drifted away in the ether.

Dane grabbed my arm, we walked down an alleyway and he found a bench. Argo sat next to it.

"Good boy, Argo," I said, resting my hand on his head. I sat down, Dane joined me. "She has his death certificate, that means she knows, Dane, she knows."

"Knows what?"

"I can't ..."

"Show me."

The light beam widened as I pulled Dane inside my memory. It didn't feel any better knowing he was there, but, then again, it didn't feel any worse.

Yellowish lights flickered in the off-white corridor as I sat waiting. My right foot jiggled. The toe of my boot tapped rhythmically against the functional speckled gray linoleum. A single glance at my watch told me I'd been sitting there, staring at the double doors, for three hours. A hand touched my knee. I looked over into Lee's concerned brown eyes.

"Coffee?" He asked.

I shook my head.

"Water?" Sam asked. I turned my head toward him. He was leaning forward, his elbows resting on his knees, his eyes searched mine. "Can I get you some water, Chicky?"

They were trying.

"No. I'm fine," I said, swallowing the lump in my throat.

Footsteps approached. I listened to the weight in the steps. Caine.

His voice rumbled and grated its way from his mouth and into my ears.

"Conway, let's take a walk."

I rose. Rubbed my palms down my thighs and looked up into his craggy face and lined eyes.

"I am not going to the chapel," I said. "This isn't a chapel situation." Yet.

"Come on," he replied and ushered me down the corridor away from the surgical suite. Over his shoulder he said, "Call us when there's news."

Conversation eluded me. What was I going to say? The crazy bitch got away and her lacky has probably killed my husband? I swept that under the already lumpy carpet in the darkest corner of my mind.

Caine pushed the left-hand door of a set of double doors open and held it for me. I stepped into another corridor. Cooler. Dimmer. Farther away. The door closed. A rubber band squeezed my heart. I turned back to the door.

Caine's hand closed around my arm. "Walk with me."

"Mac."

Caine kept hold of my arm. Firm yet gentle. "It's going to take some time."

"I need …"

"Let's walk." His voice softened, all the sharp edges smoothed at once. "Misha is waiting."

My feet stopped moving.

Ahead of us a dark figure came into view. A long black leather coat swung with each stride. Misha Praskovya. Straight from the pages of a romance novel. As he neared his eyes locked on mine and his arms opened wide.

I don't know what possessed me but I stepped forward into those arms and felt them close around me. The subtle smell of leather mixed with his musky cologne and combined with the kiss he planted on the side of my head offered a sense of safety.

"Mac is strong man. Do not worry," he whispered in my ear, his accent giving the words depth.

"He is Swiss cheese with a thready pulse," I replied, stepping back. "I don't see a full recovery from this."

"Mac he fights. I know this." Misha's hands squeezed mine before letting me go.

Top marks for positivity. If only that was all it would take.

"Are you staying?" I moved to stand next to Caine.

"Two days, then home to Russia."

"Is this over?"

"Net."

My phone rang. I wrestled it from my pocket as running feet pounded linoleum moving toward us. The door burst open as I answered the call from Lee.

"Come back," Lee said. "Now."

I disconnected and saw Sam holding a door open. "Chicky Babe, Boss, let's go." He spun on his heels, I slipped through the door as Caine grabbed it behind me, and followed Sam.

A doctor in pale blue scrubs and an open white theater gown waited with Lee. I couldn't read his face.

"Here she is," Lee said beckoning me closer. Hesitation froze my feet to the spot. Then I felt it, the protection of my team, as they surrounded me. Shoulder to shoulder we stood in a semi-circle to hear what the doctor had to say.

"Mrs. Connelly," the surgeon said.

"Ellie Conway, Mac's wife," I replied. Could've just said yes.

He nodded. "The first surgery went as well as possible under the circumstances," he said. "Your husband is in recovery. We will move him within the hour to intensive care."

"Sorry, first surgery?"

"Multiple organs were compromised. There is a spinal injury. A head injury. Shattered ribs." He talked on.

I stopped listening and trying to follow the laundry list of horror. Sam nudged me. The surgeon stood patiently in front of me.

"I understand this is overwhelming."

If Mac were a dog we would've put him down. A smile grew in the bleakness. He'd get a kick out of the whole rainbow bridge thing. *Stop!*

I breathed.

"What are my husband's chances of resuming his life?"

"Mrs. Connelly, Ellie, there are going to be adjustments."

"What does that mean?"

"If Mac survives the next twenty-four hours we'll talk about the next step."

"More surgeries?"

"Yes."

"And his chances of surviving the next twenty-four hours?"

"Thirty per cent."

That's not enough. The energy around me faltered then surged back. Strong. Steady. A million heartbeats rolled into one.

"Can I see him?"

"When we get him settled into ICU. He'll be in an induced coma. Expect machinery and for him to be non-responsive."

I swallowed. How much settling could there be for a piece of inert meat?

A voice in my head said, "Thank the nice Doctor, Gabrielle." I replied swiftly, "Shut it Mom."

Lee spoke, "Thank you." His hand reached out and shook the doctors. The doctor walked away, vanishing through a set of doors with high frosted windows.

A bubble closed around me. Noise stopped. Life disappeared. Our life was gone forever. I knew that. We were forever changed. A gunman. The kid. My husband. The lives of the families of the stolen children. Death. Horror. Destruction. How does anyone find their footing after that?

I stuck an arm through the bubble. Breaking the surface into tiny rainbows.

"Caine?"

"Right here, kid."

"I'm going to need a second opinion."

"Doctor Kurt Henderson is on standby."

I knew that name. Hadn't seen him since Dad's heart attack in Richmond. It felt like a life time ago.

The bubble reformed. Next time it popped the rainbows fell on the carpet in our living room. The cat rubbed around my legs.

Sam's deep voice called from the kitchen, "You're nearly out of cat biscuits."

The cat ran toward his voice. I followed, slower, trying to make sense of my changing world. There was no sense to any of it. It was nonsense. Why did he take his fucking vest off?

"You doing okay, Chicky Babe?"

"I'm okay," I replied with a shrug.

Sam placed a steaming mug of black coffee on the counter in front of me.

"Thanks."

"Ellie." His warm brown eyes met mine. "He's got a fight ahead but he's tough."

I smiled. "You're tough. Lee's tough. Mac's cyber."

A deep laugh bounced off the counter top, as it receded it left behind words. "I didn't want to say that ..."

Laughter swam up from the depths and took over my body, the subsided as agony rose in waves. Tears cascaded. In danger of drowning I sank onto the stool at the counter.

* * *

The needle stuck, bouncing in a scratch of the record of my life. Static blocked the hiss and click from the ventilator. It blurred the steady blip, beep, beep of the heart monitor. With the jolt from Kurt's voice the needle lurched to the next track. His voice fell from a shadow in the room, "Conway."

"How long have you been here?" My eyes focused on Mac. Still unconscious. Drains. Tubes. Monitors. Drips.

"An hour. We're weaning him off the drugs that keep him in the coma."

"Okay."

"When we know he can breath on his own, we'll take the ventilator away."

"Today?"

"Yes, all going well."

"His legs? His brain? Is he even still Mac?"

"We'll know more later today."

"Henderson ..." I dragged my focus from Mac to Kurt. "Will he talk and walk again?"

Kurt's head turned until I could see his blue eyes. "Probably." His mouth set in s small smile. "But not without a lot of support. He may never fully recover, Conway."

Okay. I suppose that's better than no.

"What kind of support?"

"He'll need to learn to walk again. May never recover full sensation in his right leg. Expect an elbow crutch or cane to be a permanent accessory."

Handicap parking perk. Will that outweigh the anger and frustration Mac will feel? Probably not. Will Mac be able to voice his frustration. Who knows? I thought back to the day Mac and I discussed what we wanted to happen if either of us were in this position. If life wasn't sustainable, if one of us could no longer live a full and productive life. I knew what his wishes were. No heroic measures. I'd already gone against his wishes by allowing five surgeries and refusing to sign a *do not resuscitate* form. And now here we are.

"Penny for them Conway."

I smiled at Kurt. "Thinking about the road ahead."

"Stepping into the unknown isn't easy."

He returned the smile. "You're not alone. You have your team and family." He paused for a beat. "And me."

"Thank you. I appreciate the reminder and the support."

* * *

I let the images of Mac and the machines keeping him alive, or more accurately keeping his shell alive, dissolve. Once again I was sitting on a wooden bench. Argo's head rested in my lap.

Dane moved beside me. "How long did he live?"

"He never lived Dane, he lay in a hospital bed and never regained consciousness. I moved him to a hospital better equipped for long term care. His brain activity was minimal. He looked like he was asleep but he never woke up. I signed the DNR."

"How long?"

"Eleven hundred and fifty eight days."

"Over three years ..."

"Yeah."

"No one knew?"

"The team knew. Life carried on. He was the living dead. A zombie. We basically waited for his body to give out."

"And this researcher, she knows he didn't die the day of the shooting ..."

"Yes."

"If you don't tell her he was in a coma for three years she'll start speculating."

"I know. But, his mom was right. I killed him. I signed the DNR." And I had a relationship with Rowan while my husband lay barely breathing in a coma. I am a fucking monster.

"Let's go get that coffee. It's going to be okay, Ellie. It is."

"Doesn't feel like it."

"What are you worried about?"

I threw him a half smile. "Exposure of secrets."

"Is that it? Because he's dead, that's not a secret."

Dane had a point. I raised my internal shields and stopped his access to my thoughts. Maybe it's that I don't want to think about those years. The absence of all hope. The endless visitations and the way nothing changed. The constant drama and accusations from his insane mother and horrible older brother. You should be home making a life for your husband. You care about your job more than your marriage. This is all your fault. Why did you let him go with you that day? What's with adopting the kid that caused this? We should be allowed to see her, she's our grandchild now. Does she know what she did? What you did? You never bring her to visit.

Endless contradictions and bullshit. I don't want that dragged out into the public sphere. I don't want my kids to hear about that part of my life from some disgusting tell-all biography. Or worse, from sensationalized media reports of snippets from the shitty book.

"It's how he died, Dane. Slowly, piece by piece."

"I get it."

He did, I knew that.

"We had a funeral ... he was technically still alive."

"That can't have been easy. What about his parents?"

"Mac's dad handled it. He knew. He didn't tell his wife." I shrugged and petted Argo. "Wasn't the first time he'd kept something major from her."

"They didn't visit Mac?"

"They didn't, but he did. Mac's dad saw him as much as he could. Shared care. Me, him, my dad, Lee and Sam, Kurt when he could." Argo pushed his nose into my hand. "The mother spent years harassing me, she already blamed me. Smarter not to let her near Mac. He couldn't defend himself."

"She's passed?"

"Yes and the older brother, Eddie."

"Does Mitch know?"

"Yes."

"Did Rowan know?"

"Nope."

"Can you refuse to discuss anything around Mac on security grounds?"

A smile splashed across my face. Yes!

"Thank you!"

"You're welcome, for?"

"I can shut down anything to do with Mac because of his security clearance. His undercover situation just became my impenetrable brick wall."

3.

"Who is doing the actual writing of this travesty?" I wondered aloud as Dane and I walked back to the office with trays of coffee. The tray I carried had less takeout cups, mostly because I also had Argo's leash in one hand.

Dane chuckled. "And why aren't they doing the research themselves?"

"Another good question."

"Must be a reason."

"I'd like to know what it is," I replied as Dane opened the door for me. "Hey Frank, come get your coffee."

Frank hurried over and met us just before the stairwell door.

"Thanks for this SAC," he said, removing the cup that said, 'Frank' on it. "You're a Champ."

I smiled, Dane opened the stairwell door, Frank vanished as the door closed behind us. Our footfalls filled the empty space. The hollow sound echoed. No running with coffee. It'd be like running with scissors but wetter.

At our floor, Dane turned to me before opening the door.

"Are you asking now?"

"Yes."

He opened the door and took the tray from my hand. "I'll leave yours on your desk."

"Thanks." Argo and I carried on up the stairs.

I opened the door to Caine's outer office. Reed looked

up and wrinkled his nose when he saw Argo. No idea why he reacted like he did to Argo but there was zero love there.

"Is he in?" I said and indicted the door to the inner sanctum.

"Yes."

"Busy?"

"Yes, but not with anyone, if that's what you are meaning, SAC."

I nodded at Reed, knocked once then opened the door to Caine's office.

He looked up from his screen. His lip twitched. "Agent Argo, come on in here boy," Caine said, his gruff voice grated across the floor.

I unclipped the leash letting Argo join Caine. I stood witness to the petting, happy whining, and licking. When Caine looked up at me he was back to his usual grumbly self.

"To what do I owe this visit?"

"This book thing."

"What about it?"

"It seems a bit much. There are plenty of agents who should have their story written, I am not one of them."

"Ellie. It's time. Before you leave, before the embellished stories become entrenched in our history, we need a record of how it really was. Not a whispered secretive highlight reel."

"It'll inspire no one."

"This reaction is exactly why the decision was made to tell the story of Special Agent in Charge Ellie Iverson."

"What if I've changed my mind?"

"That's your right. But be aware the story will still be told with or without your input."

"Then how true will it be?" They can't exactly turn over case notes to a researcher and that led me to the next question. "Who is really writing this story?"

Caine paused. His attention drawn by an alert on his screen. A moment later he lifted his eyes to met mine with slow a growl he said, "We have a problem."

"Continue ..."

"The researcher requested an interview with Grange."

"How is Rowan Grange part of this story? And do all her requests come through your office?"

"Yes, they do and she stated the reason for the request as 'background'."

Good to know Caine handles all requests, but she can fuck right off.

"Into what exactly, this is supposed to be about me the *FBI agent* not my private life."

Caine's eyes softened as he watched me.

"It's all intertwined Ellie, you know that. You and I, we were cut from the same cloth. There is no real line between private life and work life."

I swallowed a lump in my throat. "She wants to talk about Carla and Mac. Who the fuck is really writing this story?" I sat in the chair. Argo left Caine. He leaned on me and pushed my hand until I rubbed his head. "Can't I just toss her my commendations and be done with it?"

His lip twitched with unaccustomed violence. "That would certainly keep her busy for sometime. The point here is to tell the stories behind the commendations, behind the times you were hauled over the coals, to unravel the complexity of life as an FBI agent."

"That sounds like a fancier way of saying they're digging into my life like the paparazzi." With a big shovel that'll turn up the skeletons.

"No, Ellie. They want the truth not the sensationalized bullcrap that was floated by the media and paparazzi over the years."

"Maybe I don't want this. Maybe I don't want to talk about my life."

Perhaps I was a four year old about to lose the plot or perhaps I was about to take Argo to the nearest bar and drink my blood volume in tequila.

"When the publisher first approached me I warned them that you would not like this. So I can't say I'm surprised by your reaction now that the research phase is underway."

"Who is the writer that is going to tell my life story? Who is it that sold this to a publisher?"

I had an awful feeling I wouldn't like the answer.

"Randal Hopkirk."

That felt familiar. I let the name sit for a moment. Then I had it. "He co-wrote a book with Mikki Kennedy.

The story of Director Cait O'Hare."

"Yes."

"Does Mikki know about this?"

Caine shook his head. "I don't know. You'd have to ask her."

Oh, I will.

"Why isn't he doing his own research?"

"I have no idea."

Something else for Mikki or the publisher who bought this story idea. They bought the idea. Our Director signed off on it, or it wouldn't be happening.

"What do I get out of this?" Surely someone can't just expect my cooperation with no compensation. This isn't part of my job.

"All the glory, I suppose, like the FBI."

"I hate this."

He nodded. "I'm not thrilled myself, kid. Director Thomas, however, wants this to happen."

Fuck him.

"Here's your heads up - anything regarding Mac is off-limits and if I have to I'll use his security clearance and get the CIA involved."

The upper lip twitched twice in the right corner, then his lower lip joined in. He gave a frightening rendition of a lopsided smile.

"I'd expect nothing less," he said, and a lighter than average growl punctuated his words.

"I'd appreciate it if you could let Carol know."

He picked up his cell phone from his desk. "It's my pleasure."

4.

Carol dropped her empty cup into the bin in my office. My coffee was tepid and wouldn't take me long to drink. Argo settled back on his bed.

"I've been told not to ask you about Mac."

I said nothing for a beat and leaned back in my chair. Watching. Trying to read her expression. Thwarted. Wonder how many times I can force that expression before she gives up?

"I hear you want access to Rowan Grange," I said.

"That's correct," she said, and positioned her pen over her notepad.

I said nothing else about Rowan. Just left it there. Not like I could facilitate access anyway. Our relationship was long over. I wasn't about to dig around in that quagmire.

"It's well known you had a strong working relationship with an FSB Officer. Officer Misha Praskovya. How did that come about?"

"Officer Praskovya came on board during the Hudson Hawk case. He proved himself to be a valuable asset to the FBI and especially to my team."

"Was this a work relationship or was there more to it?"

"What are you asking?"

"How close were you?"

No blue dress there either. Dig away, lady.

"We became friends."

"Was there an exchange of information?"

"In what way?"

"Did you and Praskovya exchange information about other cases?"

I took a sharp inward breath. "If you are trying to imply there was something sinister in our friendship or that we were in anyway compromising our respective agencies security or committing treason on any level, then you can take your notes and leave. I have friends all over the world in all manner of roles and that doesn't mean we talk shop or exchange information that is not strictly need to know at the time."

"He was the Godfather to one of your children, was he not?"

"Yes, he was. He also helped us on many occasions professionally."

"Why choose a Russian to be Godfather?"

"Godparents were chosen by Mitch and I as a couple on merit, not on nationality," I said, keeping my tone even and light.

"But wouldn't that give Praskovya unparalleled access to your life?"

"No." He already had it. He was my friend. He was our friend. Stick your spade somewhere else, lady.

My phone alerted. Saved by the bell. I checked the message.

Kurt Henderson: A case just landed.

"We are going to have to leave this here. No doubt you can continue snooping without me for a while. I have work to do." I rose from my chair and pointed toward my door. "Goodbye."

"You are making this more difficult than it needs to be," Carol said. She stood and smoothed her skirt with one hand. "Research is not snooping, Agent Iverson."

"I have a job to do and this interview and your *research* cannot and will not interfere with that." I smiled. "You can reschedule with Sandra. I'm afraid Delta A is incommunicado for the time being."

"How about Rowan Grange?" She asked from the doorway.

"I have no idea where Mr. Grange is or what his schedule is like. Perhaps you could talk to his management." Good luck getting through the gatekeepers and that pain in the ass manager of his.

"Isn't he linked to your foundation?"

"Yes."

"Then surely you could help me to get me the access I require."

If only you did *require* it and weren't just being nosy in all the wrong places. Stay in your lane, lady.

"Afraid not. Now, my team is coming in for a meeting so ..." I flapped a hand to shoo her away.

"Would your father be able to help me?"

"You can ask him."

With my blessing. Go right ahead and try and get anything out of my father that isn't a broad brushed overview.

Carol left the room and was replaced almost instantaneously by Kurt, Lee, and Dane. Dane and Lee grabbed chairs and placed them near my desk. Kurt closed the door and sat in the chair vacated by Carol.

"You said a case landed?" I rocked back in my chair with my head on the headrest. "Did it?"

"It did," Kurt replied and tapped on the screen of his iPad. "I've sent you the link."

My phone pinged. I opened the link. It was a surveillance video.

A male dressed in black carrying what looked like an Armalite M-15 walked into a clothing store and came out with a woman held at gun point.

"Okay, is this a hostage situation?" I looked up at the team. Heads semi-shook. "What's going on?"

"Over the last four hours a male dressed in black carrying an M-15 has taken four women at gunpoint to unknown destinations," Kurt said. "We got the call from Metro asking if this might be in our wheelhouse."

I nodded. "Sure looks like it could be. Where is this man taking these women and why?"

"We tracked him via traffic cam. He put that woman into a dark colored Ford Transit van." Kurt fired up more video footage while talking. "We lost him heading toward Fort Totten."

I opened a satellite map on my laptop and zoomed in

300

on the Fort Totten area. "Probably didn't take the Metro," I muttered. "Mostly houses up there ... Aggregate Industries is there, a solid waste transfer station, cemeteries, schools, old soldiers home."

"He could've kept going," Dane said.

"In four hours he took five women and stashed them somewhere." I leaned back in my chair. I doubted he went much further. "Where were they all taken from?"

Lee stood and walked over to the smart board on the wall. He swiped left and chose a map of D.C. Then added pins to indicate where the women were working before they were taken."

"That's a pretty tight cluster," I said. "He must be using more than one vehicle. The minute a gunman steps foot in a store and takes someone hostage everything changes. He can't just waltz back into the same area and do it again."

Lee zoomed in on the area. "Adjacent streets and nearby streets, but look." He pointed to several ways in and out. "He'd still need multiple vehicles because everyone would be looking."

"Not just looking but stores would be on high alert," I said.

"Yeah," Dane said, and joined Lee at the map. "How many cameras can we access near those stores?"

Lee added cameras to the map. They popped up all over the place. Many of them were traffic, red light, and general city surveillance.

"Enough that he'd be on several."

"He had to know that, right?" Lee said. "This is D.C. The most surveilled city there is."

"So he purposely chose to commit crimes while being watched?" I said. "That sounds like it's part of his MO. Do we have victim photos?"

Kurt leaned closer to me. "Check your inbox. Photos should be there."

Sure enough they were. I sent them to the smart board. Lee saw them in the upper left corner and enlarged the set of images over the top of the map. Four women all between twenty-five and thirty. Two black, one white, one possibly of middle eastern decent.

I search my email for anything else from police. Hoping they had found something other than 'retail assistant' to connect them. No more emails. No more information.

"We need boots on the ground. Let's get everything we can on these women. While we are at it, I want a SWAT team on standby and a Delta team on the move to the Fort Totten area." I looked at Kurt. "B or C?"

"C. B is on a case and too far south to help us today."

"Okay."

I picked up my phone and called the new SSA of Delta C. "Hey, Christian. I need you and Delta C in the Fort Totten area." I typed fast sending him all the information he needed.

"Yes, SAC." His email alert pinged. "Got the information."

"Keep in touch. I want to find these missing women and the Unsub A-sap."

"On our way, SAC."

I hung up.

The smart board on my office wall sprang to life as Lee started adding more details about each woman while reading from his phone.

"Lee, what've you got?" I asked, intrigued.

"Sandra did some digging. We have commonalities," he said without looking over. "You're going to love it." His voice bottomed out.

I very much doubted love would be my response. I read the additions to the board. Yep. Love wasn't the response at all. More like gut-churning borderline fear.

"Our ladies all attended the last Grange gig at Wolf Trap?" I watched him write.

"And ...," Kurt said.

"They belong to the Grange backstage fan club and that's how they got tickets to a fan club only event like the one at Wolf Trap," I said as Lee finished up. I turned to Dane. "Find out who runs the backstage stuff and get Rowan in my office A-sap."

I picked my phone up and called Sandra. "Going to need a warrant for the Backstage with Grange fan club, Dane will be with you shortly with the names of the band management. I need access to their membership database and a list of everyone who attended the Wolf Trap event last month."

"Judge?"

"Hartwell. We have women being abducted from their places of work, the strongest link is the Grange fan club. All details are in SENTINEL. I'll link you to the case files."

"Standing by, O Leader of the Pack."

Shitballs and whatnot. I typed a message and sent the link to Sandra.

With an absence of thought I reached for my desk phone and dialed a phone number I hadn't called in a long time and never imagined I'd call again. Rowan's personal mobile number. So shoot me, I lied to Carol. But she really does not need to stir up the mess we left behind. The world doesn't need to know about his infidelity or mine for that matter.

"Hello," said the familiar voice ringed by a hint of New Jersey.

"Rowan, it's Ellie Iverson." I paused for a breath.

"Been a while, El ..."

"Yes, it has. We have a developing situation and the only link so far is to the Grange Fan Club and that gig you did at Wolf Trap."

"That ain't good."

"No, it's not."

"How can I help?"

"We'd like to talk to you."

"Okay. I'm not far away. I have a meeting with Simon and the board at The Butterfly Foundation at two-thirty. I can swing by now?"

"Yeah, thanks, that'd be good." Then my brain kicked in. "No, not here at the office. Meet me at the house." Couldn't guarantee Carol wasn't still in the building. Lurking. Hoping to catch someone unawares.

"Half an hour? Still take your coffee the same way?"

"That works. Don't worry about coffee."

I hung up, leaned my elbows on my desk and rested my chin on my clasped hands.

"Where do they live?" I asked. "Can we have conversations with next of kin?"

Lee nodded. "We have home addresses for all victims and next of kin. Who do you want to handle this?"

"You and Dane. I need Kurt with me."

"Okay, Boss. We'll make contact and set up interviews."

"Go to their homes, Lee. Don't drag those people away from their comfort zones. This is scary enough."

"Got it."

I rose from my chair and moved around my desk. Argo joined me at the door.

"Your place?" Kurt said, swinging the office door open and holding it.

"Yeah."

There was no sign of Carol in the hallway. I waved to Sandra and pointed to my office. "Lee and Dane might need a hand."

"On it, O Leader of the Crime Fighters." She waved us

on our way.

5.

Home.

Peace.

No one asking invasive questions.

Maybe I should work from home for a few days. Call in sick. Or maybe just be unavailable to anyone not on a Delta team.

I unlocked the front door, Argo walked past me and into the house. Kurt waited for me to step inside and then followed, closing the door behind him.

In the kitchen, I put a pot of coffee on, refilled Argo's water bowl, and then sat at the counter on a barstool waiting for the coffee.

Kurt perched on a barstool on the other side of the counter.

"Quiet without the girls," he commented.

"Weirdly so."

They were at Mitch's parents for the day. They spent four days a week with his parents and one day a week with my Dad. Shared care of *double trouble*. Was the best way to make it all work. The intercom buzzed. Argo started to walk down the hall then paused and waited to see who would go with him.

"He's arrived," Kurt said. "I'll let him through the gate and wait at the door."

Kurt and Argo walked down the hallway and out of sight. I listened to the coffee maker gurgle and set three cups on the counter. It'd been a long time since I'd seen Rowan. Even longer since he'd been in my home. Feelings around our last encounter percolated in the shadows. They knew not to show themselves. This was business. Whatever he'd done in the past was just that, past. He was an idiot. End of story.

Voices wound toward me on the warm breeze from the open front door. The door closed but the voices continued and grew louder.

I poured the coffee. Kurt and Rowan walked into the room. Argo trailed behind and went to his bed.

"El, good to see you," Rowan said, and leaned across the counter to plant a kiss on my cheek.

"You too." I pushed a cup in his direction then inclined my head to let Kurt know which was his.

Staying in the kitchen worked better for me. Anything that meant it felt less like a *Rowan's in my home* situation. Kurt took his cup to the kitchen table, Rowan and I followed suit.

"What does your case have to do with my last gig?" Rowan lifted his chin and looked me in the eye.

"We're not sure, but that's a commonality. That and your fan club."

"There's nothing else?"

"Not so far. That gig was fan club only?"

"Yes."

"Do you have records of everyone who attended?"

"Not personally, but the fan club does. We sent actual

invitations or tickets if you like. Usually it's an e-ticket but this time they opted for paper."

"So you'll have addresses too?"

"Yes."

"Can we access that information?"

"Get a warrant and you can do whatever you want."

"Oh, that's on its way." I glanced at Kurt who was texting. I knew who and why. It was Sandra to organize a warrant. "Anything unusual about the concert?"

"No, everything hummed along nicely."

"You're sure?"

He nodded. "Of course. It was a concert for fans, club members. They're quite intimate shows with a lot of audience participation."

"No one got out of line?"

I'd been to a couple of gigs when we dated and there was always one nut job trying to climb up on the stage or climb Rowan. Just because it was a club event didn't mean the nuts weren't there.

"Nothing that wasn't expected."

"What was security like?"

He shrugged. "Normal. Jed's department."

Jed was Rowan's bodyguard I didn't recall him running concert security.

"Why Jed?"

"I trust him. We've had our fair share of trouble over the years and I asked Jed to step into the roll two years ago."

"Is he still your private security?"

"Yes."

Good for Jed. Two pay checks.

"Any problem with me talking to Jed?"

He shook his head.

Kurt cleared his throat. "We got the warrant, it's electronic, who needs it?"

"Management of the fan club." Rowan pulled his wallet from his jacket pocket, opened it and searched the contents. He then handed Kurt a card. "Contact details for the fan club management."

"Thanks."

Kurt walked away tapping on his phone.

"How've you been, El?" Rowan asked with a smile.

"Pretty good. You?"

"Ticking along. Miss you more than I expected I would."

A small laugh escaped before I could stop it. I miss a lot of people but Rowan never made the list. "I don't have much time to miss much."

He lifted his cup and took a sip. "This is good. You always did make good coffee." A twinkle of mischief sparked in his eyes. "And pancakes."

"I still make plenty of pancakes for our *family* breakfasts."

Argo's tail swept a toy block across the floor, it clonked against a chair leg.

Kurt caught my attention with a wave of a finger from

the doorway. "All the information we want is going direct to Sandra. Two more women have vanished."

"Same as the others?" Rowan asked, a frown deepened, knitting his brows together. "Fans?"

"We need a minute to determine that, but now we have a database to run the names through, it'll definitely help."

"Rowan, is Jed with you?" I said, refilling my cup.

"He's at the hotel."

"Gimme his cell number." I unlocked my phone with one touch, opened contacts, and passed the phone to Rowan. He obliged by adding Jed's cell number and name before passing the phone back. I took it from his hand, avoiding touching any skin.

A wisp of the past floated on an ethereal strand between us.

My phone rang as Kurt's phone rang. That's never good.

Dane's image sat on my screen. With a swipe a video call started.

"When were you last in a chat room?"

"A couple of weeks ago."

"Was it another poetry chat room or your old poetry room?"

"No. It was the Butterfly Foundation chats."

"Have you been in any chat rooms other than those?"

"No."

Dane frowned. "You need to be back here. We have a situation."

I glanced from the screen in front of me to Kurt. He ran his hand through his hair. That wasn't good either.

"What's all this chat room talk?" I asked Dane and watched his expression change from a static frown to animation.

"The Unsub is sitting in a chat room demanding OtherwiseCat join him."

"What's his nickname?"

"DHS."

"He's dead. DHS was killed by Charles Boyd. We're coming. Ping him, find out where he is."

Dane sighed. "We have him in London, Berlin, Quebec, Calcutta ..."

"Okay, get cyber onto it, someone must be able to locate this fool."

"What chat room?"

"He's in Cobwebs."

"That's not possible. Only Mac and I can open that room, those servers don't even exist now." My mind spun. No way could it be the same room. "Find the server that's hosting the room he's in."

He sent a screen shot. Shit. It looked just like Cobwebs. I knew it wasn't.

Rowan's cup bumped the counter as he put it down. Okay, think, El. How can this be happening?

"Dane, we're coming." I hung up and shoved my phone in my pocket. Kurt did the same.

"Lee is getting the files," he said. "What happened to

Charles Boyd?"

"He was executed."

"Probably not him doing this then."

"I hope not," I replied and rinse my cup under the faucet, then left it upside down next to the sink. I reached out for Rowans. He handed it to me. I did the same with his. Kurt came over and rinsed his own cup.

"Do you still need access to the fan club?"

"Yes." I headed for the front door then stopped and turned around. "Rowan, does the fan club website have chat rooms?"

"Yes."

Kurt tugged his phone from his pocket. He had his finger poised ready to text. I guessed it was Lee he was about to text.

"Can the members create their own private groups or rooms?"

"Yes."

Kurt sent a text.

I closed the front door after us. Rowan left with a wave. Kurt, Argo and I followed him out.

Silence pushed into the airspace around me as I sat in the passenger seat. Kurt drove. I couldn't hear the tires on the road, or the tick of the turn signal. There was no sound. My heartbeat faded into the leather.

Breathe.

It's not him. Boyd is dead.

My eyes closed. What the fuck was going on? A pencil

sketched lines on a blank page. A soft voice followed the lines until an image formed. Chance climbed out of an elevator that didn't make it all the way to the floor. He dusted himself off and grinned at me.

"What kind of half-assed call was that?" He pointed at the elevator doors open but still a good three feet from the floor proper. "Usually I get a door and make an entrance."

"You definitely made an entrance," I said with a smile. "There's a problem ..."

"No kidding."

The magic pencil raced to draw a couple of chairs. Nothing fancy, just wooden dining chairs. We sat facing each other.

"I think someone is copycatting Charles Boyd, only this time the targets are not my friends."

"Okay, who are the targets?"

"Not who is Charles Boyd?"

"That too."

"Someone who was at the same high school as me. We were the same year. He played the long game when it came to getting his revenge on the wrongs I supposedly did him."

"Why do I get the feeling there is more to it than that?"

"He killed my mother. It was nearly thirteen years ago. Boyd was executed by the Commonwealth of Virginia a few years back.'

"Death row, then he shouldn't have been in general

population or had a cell mate. Or even many visitors."

"Yeah."

"All right, so it might not be a criminal who heard his story directly."

"Not that it matters, but if it is, might be easier to track. We'd have less names than, say, the entire eastern seaboard."

"Good point."

"He's kidnapped six young women from the middle of the city. I don't think he's working alone. So far none have turned up in pieces, which was Boyd's thing."

Movement made the scene shimmer. I blinked and re-focused. Chance vanished.

"Iverson, we have a problem," Kurt said, reaching forward he turned on the grill lights and the siren. "You okay?" He glanced at me then back at the road.

"Sure, I'm okay. What's the problem?"

"Check your phone. He's dumped a body."

I opened a message with an attached photo from Lee. Hard to recognise the jumble of flesh and bone as a body. I tipped my phone sideways, hoping the image would be bigger and easy to see. It was. Still didn't look like a person.

A quick reply to Lee garnered a response.

Lee: Someone sent it from a burner phone.

Me: Of course they did. We'll be back soon. Do we have a location on that body?

Lee: Pulled data from the image. You want me to wait for you before sending a forensic team with an escort?

Me: Yes, wait. Delta A will provide escort service.

Lee: I get the feeling that's what the Unsub wants. Don't think any of us should attend.

I closed the message app. Leaned back in the seat and took a breath. And we're here again. Full. Fucking. Circle. Lee had a point. If this is to get us at the scene ... but then if we don't go, he could escalate. "Henderson?"

"Iverson?"

"The interviewer was keen to talk about Charles Boyd this morning. Annoyingly keen." Another deep breath followed as I tried to settle the unease in my gut. "You know how I feel about coincidence."

And Dane said someone was in a chat room pretending to be DHS, and the chat room was called Cobwebs. The DHS poser was waiting for me. Now we have a dismembered body. My mind spun. Faster and faster with each revolution.

"Pull over!" I zapped the window down hoping fresh air would stop the rising bile and spinning.

"What's going on, Iverson?" Kurt asked, as he pulled onto the shoulder, leaving the siren and flashers running.

I unclipped my seatbelt, flung the door open, and vomited onto the roadside. Kurt was out his door and leaning in mine within seconds. He handed me a wet wipe, as he re-positioned his feet careful to avoid the mess in front of the door.

"Feel better?"

"Not really," I replied, wiping my mouth and attempting a smile. Kurt reached around me and hooked a water bottle from the footwell.

"Small sips, Iverson. You know the drill."

I took the bottle, unscrewed the lid, and did as I was told. A few moments later I looked up at Kurt. "We have to find those women."

"We're working on it, Iverson." His eyes scanned my face. "You all right?"

I shook my head. "Yeah. Let's go."

Half a smile tweaked his lips. "Good enough. Buckle up."

He closed the door.

6.

Argo and I walked into my office to find Lee, Dane, and Sandra waiting. Lee was on the sofa. Sandra sat at my desk and Dane in a chair in front of the desk.

"We have the location of the body. Metro PD are at the scene. It's secure," Dane said, he swivelled in his chair to look at me. "Ready to go when you are."

"Thanks. And the chat room?" My eyes hit Sandra's. "Can you get me in there?"

"Already done O Protector of Artists and Vagabonds. You are waiting in the wings ready to jump into the room as OtherwiseCat."

Oh, man. A ball of barbed wire formed in my gut.

Sandra stood came around the side of the desk.

"Thank you," I said and took my seat.

Kurt hurried in, grabbed a chair and pulled it up beside me. "Right here, Iverson. We're all here. This freak can't touch any of us."

Argo yapped once from his bed. Yep, we're all here.

"Don't let those be famous last words, Henderson." I moved the cursor and entered the room.

It was identical to Cobwebs. A piece of wire pinged into the wall of my stomach. Pain hit so hard I gasped.

"You all right?" Kurt asked, his hand touched my arm. "Iverson?"

"I'm okay."

I scanned the right side of the screen looking for the

dead. There was an occupant list. Ten people. No names that I recognised apart from DHS. And he *was* dead. I knew that. One hundred percent. That was not the real DHS.

I spoked to Sandra, "Can we track him through this?"

"He's all over the map, literally, I can't get through his VPN."

"Do we know what he's using, is he mobile?"

Lee replied, "We have to assume he is, he could be on a phone. He could be with the rest of the women."

Could be and assumptions. Not how I liked to operate. At all. I saw three dots appear next to his name. "He's typing."

DHS: *You're gonna die, bitch.*

OtherwiseCat: Not today motherfucker.

DHS: *I'm serious, you're gonna die.*

OtherwiseCat: It's been tried, didn't stick.

DHS: *He said you were cocky.*

OtherwiseCat: What is it you want?

DHS: *Your death.*

OtherwiseCat: Anything else? Money? Infamy? A plane standing by? A date with Rowan Grange?

DHS: *I want you dead.*

OtherwiseCat: You're not the first and I doubt you'll be the last. Can't wait to see how this pans out for you.

Someone else entered the room. Nothing was said for a

moment then the newcomer typed.

Squirrel: Thought this was supposed to be a Grange chat room. Not very friendly DHS.

Dane!

He caught my eye when I looked up. He grinned and said, "I'm here to get everyone else out. I'm going to PM them all and suggest another room. We've created a link for it. Better if they aren't in this one, around this dick."

"What's to stop him following?"

"Me," Lee said. "I'm in the new room, ready to ban his ass the minute it appears."

Okay then.

Someone else tried to join the conversation. Someone called Grange4eva.

"Flick me the link in a PM, Lee."

My private messages alerted. I grabbed the link and opened a private chat window with Grange4eva.

OtherwiseCat: For your own safety do not respond to anything DHS says. This chat room is monitored by law enforcement.

Grange4eva: This is supposed to be for Grange fans only!

OtherwiseCat: My name is Ellie Conway. I am FBI. Please go into another room.

I dropped the link.

Grange4eva: You're her. The one who dated Rowan!!
OtherwiseCat: Yes I am. Please leave this room.

Grange4eva disappeared.

"Dane, did that person land in the new room?"

"Grange4eva is in here and already talking about how you're in the other room. Stopping them all going back to watch the carnage is going to be hard."

Sandra piped up, "I got this. Watch." She appeared in Cobwebs as herself. "Anyone who comes back will get a gold hammer to the head. Banning them this from this room."

Good thing we all knew she meant a figurative gold hammer to the head.

"Good thinking," I said.

DHS was in full rant mode about what an awful person OtherwiseCat was and how she was going to pay but not before he had some more fun.

"We need a location," I grumbled. "I don't want any more bodies."

DHS: *I know what you did to Charles.*
OtherwiseCat: I arrested him for multiple murders.
DHS: *You ruined him.*

I circled my hand in the air. We needed to wrap this idiocy up and get to the body.

OtherwiseCat: Why don't you come talk to me like an adult. Message me when you're downstairs and I'll come get you.

Dane chuckled.

DHS: *That's not how this is going to work, Bitch. You're going to do what I want or I'll kill another one.*

OtherwiseCat: I thought you wanted me dead.

DHS: *That'll happen. Maybe I want other things. Maybe you gave me ideas.*

Wonderful.

Lee spoke, "Ideas are good, anything that keeps him talking is good."

"Yeah, but as long as he's bouncing country to country using a VPN … it get's us nowhere."

"It buys us time. It buys those women, time."

"I need to get to that body, can we take this on the road?" I glanced at Sandra. " Can we?"

"Yes, O Leader of the Road Trips."

"Make it so."

Sandra moved to my desk and picked up my iPad. "I'll need a minute, and I'll get you set up in the chat room on this via a wee trick I have that will only ping back to our IP here, don't want our new friend realising we're on the move."

7.

After twenty-minutes of negotiating traffic and keeping the Unsub engaged, we arrived at the crime scene.

"Stay in the car, Argo," I said giving the dog's ears a rub.

It was Crime Scene One but we knew it was not the original scene. The woman was not killed and dismembered there, she was dumped. Lee and Dane double checked with the police on scene and secured the area. A forensic team waited in their cars and the Medical Examiner waited behind them.

I walked back to the ME's car. Susan zapped the window down.

"Ready for me?" She asked.

"Yes. Thought you and I would go together."

She opened her door, reached for her bag from the passenger seat and followed me. Kurt met us and shook Susan's hand.

"We never know who we'll get when we call for an ME," he said with a smile. "Good to see you, Susan. This is a messy one. Hope you don't have dinner plans."

"Been doing this a long time. Nothing's interrupted my devouring a good meal yet," she replied with a smile. "Let's see what we have."

Lee lifted the perimeter tape so we could all duck under. I could see from where I stood. Pieces of flesh. Undetermined chunks.

Susan nudged me. "Bad?"

"Yep." She was a bit shorter than me and didn't have the view I did.

"Give us a moment, Susan," Kurt said. "We need a quick look before you do your thing."

"Go ahead," she replied.

She hung back while we crossed the muddy ten or so feet to the body. Kurt's head swiveled as he looked from the jumbled mess that was once a person, to me, and back.

"All right?" He said.

"Fine," I replied.

"Do you want to see if you can get anything from the deceased?" Kurt crouched near the head of the woman.

"I doubt it's possible, but, I'll give it ago. Do we have a name?" I moved closer to Kurt. "Can you stay here?"

"You sure you're all right?"

"I'm okay, just, this is all a bit too familiar." I dropped to one knee, as close as I could to the woman's head and looked over at Kurt. "Was there a name?"

Kurt snapped the best possible picture of the woman's face and sent it to Sandra.

My phone pinged. It was the chat room alert. I pulled the phone from my pocket and looked at the screen.

DHS: *Aren't you sneaky? Charles said you were sneaky. What do you think? Isn't she beautiful?*

A lightning bolt shot through me. He was watching? My eyes scanned the area, looking for a concealed vantage point. There wasn't one. I looked again, a camera maybe? Then I saw it, up in the air. A small drone.

"Henderson, we have an uninvited guest, above us."

Kurt didn't look up. Instead he sent a message and spoke quietly to me, "Don't worry about it, Lee's got this. Let's keep doing what we're doing and keep that thing where it is."

I kept my head down and smiled. "I'll reply to him. Have we got that name?"

Kurt's hand moved. "This could be Shaniqua Thomas. That's the best we can do right now."

OtherwiseCat: *She was pretty. You ruined her life and the life of her family. How do you feel about that?*
DHS: *Dramatic! This is all on you.*

A sharp crack was followed by a sudden bang and the drone smashed into the ground three yards from us. I looked back toward the car and saw Lee holding a rifle. My phone alerts went crazy. I didn't look. No doubt our Unsub was complaining about his lack of vision. Well, fuck him.

"Get forensics to bag that thing, we might be able to get something off it," I said and turned my attention back to what was left of Shaniqua, I let my mind reach into the ether. "Shaniqua, if this is you, if you're there … can you show me what happened?"

My vision blurred as a cool mist enveloped me and the remains. I breathed. Darker areas of cloud formed and joined together, providing a fluffy grey backdrop for a terrifying scene. Terror seeped from the surroundings and into the woman. Her eyes were my eyes. I breathed. Male legs and torso moved across my line of sight. He had a limp. Concentrate. Something wrong with his right leg. Black boots. Navy blue cargo pants and a navy blue hoodie or sweatshirt. No logo. I pulled her head upward with mine. I needed a face. He had his back to her. She cried out. He turned. There it was. His face. Scarred and twisted. Unforgettable. No wonder he wore a mask when he took the women. Shaniqua cried out. He glared at her. That's when I saw it, one eye was gone? His left eyelid was closed, surgically but the look of it. Fire. He was burned. That's what the scars were. Burn scars. He didn't speak, he growled. In his scarred hand was a phone. Shaniqua sobbed. He picked up a sword from the ground and gave a twisted smile. Shaniqua slipped into a soft fog. Tiny rainbows danced across her vision as she vanished.

"Thank you," I said and stood up with care.

"Anything?" Kurt asked.

"Yeah, I think she was Ketamined before he chopped her to pieces with a sword. He's a burn victim or maybe acid. Scarred, twisted, very recognisable. His left eye is missing. Something not right with his right leg. He wore dark blue, navy, cargo pants with black boots. The sort of boots …" I made eye contact with Kurt. "The sort of boots fire, paramedics, and police wear."

"You said burn scars?"

"Yeah, let's look for fire service personal. Refresh my mind, which fire house is out by Fort Totten?"

"Engine Company 14," Kurt replied.

That was familiar. Lee's brother and I hightailed it into Engine Company 14 a few years back when someone opened fire on us. Memories rattled around in my mind looking for names. The Station Officer I met that day was Greg Cabot. And there was a paramedic, who was he? George Papadopoulos.

"Let Susan do her thing," I said. "We're going to Engine Company 14."

We walked together. "You have an address?"

"4801 North Capital Street NE."

"You think our Unsub has something to do with that fire house?" Kurt asked, ducking under the crime scene tape.

"I think, they'll know, if they've come across him."

The car door opened, I climbed in, told Argo he was a good boy for waiting and buckled up.

8.

Kurt parked on the road just down from the fire house.

"Come on Argo, let's go," I said as I unclipped his seat-belt. He bounded from the car with joyful exuberance. "With me." He settled and stuck close to my right heel. Didn't feel like he needed a leash in the fire house.

The right hand pump bay door was open. I could hear muffled music as we approached. Guess someone was listening to the radio. Two engines and an ambulance were in the bays. I skirted around the ambulance and walked between the engines to the back of the building.

"Hello!" I called.

A chair rolled across the floor and creaked. A tall male stuck his head out of an office.

"How can we help?"

I took my badge from my pocket and held it up. "FBI, we think you might be able to help us identify someone."

He emerged fully from the office. "Ellie Conway?"

"I was, yes," I replied. "Greg Cabot?"

"Good memory," he replied with a smile.

"Same could be said of you."

"Easy to remember people who fly in the door under a rain of bullets."

I do make an impression.

I turned to Kurt. "This is Doctor Kurt Henderson. He's an SSA with my team."

Argo stood, his tail slowly wagging.

They shook hands. "Nice to meet you, Greg."

"This is Agent Argo," I said.

Greg bent down a little and petted Argo on the head. "Pleased to meet you, Argo."

Argo's tail went into full wag.

"Come on into my office," Greg said, stepping out of the way. "More comfortable and less echo in here."

He was right, definitely more comfortable. Kurt and I sat on the sofa and Greg in an armchair.

"What can I do help the FBI?"

"We're looking for someone with major burn scars on his face, and hands. Don't know about the rest of his body. He has a missing left eye, and something wrong with his right leg."

"There aren't too many people like that," he said. "There was a man who used to hang around here. He wanted to be a paramedic. Hang on ..." Greg jumped to his feet and retrieved his laptop from the desk by the wall. He sat down with the computer on his lap and tapped at the keys for a few moments. "Here he is." He spun the laptop around so we could see a photo. "His name is Crimble. Jay Crimble. Could that be him?"

"Yeah," I said. "Is that George next to him?"

"Sure is."

"He around to have a chat?"

Greg turned the laptop to face him again and closed the lid. Sadness filled his eyes. "George passed away eight months ago. Cancer."

"I'm sorry for your loss. He was a good guy."

"He sure was. He had a lot to do with Jay. It was George that pulled him from a burning wreck."

"Tell me about Jay ..."

"Troubled is the best description. I don't know that he was that together before his accident. He used to hang around before that. He wanted to be a fire fighter but didn't make the cut."

"How'd that sit with him?" Kurt asked.

"He wasn't pleased. "Then he wanted to be a paramedic after his accident. That was never going to be his destiny."

If he was our guy what was the connection to Boyd?

"Do you know where Crimble comes from?" I asked.

Greg shook his head, then stopped. "I might have his application on file, that'll have those details." He flipped the lip of his laptop open.

My phone pinged like a crazy thing in my pocket. I took the opportunity to check what our Unsub was doing. He was filling the chat room with nonsense about how he was going to avenge Boyd.

OtherwiseCat: *Get a grip, Jay.*
DHS: *Clever little bitch.*

I showed Kurt the screen.

"And we have a winner ..." he said with a half a smile. "The question is can we find him before he kills someone else."

Greg looked up. "He's a killer? The man you're looking for?"

"Yes."

"And you think it's Jay Crimble?"

"I do," I replied. "Got that application form?"

He nodded, pressed some keys and a whir came from the printer on a set of drawers by his desk. He stood, and retrieved the papers from the printer.

Greg handed them to me. "I hope this helps. For the record, he is a really strange man. And we get our fair share of strange."

I read the first page. "Henderson, he went my high school. He went to *my* high school. We were the same year."

"Iverson, how many more people are going to crawl out of that particular swamp?"

"I don't know."

Nausea rose, I swallowed hard. Argo pushed on my leg. I touched his head and felt better. "At least we know the connection to Boyd."

I handed the papers to Kurt and stood up, Argo stood next to me leaning against my leg. "Thanks, Greg. I'm really sorry about George."

We left. From the car, I called Andrews.

"What've you got for me?" Andrews said into my ear.

"A name and an address. Jay Crimble. 5098 Rock Creek Church Rd North East."

"Rolling, you joining?" I heard scuffling and movement.

"Yes. We're closer and we have reason to believe there are five kidnapped women on the premises."

"Wait for us, El."

"No promises. Hurry up, Andrews." I disconnected the call.

Kurt let Lee and Dane know the address. They weren't far away. I looked at the map on my phone. We got this. I clipped Argo into his seatbelt.

Kurt fired up the engine.

9.

We drove past the intersection with Rock Creek Church Road. I scanned the street. It was lined with red brick houses and cars. Not an SUV in sight. We were going to stand out even more than usual in our big black Suburbans. I motioned to Kurt to find a parking space. Walking down the street was a better idea than driving. Cars would draw more attention than people. I climbed through to the backseat then leaned over into the very back and grabbed our bulletproof vests. I dragged them over the backseat. Kurt opened the back passenger door, and let Argo out then took his vest from me. I grabbed Argo's short leash from the console and exited the vehicle. Then pulled my vest over my head and fastened the velcro. Kurt locked the car. I clipped the leash to the patient dog.

Coming toward us were Lee and Dane in their car. They pulled in behind ours. We waited on the sidewalk while they geared up. The five of us walked to the corner.

"Which house?" Dane asked.

"Not sure," I replied.

Kurt looked at his phone. "I've got a street level view satellite map. Looks like it's the fourth one in on this side," he said.

I turned the sound off on my phone. DHS was still ranting in the chat room.

"Lee and Dane, find a back entrance. Kurt, Argo, and I

are going in the front. Andrews and SWAT are on their way. I don't think we can wait."

Lee nodded. He stuck his hand into the space between us all. "All for one ..."

Dane, Kurt and I added our hands to Lee's in unison we replied, "One for all. Alert and safe."

Lee caught my fingertips with his. "Alert and safe, El."

"We got this," I said with a grin. "Come on, we're good at this bit. Let's go have some fun."

Somewhere deep inside my mind I heard Sam's deep velvety voice say, 'Knock, knock, Avon calling' and it made me smile. He loved to open doors.

Lee and Dane left first. They vanished between some houses. Kurt and I gave them a minute then we walked to the house and up to the front door.

Kurt stood to the right, weapon drawn. I moved to the left with Argo and knocked three times on the wooden front door.

We listened for sounds of life from the house. Just as I went to knock again I heard something. I looked at Kurt. He nodded. We waited. I counted to ten in my head then knocked again. This time I shrugged at Kurt and called out, "It's Sally-Anne from down the street, you got any milk?"

Footsteps closed in on the door. Kurt pressed the send text button on his phone. I knew it was to tell Lee to go. I moved back a step so whoever opened the door couldn't see me or Argo right away. I took the opportunity to check my phone. Nothing from the chat room. The ranting had stopped about when I first knocked on the door. Good sign.

The door opened a crack. "Where you from Sally-Anne?" A male voice spoke.

"Down the street, just need a cup of milk for goodness sake."

Kurt wrapped his hand around the door handle and silently moved closer. Ready to give it a sharp shove into whoever was on the other side.

"You got a cup?"

"Yeah," I replied.

Kurt shoved the door, catching the man behind it off guard. We heard him grunt then fall. A voice bellowed from down the hall, "FBI. Lay face down. Do not move!"

The door wouldn't open properly for a moment, then it freed, Argo and I stepped past Kurt into the dim musty hallway. Face down on the ground was a male. His hands were cuffed behind his back. I could see scarring on the side of his face. The edges of his hair lifted, it was a dirty blond toupee. Argo growled softly. He didn't like hand-cuffed people.

"What do you want?" He said. "This is my home. What the hell?"

I looked at Dane and flicked my head. He hurried away to search the house. "Lee, you too. Look for a basement entrance."

"On it, boss."

"Jay Crimble?" I said, rolling him over and helping him sit up. Argo positioned himself for maximum intimidation. He stood, teeth bared, watching the man. I got a good look at his face and he was the same guy I'd seen through Shaniqua's eyes. "Are you Jay Crimble?"

His mouth twisted into a grotesque smile. "Gabrielle Conway."

Lee waved from the end of the hall. Then signed fast with his left hand. I nodded. They had found the women.

Andrews called out from the street. "Coming to you." He appeared next to Kurt. "All good?"

"Yeah. Can you take this person out?" I said, indicating to Jay.

"We got him, you go do what you do," Andrews said, his weapon trained on Jay's head. "You just sit nice and still until we're ready to move you, got it? Don't want to give Agent Argo a reason to bite."

I dropped the leash. Kurt and I moved past the man and joined Lee. I called Argo to me once Andrews gave me the all clear.

"Show me," I said, wrapping the leash around my hand. "Good boy, Argo."

We followed Lee into the kitchen, through a door, and down a flight of stairs. The smell hit me five stairs down. Cloying metallic and something rotten. I covered my mouth and nose with my elbow, breathing into my shirt.

Lee waved a hand at a closed door. "The smell is coming from in there."

Kurt nudged me. "Step away. I've got this."

Argo and I moved closer to Lee. I could hear voices from deeper in the dingy room. "Dane?"

"I'll stay with Kurt. Follow the voices," Lee said.

No argument from me. Argo and I strode deeper into the cave like room, using my phone as a flashlight.

"El," Dane said. I shone the light toward the voice, then turned it off as Dane pulled boards off a small window at the top of the wall and a little bit of light tumbled down. Enough that we could see. Four women huddled together. One looked up, defiant.

"I'm SAC Ellie Iverson with the FBI. This is Special Agent Dane Smith. You're safe."

Tears trickled from the defiant woman's eyes. "This is Argo, he's here to help keep you safe while we get you out of here."

"Go to work, Argo," I said, softly, and unclipped the leash. Argo bounded across the room then slowed and sedately walked to the women. He sat within arms reach and waited. The one who appeared so defiant reached for him. Moments later Argo was laying where they could all reach him and lapping up the attention. Dane broke more boards away from more windows while I removed plastic cable ties from the women's ankles.

"My name is Sonya," the defiant one said. "There were two other women but he took them somewhere."

"Shaniqua?"

She nodded. "He took her before the other one. She's

dead isn't she?"

"Yes, she is."

Another of the women let out a sob. Argo moved closer to her.

"Was anyone working with him?"

"We only saw a dark haired man," Sonya said.

Jay was blond.

"Did he have scars?"

"No." She petted the dog then looked at me. "I don't remember seeing skin."

Okay.

"Dane."

"I'm on it boss." I heard his voice as he spoke into his phone asking Delta C for a sit-rep. A few seconds later he pocketed his phone and turned to me. "Christian is outside. They found nothing. There is a cordon. No one else was seen in the area."

"So a dark haired man ..." Just in case there was someone else, I needed to talk to Jay. "Stay here with Argo and these ladies. Lee and Kurt will be in once they finish up in the other room. I'm going to be up top with Andrews."

I stopped outside the stinky room, the door was closed. "Henderson?"

"Don't come in," he said. "We know why there are only four women in the basement. He was planning on dumping another one."

I wasted no time leaving the basement and the house. Andrews waved to me from outside his truck.

"Where is he?"

"Inside."

I swung the door open and climbed the steps. Dixon stood opposite the prisoner. I acknowledged him with a smile then gave Jay my full attention.

"Who was the dark-haired guy who grabbed the women for you?"

His lips twisted into a distorted smile. "I thought you were clever enough to figure that out. This is a disappointing moment." I took note of Jay's clothing. Black boots, navy cargo pants, a very dark blue hoodie. That was what the killer wore.

"Enough games, Jay. Who is it?"

"I'm not finished playing."

"Shame, because I am." I stepped forward and looked down at the seated man. "I'll be back. Stay put."

I winked at Dixon and climbed out of the truck, shutting the door behind me.

Andrews waited. "Now what?"

"Now we rip the house apart. There's no one else. I think we'll find a dark wig and possibly some masks."

"What makes you think he worked alone?"

"He wants us chasing our tails. What better way to do that than a fake helper?"

Andrews smiled.

I pointed to Christian and two Delta C agents then beckoned them over.

"With me, we're searching for evidence of a second

Unsub."

* * *

Half an hour later, we had dark wigs, skin coloured gloves, and latex face masks that were creepily real looking. And nothing to suggest Jay worked with anyone. Nothing on his phone, his laptop, nothing in the house. We were thorough. No way did anyone want someone crawling from my distant past again.

Four hours after we found the remaining four live women, Jay was in custody sitting in a holding cell, waiting for his attorney. The women were home with their families.

My phone rang. Rowan's name sat on the screen.

I answered. "Hey, everything's fine but maybe you should look at some more intensive security measures for the chat rooms and the fan club site."

"We've decided to close the chat function down. If people can't talk openly in the forum then we don't want them using our system," he said. "Seems like if you can't say it in a semi-private forum, you shouldn't be saying it at all."

"I agree."

"Thanks, El. For sorting this out and not letting it become a media circus."

"No problem. I'm sorry my past intersected with your present and caused shit."

"Hey, what's this about a biography?"

The feeling of cold dread from earlier returned with vengeance.

I tried to keep my voice level. "Why?"

"Some women contacted my management and wanted to interview me about you."

Fuck. Just breathe.

"And?"

"I declined."

"Good call."

"Don't be a stranger, El."

"See ya, Rowan."

I hung up just as a problem walked through the door.

"Can we resume our interview?" Carol asked, her notebook clutched in her hand.

"No," I said. "We cannot."

"I was assured you'd be free to answer questions now that the women are safe."

"I'm going to be busy with the paperwork for the foreseeable future. Sorry, looks like we'll have to reschedule." I flicked through my day planner, shaking my head as I did so. "I have two clear hours on the thirteenth of December."

Carol frowned. "It's April."

"That's the best I can do."

Argo grumbled from under my desk.

Carol's face fell. "Would you pencil me in for December, please."

"Of course." I picked up a sharp pencil and pretended to write in the planner. "Goodbye."

The End.

Acknowledgments.

It's not always easy to write but it's absolutely fantastic to have written. This compilation/collection came together quite quickly once I decided to do it. Bit of tweaking here and there, and a new story. The process was ringed by swearing. That's perfectly normal. Editing and formating can be very frustrating endeavors.

(Page numbers are the devils playground!)
I'd like to thank Geoff for always believing in me.

Mark for listening to my bitching and complaining during this process.

Chrissy and Mike for providing much needed breaks and amusement.

And of course, the youngest two kids for putting up with me and ignoring everything I do and say. (They won't read this, so no worries there.)

About the author:

Cat Connor is a prolific crime thriller author hailing from New Zealand. Her expertise in the genre is reflected in her engaging and suspenseful narratives, which have garnered a loyal following. Her work is known for its intricate plots, dynamic characters, and relentless pace, keeping readers on the edge of their seats until the very end. She has authored multiple books, including the popular "Byte" series, which follows the exploits of an FBI unit that investigates serial crime.

Cat's passion for crime and espionage is evident in her writing, as she strives to create a world that is both authentic and thrilling. Her meticulous attention to detail and extensive research have won her critical acclaim and accolades from readers and peers alike. In addition to writing, Cat enjoys speaking on topics related to writing and publishing. Her talks are known for their candidness, humour, and practical advice. With her unique blend of talent, expertise, and passion, Cat Connor has established herself as one of the most exciting and accomplished authors in the crime thriller genre.

Her other passions include music, reading, tequila, red wine, coffee, and chocolate. When she's not writing she can be found binge watching TV shows and spending time with her much adored animals; Diesel the mastador,

Patrick the tuxedo cat, Dallas the tortie Birman, and Jimmy the thug.

You can follow and contact Cat at the following places:

Website: www.catconnor.com
Twitter: @catconnor
Facebook: @cat.connor
Instagram: @catconnorauthor
Bluesky: @catconnor.bsky.social
Threads: @catconnorauthor

.

www.ingramcontent.com/pod-product-compliance
Lightning Source LLC
Chambersburg PA
CBHW020422030726
47495CB00006B/1625